VENOMOUS

VENOMOUS

CHRISTOPHER
KROVATIN

With illustrations
by Kelly Yates

ginee seo books
Atheneum Books for Young Readers
New York London Toronto Sydney

Atheneum Books for Young Readers
An imprint of Simon & Schuster Children's Publishing Division
1230 Avenue of the Americas, New York, New York 10020

Book design by Sammy Yuen
The text for this book is set in Bembo.
The illustrations for this book were rendered in pen and ink.
Manufactured in the United States of America
First Edition
10 9 8 7 6 5 4 3 2 1
CIP data for this book is available from the Library of Congress.
ISBN-13: 978-1-4169-2487-6
ISBN-10: 1-4169-2487-6

For Quin, my hero,
and Maria, my savior.

ACKNOWLEDGMENTS

A HEAP OF GRATITUDE goes to my family and friends, for loving and supporting me unconditionally, sometimes against their better interests.

A mighty hail goes out to Ginee Seo, queen of editors, who wouldn't let me publish this book until it was the best novel it could be. Ginee, I couldn't have done it without you, and if I'd tried, it probably would've sucked. Also, thanks to all those at Simon & Schuster for helping me publish this book.

Cheers go to Kelly Yates for his amazing artwork. You've warmed this old-school fan's dark heart with your illustrations, sir. Kudos. Horns to all of the bands and musicians I love, but especially to the World/Inferno Friendship Society, for inspiring so much of this book, and to Slayer, for all the blood.

This book couldn't have been made possible without the friendship of three people—the incorrigible Andy Michaels, the inimitable Zach Smith, and the indomitable Lola Pellegrino. These three people have always reminded me that there's magic in this world and that sometimes you need to take the good with the bad. Kids, the road is long and life is short, so drive like hell and don't look back. Let's do it.

Big props go to Amanda Urban and Ron Bernstein, the most metal of agents.

To Emily Boyd, queen of the dragons, friend to the friendless—thank you.

Special thanks go to Satan. What a mensch.

VENOMOUS

CHAPTER ONE

THIS CITY IS absolutely gray today. Gray all over. The sky is a perfect shade of miserable gray that manages to emanate a coat of gray over all else—the buildings, the stores, everything. Somewhere in the distance, I see an American flag waving on top of an apartment building, a glaring peppermint-red-and-white in the overwhelming gray. I think of the Towers. I think how if they were burning now, everything might not seem so gray, and then I hit myself for that thought, because it's incredibly uncool of me to think something like that. Venom talking.

My trench coat flaps a little bit in the breeze, and I smile. It's nice. It makes me feel like Dracula or Moriarty or something. The cigarette in my hand helps, too—just that much more dramatic and badass. It's a Marlboro, though. I don't think either Dracula or Moriarty smoked Marlboros. So I dunno, maybe I'm looking like a vampire James Dean.

Heh. Vampire James Dean. That's good. That could be a band name.

I wipe ash and a little roof grit off my glasses with the back of my hand and take another drag from my smoke. The breeze blows a little harder; my coat flaps a little more. I feel the venom bubbling somewhere between all my organs, deep in the core of me that's mental and emotional all at once. It rises up just a tiny bit, swimming around behind my eyes before settling back down. It's a whale breaking the surface, coming up for air to remind me how huge things can get when they live somewhere so deep. Gray days always make the venom churn, but in a surprisingly good way. On gray days the venom makes me feel immortal.

"Locke?"

Mom grunts as she comes up the fire escape ladder, and then pads over. "When are you going to quit? You told me you'd quit." She sounds tired.

"I thought we were both going to quit."

"Don't get smart. Nobody likes a smartass. Give me one." She takes the smoke and provides her own light. We both stare out over the city in all its depressing glory, her beginning a cigarette and me finishing one.

"What a miserable day," she mutters.

"I kind of like days like this. Dark, but no rain."

"Yeah, you would, kid."

We keep staring until I have an infinitesimal line of white between the ember and the filter. I flick my cigarette off the edge of the roof in a perfect, high arc with a slow, relaxed spin. As it disappears, I wonder what would happen if it landed in a baby carriage, and then I have to mentally slap myself for thinking it. It's the venom again, the worst kind of impulse. Uncool.

Mom glances at me out of the corner of her eye. "How you feeling?"

"I'm doing okay. Just . . . thinking about things. You know?"

"Yeah."

Mom rubs my shoulder in that way that rocks my entire body back and forth. It signals the end of our checkup—I'm keeping myself sane, she's keeping herself informed, all is right in the world, let's have a Fresca. I've been okay with the venom lately; my mom understands that that's not necessarily a good thing. The venom doesn't really go away but sits and broods, festers, considers its options. Of course she worries.

"You want a quesadilla?"

"Yeah. Can I have some soup, too?"

"Kidlet, you can have whatever you want. C'mon."

Following Mom downstairs, I try to ignore the sinking feeling in my gut, the nagging sensation of doom at every turn.

After quesadillas, my mom lights another cigarette and asks me what my plans are for the rest of the day. "Why?" I ask, mid-soup-slurp.

She shrugs. "It's a Saturday. I figured you'd be going out or something."

"Well, not until tonight, no," I say, taking my dishes to the sink.

"Oh. Who're you going out with tonight?"

"Randall. He wants his outside-of-school friends to meet me."

"That should be fun."

"Yeah."

My mom smiles and says nothing. I can almost hear her thoughts from where I'm sitting. *Oh my GOD, you have a SOCIAL LIFE! Other kids your age! GIRLS, maybe!* "Well, as long as you're not busy today, will you take Lon out to get some books? He has a project for school he needs to research."

"Library?"

"Chapter and Verse down the street, actually. He's been scouting out books for a week. Just wants to go pick them up."

"He already knows what books he's getting?"

She nods, smiling even wider. "Just needs to pick them up."

I shake my head in disbelief. "Smart kid," I mutter, and skulk into my room to get my coat.

Lon's standing by the bookstore's door, bouncing around like he desperately needs to pee. "Come *on*, Locke," he whines. "What if someone already *got* them?"

"Calm down. Nobody took every book you picked out." I flick my cigarette end into the gutter. "Now, if you'd put them on hold like Mom told you to, they'd be sitting safely behind the counter."

Lon makes a face. "I thought you and Mom were quitting."

Poor kid. We'd both promised him that we'd quit sometime around July. It had started pretty well, too: Mom and I happily going around the house, crushing our hidden packs, patches latched firmly onto our biceps. Our resolve was short-lived, though. Mom had to start working overtime here and there, the stress got to her, and she started up again, and being a recovering smoker in a house with an unrecovering recovering smoker is somewhere between agonizing and impossible. But this here was the first Lon had said about any of it, at least to me.

We make our way up to the biology section, and Lon starts

pulling out books about sea turtles left and right. My little brother, the genius. The scholar. He gets things done while I daydream and fade into my own fucked-up world. He knows what needs to be done and how to do it, so he does it. Always in control. Unlike me. Unlike the venom.

He glances up at me. "Hey, Locke, do we have enough money? I don't want to be wasting any of your money on—"

I pat him on the back. "Don't worry, Leonardo. Mom gave me her credit card for these." Physical contact: opiate of the younger sibling.

Lon turns pinkish. "Don't *call* me that. What if someone was listening?"

Who would be listening in on Lon? He's ten years old (although if you ask him, he's almost eleven), and while he knows quite a few more people than I do, I doubt one of his best friends is hanging out at the bookstore, trying to hear his full name. Not that I'm an expert or anything. Having friends is not my strongest suit.

We get to the counter and load up the books. The checkout lady, a wrinkled old woman who looks like the procreative result of an elephant and a corpse, looks at the books, then at the credit card, and then back at us. "Photo ID, please." I pull Mom's passport out of my bag as well as mine. It's a standard family rule: When you've borrowed the credit card, bring

Mom's passport and your own, to show that you're family of the cardholder. Except that doesn't work this time, because the lady glances at the passports and scoffs. "I'm sorry, but I can't accept these pieces of identification."

"What?"

The checkout lady looks up at me as if I'm a salty pain in her ass and sighs. "Look, sir, just because you have this woman's ID doesn't mean anything. You could've stolen it."

A flash of cold goes through me, red-hot and persistent. "But that's my passport there. Locke Vinetti and Charlotte Vinetti. Same last name. I'm her son." But then it hits me: Mom changed her name back to her own when she and Dad split. This could be a problem.

"Names look different to me," she says, pushing the books back at me with disgust.

I despise this kind of shit. This woman spends her whole day cooped up in a bookstore, laser-scanning barcode after barcode, and the minute she sees something that, through countless idiot technicalities, does not meet company standards, she uses it to screw someone over, just to add a little excitement to her life. And if you call her on it, she can just smile and apologize and say it's her *job*, and she can do it too, because we're *kids* and she's an *adult*, right? "You have to be kidding me." I start sweating, profusely. This is not a good sign. The entire room seems to push in on me. "I mean, our addresses are the same. Look at us. She and I even look alike."

"Young man," she drawls, "I cannot sell you these books. I'm *inclined* to believe this credit card and ID were stolen or are fake." She gives me one of those tight-lipped smiles and looks away.

Because we'd do that, right? Because this kid here, this quiet little kid clutching a handful of books on fucking *sea turtles*, he's the kind of kid to tug on his older brother's shirt one day and ask if they could steal or forge both a credit card and a U.S. passport so they could go on a *Zoobooks*-themed shopping spree at the local bookstore. That's exactly what he'd do. Makes perfect sense. Jesus tap-dancing Christ.

I point to Lon, gritting my teeth. "These books are for him. For a school project. Please."

She sighs again, as if to say, *I got out of bed for this*? and waves her hand to the side. "Next customer, please."

My eyes shoot to Lon, then back to the hag. How dare she? How can she do this to a fucking kid? She won't let a *ten-year-old kid* carrying two passports and a credit card that 99.9 percent prove that he is, in fact, the son of the cardholder. Because of some *procedural* bullshit. She's doing this to ME. *TO* ME.

No. She's doing this to my little brother.

I break. I feel something in the back of my head flex. It's

slightly painful, like I've pulled a muscle, but the next thing I know, my veins are alive with fire. Every muscle's taut, and my eyes glaze over with bright crimson. My blood turns black. And it feels fucking *fantastic.*

Venom is go.

Both of my fists come slamming forcefully down on the counter. "LOOK, LADY," I bellow, "JUST BECAUSE I DON'T HAVE A PORTRAIT OF THIS WOMAN TATTOOED ON MY *DICK* DOES NOT MEAN SHE'S NOT MY FUCKING *MOTHER*!"

The wrinkled lady looks at me like I've just punched her in the uterus. A hush sweeps through the room, and all eyes, ears, and furrowed brows are on me. It doesn't faze me, though; I'm too far into it. There's no going back on this now.

A large clerk, Asian, concerned, walks over to me and calmly asks, "What seems to be the problem, sir?"

"Me? My problem," I spit, "is that I have produced valid, government-issued ID that proves that I am allowed to purchase items on this credit card, which I have done at this very store in the past." I begin to get slightly choked up, the first wave of venom wearing off. "Now, apparently, this senile old *bag* here believes that I've stolen this credit card and passport. However, if you'd like to call this phone number, which the credit card company will verify, you can speak to this woman who will assure you that I am her son. I don't think it's *necessary* to do that, but hell, this woman here, whose goal it is to make my life an obstacle course, seems to think it's completely warranted. That is my goddamn problem."

The clerk puts up his hands in defense and swipes the card. I sign the receipt under Mom's name and storm out, Lon's books in hand, the glare of the old woman burning a hole in the back of my coat.

As we walk away from the store, the venom crawls back into hiding, leaving me reeling. I begin to get the shakes. A lump catches in my throat. I start panting. I reach for a cigarette and can hardly fish one out of the pack; the first one twitches out of my fingers, and I have to pick it up and jam it into my mouth. Maybe . . . okay, maybe, for the sake of argument, I did just overreact in there a little bit. It's no big deal, right? I'll probably never see that woman again, and they were kind of asking for it, and—

—and then I see Lon. He's walking next to me with his head down, his face as red as a beet. His brown hair is matted with sweat, and he has his hands jammed firmly in his coat pockets.

"Lon? Are you okay?"

He won't even look at me. "Jeez, Locke. Why'd you have to go and do that?"

I try to say something and can't. Jesus, what the fuck *did* I do that for?

Why is the venom doing this? What more can it want?

THE CITY called to me with a funeral dirge.

As I stared over the edge of the skyscraper, some seventy stories above the frenzied New Yorkers squirming like insects below me, I heard the city call me out to play, in the form of an orchestra of sorrow and anger, a symphony of enraged madness. Every twisted little deed, every back-alley deal and big-budget brutality of this fine city, added its voice to the choir of the damned and the desperate. The city's song was the closest thing it had to a soul, tortured and scarred though it was; it was the sound of energy and emotion pulsing through the very core of this place, the invisible heart of darkness that beat its killing rhythm through the sewer, skyline, sidewalk. I heard it in the back of my head, like a buzzing hornet whirling angrily in a jar, begging its captors to let it out so they can see what it's made of. It was miserable, yes—the core of this city was rotten, to say the least—but also inviting, impressive. I focused on it, let its words and melody billow in my brain until the tone became deafening. It fed me power unthinkable and thoughts unspeakable.

All the song needed was a vessel, and that was my use. It was the paint, and I, the canvas.

There was the prickle of apprehension as the doors to my mind and soul flew wide open, the transformation setting off my basic reptilian defense system; then the becoming began.

From my eyes, my mouth, the tips of my fingers—the song of the city wrapped its inky cloak around my body. Pure negative energy, the physical form of hatred and pain, twisted around my body and clothes, coating me in a suit of shadows. I became a corporeal conduit of every twisted deed done around me, a well of free-floating malevolence and misery. I could control the energy with my mind and body the way an electrode would control electricity. Soon my entire body was cloaked in pure ink black, leaving me a walking silhouette, an animate shadow. This power was my curse and my tool. With it, I could use the pain of others to right the many wrongs that plagued this place and the people who dwelled in it. The venom, my parasitic dark side, had given me one incredible power: that of channeling negative emotions into physical energy, creating darkness that was as real and powerful as light. I was a fallen guardian angel, the gargoyle upon a church of sin and despair, a cathode ray for desolation.

The glittering lights of Manhattan twinkled red, like bloody stars in the night sky. Now, dressed in the city's darkness, I could respond to its funeral song, soar out into the night on wings of rage, and enact vengeance on those who deserved it.

"I am Blacklight," I bellowed into the rank night air, "and the night is mine!"

I leaped from the edge with a laugh and soared down into the degenerate streets below me.

CHAPTER TWO

I FIRST REALIZED that there was something poisonous inside me when I was eight years old.

I'd always been cut off from everyone else, the quiet kid building little houses out of wood blocks or driving toy trucks around on my own. My world was what I made it. When being Locke Vinetti was too hard, I could be Indiana Jones or Batman or, fuck, I dunno, Usagi Yojimbo (he's the bunny from the Ninja Turtles). Even when other kids picked on me, I just kept quiet, no matter how angry I got. There wasn't any of that after-school-special nonsense about being the one kid who the bullies picked as a goat; I got bullied just as much as anyone; I just didn't respond to it. Other kids bawled or spat insults or threw punches, which seemed about as effective as not doing anything, and the latter option involved a lot less futile effort. I wondered, later, if maybe that's how the venom was first birthed—through my silence, through the containment of my anger. Y'know, like Michael Douglas in *Falling Down*, only without any of the political commentary crap.

Anyway. One day in gym class, a basketball knocked me to the floor mid-layup, landing me right on my tailbone. At first I thought it had just bounced from the backboard to my head, but looking up, I saw three of my classmates baring three hyenas' grins. I nearly started crying—my head, ass, and pride were in a state of stubborn agony—but if there's one thing any elementary school kid knows about bullying, it's that crying is like stapling a KICK ME sign to your forehead.

The second ball hit me in the face. I saw it clear as day: One of them, Tommy Ferraro by name, called out "Yo, Locke!" in a jovial enough tone, and when I turned around, the cretin chest-passed the ball straight into my nose. The world went white, the ground went unreliable, and my nose went gruesome. I touched my face, and once I saw the crimson smear on my palm, the tears just came.

This, as I had predicted, didn't help the situation. Tommy jabbed one of his little sausage digits at me and brayed, "Oh, wook! He's gonna stawt cwying! Pwoor baby!" He laughed again and reached for another basketball.

At this point, something just . . . broke free.

And it was overpowering. Irresistible. It welled up inside me, like tears well up in your eyes—only this thing was pure, liquid hate, anger and rage and depression, all in a physical manifestation. This was no simple emotional response; this was a real, honest-to-God, all-over *change.* It percolated up in my head, bubbling, bubbling, and then bursting, overflowing. I felt it burning in my veins; every part of my body was so alive, more alive than I'd ever felt it before. And once the feeling, the substantial emotion, had filled me and solidified, it took control. But the worst part about it was that I enjoyed it—Fuck, I *loved* it. This thing took me in its smooth, warm, black embrace and guided my limbs, and there was something, a voice without any sound or words, soothing and quieting. The insecurity and instability of what was happening seemed to vanish. I didn't worry about what to do next, because it had been decided for me. Everything fell into its wicked, brutal place, and all was well.

So then I tackled Tommy Ferraro and bit off the tip of his nose.

Now, in the years since it went down, this story has been *greatly* exaggerated. People have claimed I did everything from bite off his entire nose to spit the piece back at him. Tommy Ferraro himself spouted some ridiculous yarn about me having razor-edged teeth and lapping the blood off my fingers as I rose up off of him. The true story is sort of lost to time—I was somewhere else entirely, Tommy was pretty caught up in the moment, and his friends just stood there stupefied, so all accounts are questionable. The fact remains that I managed to take a small chunk of nose off Tommy's face with my teeth. He lay back, screaming, clutching his face (which was bleeding far worse than mine was) while I stood over him and barraged him with swear words and monstrous laughter. I know it sounds sadistic, taking the time to stand there and laugh at him, but it all felt so rapturous that I didn't give it a second thought.

When the teachers finally found us, I was huddled in a corner, a blubbering mess. They kept asking me what was wrong, saying not to worry, Tommy would be fine. I didn't care about Tommy. Fuck Tommy Ferraro. Even through the weeping and shivering, it never occurred to me that what I had done was wrong; that little cretin got what was coming to him. It was just that once that pure, black energy had gone back into hiding, I was left with the sludgy residue of it. I felt empty, worthless, overexcited, depressed. I wanted to go home and go to bed.

My mother had to get off work to pick me up, which, let me tell you, was a huge pain in the ass. She kept asking me questions about why I did it and whether or not I liked my school. Answering wasn't an option, as my face was just flushed creases and snot. The minute we got home, I climbed into bed and passed out until ten o'clock the next morning. From what I've read and seen in movies, it was like recovering from your first shot of smack: Once that first blinding feeling had run its course, the rest of my body just sort of shut down for recovery. And just like with a drug, the thing that most irked me was how much I adored that raw, powerful feeling, and how deeply sad I was that it was no longer there. The best sensation I'd ever experienced, and the only thing that could spark it off was utter fucking misery.

From that day on, my life was peppered with outbursts of the venom and its sickly influence. Almost overnight I went from easy pickings for the bullies at my school to someone the new kids were warned to stay away from. Circles of whispering kids went silent as the grave when I passed. Which was cool at first, I admit. Like I said, I had never been THE target for torment—you know, That Kid? I wasn't That Kid—but now I was a social Typhoid Mary. I'd made it clear that I didn't want to be messed with, and I was left alone. Whenever new kids came by and tried to show how tough they were, I'd have an outburst and they'd go home to their parents, and the next day the school would get an enraged phone call, asking for my head. It was sort of like prison that way, just not with the whole selling-ass-for-cigarettes and the like.

The first time was indicative of the venom's style, though, and that was definitely a problem. My books would get slapped out of my hands, so I'd whale on the slapper with my backpack. If someone spat in my face, I'd punch 'em in the throat. If someone shoved me into my locker, I'd slam their hand in the door of theirs. People would constantly ask why I had to go "that far" when someone was a bastard to me, and truth be told, I hadn't the foggiest, because it wasn't me doing it. Even if *I* wanted to beat someone down, it wasn't a simple punch in the nose or a knee to the balls; something uncomfortable and effective. The venom saw things along the lines of nerve clusters and necessities (fingers and eyes, mostly, but basically whatever would be really difficult for someone to have wrapped up for a couple of weeks). The venom liked extremes—the crueler the better. This wasn't about getting even, it was about causing the worst pain in the weirdest way possible. It was about being unforgettable.

Over the years, I managed to build up some tolerance for the venom. Sure, after an outburst I'd still vibrate and mumble as though I was attending synagogue, but nowhere near as bad as I did that first time. It helped that the vessel for the hate had been expanded: The level of rage has stayed the same, but I've grown enough, both physically and emotionally, to be able to deal with it now. The anger was the same, but recovery time shortened significantly. So the venom got creative and started reworking its game plan. Starting around eighth grade, I found out the venom's other talent: It made me poisonous.

I had the Midas touch, if old King Midas had a penchant for decay rather than gold (stupid analogy, I know, but you know what I'm talking about). Everything I became a part of turned to shit before my eyes. My growing depression and antisocial tendencies were definitely a few of the things that caused my dad to leave us around then. (The question has always bothered me: Was Dad always a dirtbag, and did the venom just reveal him; or was Dad fine until the venom drove him out?) I remember hearing the fights he and my mom had right before they split; her side was always sympathetic and nurturing while his was always authoritative and dismissive—I was "nothing more than a punk." (He's the kind of guy who likes that word, "punk," when talking about people he considers insolent.) The fights centered around the venom a lot of the time: He kept saying that it must be her fault, that she kept letting me get away with it, and she kept insisting that I needed a sense of unconditional love and sympathy. He was honest-to-God *scared* of the venom, too, which was . . . interesting. One time, in fifth grade, a kid named Alan Raskowitz pulled out a chunk of my hair during art class, because he thought it was funny, so I beat him to a pulp. Just got on top of him and started pounding him with the fuchsia plastic handle of the scissors I was holding. My mom couldn't be reached, so my dad had to pick me up from school, and the entire car ride, he just kept glancing over at me and shaking his head with this terrified look in his eyes (although it might have been 'cause I looked sickly and miserable and had blood on my shirt, but I was still his son). In any event, point is, Dad left right before I turned thirteen, and I definitely had a hand in it. He said goodnight to Lon and me one night, and the next morning he and his stuff weren't there, and Mom couldn't stop crying. He lives in Westchester now with a very nice woman named Millie, who smiles constantly. They have two well-adjusted little blonde kids; a daughter and a new baby boy. I met them at a Christmas party when I was fifteen. Lon seemed to think Millie was really sweet.

I hope they all die in a fucking fire.

My romantic life? Right, okay. I'm like an owl: From a distance, I seem graceful and deadly in a stylish way, but up close it's all claws and fleas and coughed-up pellets of hair and bones. Either the girl gets scared away from me or the venom works its magic and her life begins to slowly spin down the toilet. Don't get me wrong, I'm not too ugly a guy—I get "handsome" a lot, and sometimes "cute in a certain way," which makes me think I look like Nick Cave, so I've had experience with getting to know and spend time with girls. But every time I enter anything resembling a relationship, the venom makes an appearance—an obscene comment, a violent opinion, a depressed sigh, you name it—at just the right time to leave me embarrassed and my date terrified. One girl, Clarice, even casually mentioned that nights out with me and her other friends always seemed to be a lot less fun than the nights with just her and her friends; she told me she'd been observing this, like a science experiment, for a couple of weeks, and all the evidence pointed to me being a social bad-luck charm. I got the point, paid for my half of dinner, and went home to drink about a gallon of chocolate milk. So after a while, I just stopped giving a shit. My reasoning: better to be terribly lonely than screw up someone else's life. Girls sometimes shoot me a smile or a glance, and I can't even look at them, because there's no fucking hope. That's it in a nutshell. Hopeless.

My friends? Make it friend. Randall Elliot seems to be the one person who isn't affected by the poison that is me. One day in eighth grade, Randall watched a kid tormenting me until I slammed him in the ear with a lunch tray. When the teachers began screaming at me, Randall intervened on my behalf (I believe his actual opening comment was,

"Oh, this is some BULL*SHIT* right HERE!"). Since then, we've been inseparable. He's one of those popular misfits, the quirky kid who still has a lot of friends and a decent social standing. Like . . . he *LOVES* Weezer. Which sort of tells you everything you need to know. He still considers me his best friend, which makes no fucking sense considering that I weigh him down more often than not. People always ask him, "Why do you hang out with that kid?"

He always has the same response: "'Cause he's awesome."

I don't get Randall a lot of the time. But then again, he doesn't always get me. The one time I tried to explain the venom to him, he shook his head at the right places and nodded when he needed to, and finally whistled and said, "Heavy stuff, Stockenbarrel." (That's his idea of a joke, by the way.) Just like everyone else, he doesn't understand the venom, because that'd be like understanding God. Unlike everyone else, though, he accepts the venom as a part of his best friend. "The way I see it," he told me, "I won't encourage it, but I guess I'll just learn how to deal with it, y'know? Now can we eat?" And he has. Dealt with it, that is. He knows the tricks to calming me down, can see an "episode" long before it hits. To him it's a strategy, a way of working around things. Which I thank God for. Every day. Because if he reacted logically, if he eventually just threw up his hands and walked off, I'd be alone. It's one of my big fears: the day

Randall doesn't understand. But until that moment arrives, I owe him everything.

When all's said and done, my problem is simple: The venom is my own. They get the concept but can't grasp the curse. Because no one else could be me, no one could have any idea what it meant to be poisonous.

OH GOD, STAY AWAY FROM ME!" screamed the kid, skittering nervously across the filthy concrete.

Fear. Music to my ears.

Thugs and criminals had some strange theory that since they're morally reprehensible, they're the prime specimen of humanity this side of the planet. They assume that they live in a state of invincibility, because they're twisted enough to be horrible. Nothing could be farther from the truth. Being tough is one thing—anyone can be tough, so long as they have enough time to go to the gym and enough gall to act like they're God. But being invincible is an entirely different beast altogether. And when a person proves himself unworthy of their humanity, they assume it's a triumph and revel in their so-called victory, right until the power of true justice wraps its steely blue fingers around their scrawny necks.

"Nowhere to go," I said to him, walking calmly down the alleyway toward him. His victim, some poor girl with a swollen wallet and a little red dress, huddled crying next to a Dumpster by my side, her wide eyes focused on my wraithlike form. "Nowhere to run. Nowhere to hide. Just admit it, scum. This is a long time coming. Take it like a man." My footsteps echoed through the alley like the ticking of Satan's clock. I loved my job.

"BACK OFF!" he shrieked. He waved his knife at my face,

a little silver thing that glittered like tinsel. "YOU HEAR ME?! I'LL CUT YOU! I'M NOT AFRAID OF YOU! DO YOU HEAR ME?! I'VE HEARD ABOUT YOU, AND I'M NOT AFRAID OF—"

I flickered out my claw, and in a crackle of black lightning, the switch flew from his fingers into mine. I clenched my hand together, and the knife was scrap. The kid made a noise, like a kitten, in the back of his throat.

"You could have fooled me."

"Oh Jesus." He shuffled backward on his ass, clawing his way behind him until his back pressed against the brick wall at the alley's dead end, newspapers and food wrappers bunching up behind him. "Oh Jesus. Please, no. I didn't mean it. I really didn't want to hurt anybody, man, please, you gotta understand—"

"I understand you're a liar," I said. "I can feel your lies. They give me power, they make my soul burn darkly with your weakness and pain. So don't tell me you didn't mean to harm anyone tonight. Because that pain is my strength, and your dishonesty . . . Well, that just adds flavor.*" I reached out my hand again, letting the dark energies I controlled whirl in my palm, blazing diabolically in the alley's shadows. "Your time has come. Take it like a man. It'll all be over shortly."*

Before I could wreak vengeance, a strip of flesh, a tentacle of dripping black, descended from the rooftops above, wrapped around the thug's neck, and yanked him upward. His hands went to his throat as his face turned gray and his eyes bugged out, and for a while I watched as he twitched at the end of the tendril. His face bloated, his tongue swelled, and with one final gurgle, he hung limp. The tentacle loosened from his neck, and his body dropped with a crash back into the refuse that filled the alleyway.

From the roof above me, something slithered into the night with the sounds of scales and slime.

Well. It appeared I had a cohort.

CHAPTER THREE

WE GET HOME, and Lon beelines it for his room while I sit down on the couch in the living room and let my head drop, like it was made of steel. Mom steps out of the kitchen and smiles. "Got everything you needed?"

"Yeah," says Lon with a sigh.

Mom's ears seem to twitch as her Mother radar picks up the vibe in the room. "What's wrong?"

Lon shakes his head and tries to say something nice, but finally just throws his arms out at his sides. He's like a little adult when he's angry. It's almost cute. "Locke flipped out. I'm never going to be able to shop there again."

"Hey, Lon, I'm really sorry." I am, too. He's the last person in the world I want to hurt. But what the hell was I supposed to do, with that woman pulling shit like that? Should I have just shrugged and told him that we'd have to get his books later? How else *could* I react?

"Whatever," he says, slamming the door.

My mom slowly ambles over to me and sits. "Dare I ask?"

I shake my head, catching a sob in my throat while I take off my glasses and begin to rub my eyes furiously. I will not cry. I'm a big kid. I will not cry.

She pats my back with the hand that still has the wedding ring on it. "Want to talk?"

I nod, and then whisper, "Um, can I have some chocolate milk?"

Chocolate milk is the antivenom. I have no idea why.

My mom goes to the kitchen and comes back with a big glass of Nesquik, and I toss it down my throat like it could save the world. The cool settles in my stomach, pervades my being, until I'm feeling fit as an athletic fiddle.

Seriously, I have no clue how it works, but it does.

"I'm just really upset about losing it in front of him," I gasp after swallowing. "He shouldn't have to deal with that."

She nods in agreement. "I know, kidlet," she says, "and I know sometimes the bad stuff just forces its way to the surface, and it's hard to stay in control. But it's not just him, y'know? You should be trying not to blow up like you do in front of anybody. It doesn't help at all. Nothing improves."

I nod and keep my mouth shut, and it feels like lying. In the past, the venom has always been reliable when it hits me—controlled chaos, a limited outburst of pure rage. But lately there's been a jagged edge to the venom. There's no black-and-white anymore. The venom is present all the time; even when I'm feeling okay, there's a persistent sense of hurt in the background, like a rash that won't go away. Its voice is clearer and constant. The full-on attacks come closer to the surface every day. The little show I put on at the bookstore wouldn't have happened a few months ago, but today the venom took over quickly, like it was the most reasonable solution in the world.

What worries me is that the venom is growing restless, like it's tired of the passenger seat and wants to take the wheel for a while. It's always been an impulse, but I'm beginning to wonder where Locke ends and the venom begins. This concept terrifies me, sure. But if my mother knows about it, there'll be more therapy. More long talks, more warnings to my teachers. Plus, Mom might cry. I can't let that happen.

"You haven't had an angry in a while." An "angry." I used the term maybe once when I was nine or something, and it stuck. Moms. "How'd it feel?"

"Like it always does. Really good and then really, really bad."

"You know, if you wanted to go back to seeing Dr. Reiner . . . ," she says softly. That's a laugh. Dr. Reiner was a shrink I saw, who was convinced that the venom was a product of some sort of sexual repression, a projection of my inner kink. He'd ask me about what I liked "to do" to girls, and whether I ever wanted "to do" things to other boys. When I told him that I knew I was straight and that gay sex never appealed to me, he asked me why I wasted his time by closing my mind. Well, he didn't say it quite like that, but I'm no moron, and he wasn't the champion of subtlety. You can always tell with people like that, whose sole purpose in life is to explain away what's wrong with other people. So I broke one of his windows, and we don't talk anymore and everyone's peachier for it.

"Dr. Reiner was a chump, Mom. I think I'll be okay."

"Honey, maybe you should just give him another chance—"

"I gave him a chance. It didn't work."

She pats my knee again and gets back up to continue fixing dinner. "Whatever you want, honey. I'm just worried about you, is all. No harm meant. Whenever you need me, I'm here."

I love my mom and my brother more than life itself. It's not fair that they have to deal with the utter fucking mess that is me. I'm not even sure I could put up with it.

I wake up to the sounds of the doorbell and realize that I've fallen asleep. I take a quick look at the clock. Shit. Eight thirty. Randall's here.

"Mom, I'm going out, okay!" I yell as I yank on my coat. "I'll make curfew!"

From somewhere in the apartment, there's a muffled, "Have fun, sweetie!"

I throw open the door and there's Randall, all spiky blond hair and vintage suit. He has his acoustic slung over his back and a big Cheshire cat smile on his face. He's shabby but stylish, awkward yet handsome—the kind of boy most skater girls dream of. He could be playing either the owner of a casino or a punk rock troubadour. I envy the whole dichotomy of it all.

"Why do you always wear black, Stockenbarrel?" he asks. It's a Chekhov line; our joke.

"I'm in mourning," I say dramatically, "for my *life*."

He throws his head back and brays, his face all squinting and teeth. I think that's what gets Randall so much attention—even I can't deny that smile. When he smiles at you, you feel chosen. "You ready to go?"

I nod and we walk slowly down the stairs and out onto the street. I give him a smoke and light one myself.

"I thought you were quitting."

"What are you, my mom?" I sigh.

He shrugs. "Just wondering. Didn't mean anything by it."

"Sorry. Long day. So remind me of their names again."

"They'll be a bunch of folks there, but you're thinking

Casey and Renée. This'll be nothing big, just hanging out. But they really want to meet you."

"Well, I've heard the names enough, I guess. It's totally okay that I'm coming, right?"

"A small gathering, dude, nothing more." I know this tone of his. He's making sure I don't get scared away, thinking this is, God forbid, a *party*. It's somewhere between sweet and infuriating, but I let it slide. I've flaked out on meeting Randall's outside-of-school friends enough times for it to be unfair. I owe him one. "Anyway. Why was your day long?"

"I had a venom moment in front of Lon today."

"Ah." I know what that "Ah" means, too. It means, *Ah, you did what you always do, which is embarrass those around you by going apeshit*. Randall's like that: He doesn't hide how he feels when it comes to me or the venom, so I can't blame him for expressing those opinions, even if he doesn't just come out and say them. He knows I can read his tones and movements.

We get down to Riverside, around 84th Street, coming upon the massive rock right next to a playground, what could almost be called a crag if it was a little bigger and sharper. Tonight, the rock and the entire area by it are lined with kids, but not normal kids. *Circus* kids: punks, mods, Goths, metal heads, indie kids, emo rockers, rude boys, all of that kind of crowd. (Randall uses these terms as though he were compiling a hipster encyclopedia). A bunch of them have guitars out; one or two of them have bongos. Surrounding them are about a hundred candles, all waxed to the ground, lighting up the entire area like a cathedral. These kinds of kids don't exist in my little Manhattan private school universe. Parents send their kids to my school, hoping we won't fall in with this crowd, unaware that the rich preppy kids drink and do drugs more than anyone on the planet. Randall refuses to buy it, though. He'll go to punk shows and the skate park and return with a hundred new friends from all over the city.

Nothing big, indeed: To me this isn't a party, it's a fucking gala. The strings in the back of my brain get tightened and pulled; my whole body rides a wave of twitchy anticipation. My teeth chatter a bit. I'm not one of those Music People. Yes, I have my album collection and all that, but I'm not as dedicated as this crowd here. I know what I am when it comes down to it—an awkward, skinny dude with little to nothing in the ways of social skills. What the fuck am I supposed to say to this carnival of pop culture? Lots of people. Lots of activity and talking and necessary interaction. Not my forte.

The venom shifts and itches. It wraps an agitated hand around my nerves and gets ready to explode if it's needed. An angry venom is bad, but a scared, nervous venom? I'm in trouble.

"I don't have to be, like, a social butterfly or anything, do I?" I manage through a shaking jaw.

"No, of course not."

"And I can leave whenever I want to? You won't be offended?"

"Stockenbarrel," he says, sighing, "just relax. You can do whatever. This is not a fancy dinner your parents are throwing. Have a drink. Decompress."

"Of course I'm—No, I just planned on sitting around and trying to feel as miserable as possible."

Randall raises an eyebrow and gives me another grin. "Yeah, well, it wouldn't be the first time." Touché.

We get to the rock and start climbing up the side. People are saying hi to Randall left and right; I know he has a lot of friends besides me, but it's weird to see him in action, working the special handshakes and goofy nicknames (at one point he calls a guy "Brad the Rad" and I almost want to go home right then and there). Finally he gets to the top of the rock and pulls me up next to him, standing in front of everyone, illuminated by the candles as if we had flashlights pointed up at us. It's actually a nice view of this mass of teenage insanity. This evening might not be so bad.

"Hey, guys!" he calls out.

An assortment of "Hey, Randall"s and "What's up"s come from out of the crowd of kids.

He slaps a hand on my chest. "This is Locke!"

Randall, you sneaky son of a bitch. You dirty motherfucker.

"He's new! Everyone say hi!"

A loud chorus of "HI, LOCKE!" shoots from the group.

"Locke, say hello!"

Shit.

I raise my hand as casually and say, "Hiya." I sound puny and quiet and stupid. Well done, Locke. Fucking genius.

And that's that. Randall and I sit down, and Randall starts talking to this girl next to him about Henry Rollins's neck. I finish my cigarette and flick it over the edge of the rock and onto the curb a few yards away.

"Hey, watch it!"

I glance over the edge to see a tall, beautiful black kid with a Mohawk staring up at me. It suddenly dawns on me that I'd hit him in the head with my cigarette. He doesn't look angry, just confused and a little hurt. Man, I just keep getting better and better at this making-a-complete-jackass-of-myself game.

"Oh God, I'm—I'm really sorry, I—"

"Don't worry about it, Locke. Just be careful."

I lean over and tap Randall on the shoulder. He looks over at me quizzically. "Who is that?" I say, pointing over the edge. "Tall black kid, Mohawk."

"Oh, that's Tollevin the Tower. He's on lookout tonight."

"Lookout."

Randall shrugs. "We've had problems with the cops before. The lookout keeps an eye open for them."

I nod. "And how does he know my name?"

Randall looks puzzled. "I just announced it."

"And he knows it already?"

Randall slaps my back. "People catch on quickly here, and besides, they've heard of you," he says, and goes back to his conversation before I can ask him what the hell *that* means. So, to review: Now everyone knows my name, and there's a kid who's casually referred to as "the Tower" watching out for the cops, who'll probably make an appearance tonight. Fan*tastic.*

As I'm sitting there trying to make sense of all of it, a voice beside me says, "Locke? You're Locke?"

I turn around, and sitting there is an angel. A really, really inappropriate angel.

She's a Goth girl with a spiky blue fairy cut, her face a light shade of pale with dark patches under her cheekbones and eyes. Her lips are flawless shining black with a single ring piercing her lower lip down the middle. She's wearing a corsetlike top that pushes her breasts up and outward, vinyl pants, massive death-boots, and a spiked collar. From the bottom of her right eye, an upside-down cross curves down her cheekbone, as though she's crying evil. She's beautiful in a way that I can't describe, but in a way that you can see under all the makeup and buckled-up leather. Her voice, her posture, the curve of her eyes, the way her lip ring makes her full lower lip puff up a little on either side . . . Jesus. I cannot take my eyes off this girl.

"Um," I begin, "uh, I, um, yeah. That's me."

She bows with a bit of flourish. "Finally, we meet. Randall mentions you constantly, but it seems like every time you're supposed to come out with us . . . Well, you tell me." She smiles. "Sounds like you two are pretty good friends."

"Best, actually. *Best* friends."

"Oooh. Sounds official. Let me know when you guys head up to Brokeback." My face must turn as red as it feels, because she smiles and scratches lightly at my shoulder with her long black fingernails. The sensation stays on my skin like an aftertaste. "Just messing around. No worries."

"Sorry," I say, and then, with all the eloquence of projectile vomit, "I'm just really, really, really not used to meeting new people is all, y'know? I'm a little on edge. This is a lot to take in over, like, five minutes."

She nods slowly, smiling still. I'm trying to keep my eyes off her cleavage, and I'd be failing miserably if she weren't so beautiful. "Want a Djarum?" she says, holding out a pack. I've heard about these—clove cigarettes, like smoking incense, big in the Goth scene—but I've never had the pleasure. I grab one immediately and light it on a nearby candle, an action that seems unspeakably cool to me.

One drag tells me I haven't been missing out on much. Gag. Ugh. Yech. Medic. If I wanted to inhale potpourri, I would've hit up Gracious Home on my way here.

She lights her own and glances over at me. "Good, huh?"

I force a smile. "Great."

"So, what sort of scene are you a part of?"

Well, shit. This is the music thing I'm so worried about. I have to calm down and not be a fucking nutcase. Maybe a raver? No, that's moronic, look at yourself, don't say that. Hip-hop? God, no, you're about as convincing a hip-hop fan as you are a fucking jellyfish. Classical? Country? Polka?

"Well, I don't really have a scene."

Her pointed eyebrows arch. "Really?"

Okay, work it. I've gone with the honest answer, so I might as well stick by it. "I'm a music fan, but I like a lot of different stuff. I don't fall into any scene or category. I listen to a lot of Tom Waits, if that helps."

To my surprise, she says, "Cool."

"If you say so."

"Well, it's cool that you can stay outside the boundaries of all the scenes in that way. Too many kids just buy the right clothes and go through the motions, so they can be dumped into a category, right? I mean, look at *me*, all dolled up like

Siouxsie. And some of the schmucks here . . ." She waves her hand, displaying the schmucks. "I'm impressed. Plus, Tom Waits rocks."

Locke, you are an accidental genius. You are the fucking moron Mozart.

Suddenly "Bela Lugosi's Dead" comes tinkling out of her pocket. She reaches in and yanks out a cell phone, which she flips open. "Just a second. Hello? . . . Yeah . . . Well, no, we're just hanging out. . . . Okay . . . one song? Okay . . . one song . . . okay, bye." She snaps it shut and pouts. "I have to go home after the first song, dammit. How bogus is that?"

"Utterly bogus. There is none more bogus." Wow, Locke. Just . . . wow.

She laughs. "Well said, Locke."

I repeat: moron Mozart. Idiot Einstein.

Before I can continue charming the pants off this dark angel, Randall whips his guitar out and starts a-plucking. I recognize the tune as "El Scorcho" by Weezer (him and his fucking Weezer). Suddenly the whole crowd yells out, "El Scorcho! Aye caramba!" and a frenzy begins. We sway, banging our heads, screaming the lyrics we remember and garbling the ones we don't. Kids begin dancing; soon the entire rock is a whirlwind of spikes, parkas, checkered ties, purple hair, and smiles. I've never been a part of something like this before; this is only supposed to happen in nineties teen comedies. These people, these candles, Randall as the host . . . It's like a dream. A weird, unexpected, magnificent dream.

The Goth pixie taps me on the shoulder as the last chorus becomes one huge joyous scream. Before I know it, there are soft hands cradling my cheeks, and she kisses me—she, her, *this* girl, kisses me, Locke, poisoned boy. Our arms work their way around each other (I have to do that damn awkward scoot, where you sort of hop over to someone while sitting), and soon we're in what a Victorian novelist would call a "passionate embrace." It's airtight. I want every possible part of her on me.

She pulls back and says, with her inky lips only millimeters from mine, "I'm Renée, by the way."

This is *Renée*?

Her breath smells like a church after dark, like the graveyard in Candyland. "I'm Locke."

She giggles. "I know." And with that, she leaps down off the rock, gives Tollevin a hug, and trots uptown while I stare after her and make a mental note to crown myself King of the Universe.

The feeling of eyes on me jostles me out of my girl-scented world, and I turn to see Randall giving me the ultimate shit-eating grin. He leans in like a mom and pulls his thumb across my face, then gives me a thumbs-up smeared black. Again, I swell with glee.

"You could've told me," I growl sidelong at Randall, "that *that* was Renée."

"And miss your suave-ass moves? No dice. Besides, getting between Renée and her food is incredibly hazardous to my health, and you obviously weren't expecting that kind of girl—Well, it was too perfect."

"Did you set that up?" I ask, riding the adrenaline.

"Not exactly, but I was damn sure hoping for it." There's a moment of good vibrations between us; then, with spider-like grace, his fingers go slowly across the strings of his Gibson and leap to life. And this time, there's no garbling.

"'When the night . . . has come . . .'"

The kids with the bongos howl in approval and pound on their skins, like their lives depended on it. Guitars all over the rock wake up, and pretty soon we've managed to start the biggest, coolest camp singalong I've ever heard. Kumba*ya*.

"'No, I won't . . . be afraid . . . No, I-eee-I won't . . . shed a tear . . .'"

And as I'm sitting there feeling truly cool for the first time in ages, I see this guy sitting off to one side of the crowd, with a bottle of something or other, facing toward the river. He's all curled up into a fetal position and sort of rocking back and forth, taking a swig from his bottle, and then rocking back and forth again. And his demeanor, the way his shoulders hunch and his head hangs, sets off a buzzer in the back of my head: familiarity. This kid hits me with a two-ton sack of déjà vu.

I tap Randall on the shoulder as the song draws to a loud finish. "Who's that?" I ask, pointing.

Randall follows my finger and frowns. "*That's* Casey. He's the Emperor of our little group."

"I thought you were the Emperor."

"Oh no," he says, "I'm the Fool. Casey's the Emperor." He hikes his finger back toward uptown. "Renée's the Hierophant."

"I don't know what that means."

"I'd be a little weirded out if you did, to be honest."

"I want go talk to him. I'll be back, okay?"

Randall nods like he understands. "He's in one of his funks, though. Don't push him."

"Why, what are his funks like?"

Randall opens his mouth to explain, but then gets this thoughtful look in his eyes. "Y'know what? Go find out. It'd be good if he tells you himself."

I get up and start walking through the crowd. The closer I get to Casey, the more I see that he's dressed quite nicely. He's wearing a white collared shirt and black slacks, and his hair is all slicked back and shiny. He looks very dapper, and I begin to wonder what he's doing with a crowd like this. He has a round face with chubby cheeks and the tiniest hint of a double chin, but also has very dark patches under his eyes, only they aren't painted on like Renée's, they're earned. As I stare at him, he takes another slug of whatever and holds the bottle out to me. I take it and take a very tiny sip, which burns nicely on the way down. I glance at the bottle. Jack Daniels. I've never had whiskey before.

"Hi," I manage to say very quietly. "You're Casey, right?"

"I'd prefer you not take the guidance-counselor tone with me, Locke," he says in a deep baritone voice. "Locke Vinetti, the school friend, Randall's cohort. Lovely night, isn't it?"

I nod. "It'd be nicer if you join us, sir." What the hell? Where did that come from? Maybe it was the whole "Emperor" thing.

He finds it funny enough to laugh a little. "'Sir'? Call me Casey. Or 'Emperor,' if you're into that thing."

"Thing?"

He waves his hand back to the crowd. "Locke, Tarot. Tarot, Locke." He takes another deep slug of whiskey. "It's something Randall and I came up with, which all these kids have taken a little too far. There are even gangs now." I look confused, and he sighs and continues. "The punks and rude boys are the Swords, the hippies and emo rockers are the Wands, the mods and indie kids are the Cups, and the metalheads and Goths are the Pentagrams. Mind you, in the original tarot it's actually Pentacles or Coins, but they changed it to Pentagrams, what with the Satan-loving and the angry music, and the . . . Ah, whatever, you know what I'm talking about." He spits like the idea has left a bad taste in his mouth. "The creators get to be the Major Arcana. Tollevin, Randall, Renée, myself, two or three others."

I'm absolutely amazed. I've never in my entire life heard something so incredibly wonderful. Tarot gangs. Tarot get-togethers. A youth network based on magical cards from medieval times. I couldn't have come up with that in a million years. It's all too great. This kid is fucking brilliant. "That's insane. You did all this?"

Surprisingly, he looks enraged. "*They* did it," he snaps. "I just came up with the whole idea one day after school with Randall, and it became this THING. Fucking . . . *look* at them. It's kind of pathetic, right?" I fidget a bit. Well, this is awkward. Randall's warning echoes in my head. Okay. One more question, then I'm done.

"Is that why you're sitting off to the side?"

"No, this is different. This is the heaviest shit you've ever known."

I'm about to go against my plan and ask him what that means when Tollevin leaps up onto the rock and yells, "PO-PO!"

The what now?

And like lightning, the candles are blown out and snatched

up, the instruments are packed away, and the kids are running, like stampeding cows. One kid, a hardcore-looking punk rock chick, comes running backward past us. "Didn't-youfuckinghearhimmanhesaidthepo-poareherefucking-RUN!LaterCasey!"

Casey waves drunkenly. "Later, Ivy."

I spy two policemen wriggling their fat asses over the edge of the rock, grunting stuff about permits and big trouble. A couple of the punks and metal heads start throwing rocks and bottles, which isn't helping. Suddenly there are two nightsticks in two chubby Irish hands, ready to beat some counterculture ass. Randall shoots me a frantic look, nods, and bolts into the park.

"Shit! Casey, c'mon!"

Casey slowly gets up and nearly falls to the ground in the process. "Shit," he says, giggling. "Fucking *whiskey* . . ."

One of the cops sees us and points to the other one. Two words come ringing out over the din that make my blood drop a couple degrees: "HEY, YOU!" I've never had a run-in with the cops before, and personally I don't want to. Getting picked up downtown by my mom would suck. Even worse, I don't want to start an argument with people who won't listen, which is exactly what these two fat, badged, on-edge pieces of shit look like. If the venom breaks out, there would be less Partying without a Permit and more He Must Be on PCP. So I do the only thing I can think of: I hook one of Casey's arms around my shoulder and we start running.

I expect the cops to leave us be when we sprint away, but no dice. They're on our asses from the moment we hightail it. Zigzagging, ducking through bushes, nothing works; I glance over my shoulder and they're behind me, stumbling through the park and swearing under their breath. The 72nd Street stairs come into view, and I begin panicking, because our options are down to Riverside or the Trump Pier, both of which are gonna be packed on a Saturday—

Something catches my eye. The venom twitches nervously, assuring me that it won't work, that confrontation's the only option. I swallow it down and go with the only glimmer of hope I have.

I wheel Casey like a sack of potatoes under the picnic table by the park's baseball diamond, and duck underneath it, squeezed in next to him, our breath quick and purposefully shallow.

"So gentle," he slurs.

"Shut the fuck up," I hiss.

Through the opening between the bench and the table, I see the cops, their silhouettes distinguishable only by their cute little hats. They stop, the fatter of the two leaning over on his own knees, panting.

"You see 'em? Did you see where they went?"

Pant, pant. "I think"—pant, pant—"I think we lost 'em back"—pant, pant. Goddammit, just leave—"by the restrooms."

"Ah, shit." The less fat one whips back and forth, hoping to catch a blur of frightened teenager, but no dice. "Unbelievable."

"Long." Pant. "Coat." Pant. "Couldn't'a gone far."

"Fucking kids. Let's head back, clean up." The thinner one stalks back to the rock. The fatter one follows, gulping and gasping as he goes.

A full minute after they disappear, I start breathing again. Casey and I duck out from under the picnic table. We somehow drag our carcasses up the stairs to the tunnel leading out to Riverside Drive. My brain is bobbing in a sea of adrenaline. I can barely hold the cigarette I jam into my face. The night air was never this refreshing before.

Casey laughs like a terrified madman, head back, brow glistening. "I can't believe . . . we . . . that was inten—" Before the word ends, his body lurches like it shouldn't, and a seemingly endless stream of whiskey-infused horrible gray shit comes pouring out of his mouth and over the edge of the stone balcony, down onto the grass below. The smell hits my nostrils like acid. I smoke harder.

When he's done puking, Casey sits up on the ledge a little ways from me and says, "Thanks. I owe you one for that." His torso hangs like an unused marionette.

I just nod and light my smoke. "Why do the cops hate you guys so much?"

He shrugs. "We leave candle wax and trash everywhere. That and, y'know, the drinking and pot smoking. Mostly, it's just our healthy disrespect for authority."

I nod again, still a little miffed. "I don't think I like the police."

"Good job being a teenager there," he snorts.

My mind catches up with the rest of my system, and my train of thought comes chugging back to life. "Is that the heavy shit you were talking about?"

His head wheels upward, face scrunched. "Pardon?"

"You said you were dealing with 'heavy shit.' Organizing this get-together, the cops—that it?"

His body shakes with lazy chuckles. "No, no, I have . . . sort of personal issues."

"What do you mean?"

His eyes focus on some point in the air, and he opens and closes his mouth, like a fish, before he hooks onto the words he needs. "Have you ever just . . . have you ever gotten angry to, like, the point where it takes you over?"

Wham. I'm interested. "Yes."

"Well, I have that, but not . . . not like, tantrums. I have this . . . this uncontrollable thing in me that just cuts loose when I get angry or depressed enough, like this violent . . .

beast inside of me. Like my Mr. Hyde, only worse, only it's not just evil, it's me, it's got my morals and intelligence. I don't become someone else. I just become a perverted version of myself." He shrugs and snorts out a shoelace of vomit-snot. "I know this doesn't make any sense. It's named the black. . . . Well, that's what I call it, anyway. And it sort of took over my life tonight, and so I tried to drown it in booze. That normally works." He looks at me as though he's explained this too many times, and he's used to the standard response. "It's okay if you don't get it."

"No," I say softly, "no, no, wait."

My confession ends around the same time the smokes run out. I've told him things I realize I shouldn't have. It wasn't in my control. I told him about my father, about the few girls I'd tried to be with, and about the violence. The violence was the meat of it, the part full of yelling and swearing and pulling at my hair. But he listened. He heard me, and not like Randall. There wasn't a lot of "sure" and "yuh-huh." None of the wise, thoughtful nods that suggested he was thinking deeply on the subject. He listened to me like I was telling him about himself, and then he described his problem, his situation, which was my own. For the first time, both problems were the same. For the first time in . . . in forever, I guess, I was talking to somebody who thought of the venom as a reality. Imagine that. Imagine what it's like to finally find somebody who understands not what you're getting at, but *exactly what you're talking about*, after eleven fucking *years* of people either not giving a shit or screwing up the message along the way. It's like everyone on Earth has always been blind except for you, and then one day, someone walks up to you and asks you how you feel about the color blue. I couldn't *not* talk.

And now we're sitting on the ledge and looking out at the tunnel. We've both gone silent now; we have been for about ten, fifteen minutes; a little embarrassed on top of all our massive relief. It's as though we're naked for the first time in our lives, proud of each other for facing up to ourselves. I feel more comfortable than I've felt with anyone else in a long time, except maybe my mom, but that's different, because with my mom, even though she doesn't understand, she loves me. And while I don't really know this guy, he understands.

When I turn to look at him, I realize that he's staring straight at me. He's got something slightly resembling a smile on his face, and I'm not quite sure what is going on.

"I know, right?" I say, nodding. "Incredible."

He cocks his head to the side. "Yeah, that's one way of putting it."

And then he reaches up and takes my glasses off, and

my vision gets blurry, and I start to get nervous, because I know that movement and I know what it could mean, and it begins to worry me, because if it turns out that I'm right, I'll be dealing with the most ridiculous, ass-backward thing I could ever imagine, which, given the context of the night (partying, kissing Goth girl, drinking a little bit, running from the cops, and finally releasing my demons to a kindred spirit), would be appropriate while at the same time really, really harrowing. And it means *exactly* what I think it means, because Casey leans over and kisses me really softly, on the lips.

The first thing I think is, *Mmm. Vomit.* Then I wonder if I should elbow him in the stomach and knock him off the ledge, but that's the venom talking. I'm not really pissed at him anyway. I'm just . . . surprised. And uncomfortable, sure, horribly uncomfortable. But the weird thing is, I let him do it. I sort of sit there and . . . get kissed. Not because I enjoy it or because I'm attracted to him, just 'cause . . . Well, honestly, I feel like I owe him one for hearing me out and understanding, for making me feel anything but crazy. Which feels cheap. And wrong. And easy. But I don't know . . . This is new. Everything is new. Tonight has been a series of firsts; this is just the worst one of them so far.

He breaks the kiss and I say, "Casey. Casey. Hey."

"Mmm," he purrs tipsily, "that was nice."

"Casey. Wait." He doesn't back off. Not good. This has to stop before my owing him one turns into him taking it as a go-ahead or a come-on. "No, we can't. No."

"No one's stopping us," he says slowly, leaning his face toward mine again. His breath blows hot on my face; it reeks of puke and dude.

My senses slingshot back to reality, and my hand snaps onto his shoulder and shoves him back. I snatch my glasses back and fumble putting them on.

"I'm stopping us," I say solidly. "I'm not . . . y'know. I'm not."

He stares at me for a second, dumbfounded, like a little kid. All of a sudden, I feel terrible. I shouldn't have let him kiss me. That was wrong. I should have pushed him away the minute he tried. But no, like a timid little idiot, I let him go ahead and expect something of me that I—

And then it happens. I notice a cord on his neck stick out and a vein near his forehead bulge a bit. His face goes tight. The mouth curls into an oyster of resentment while the eyes stay bugged and hard. Something inside of him goes away; what replaces it is hate. Not rage or passion but hate—cold, dead, twisted hate.

I can see the black rising inside his eyes.

"Hey, wait. Casey. Wait."

"Fuck you."

He's not listening. He shoves me hard, throwing me off the ledge and onto the concrete. My shoulder blade screams in pain, but I manage to start lifting myself up slowly, just as he leaps down from the edge. Something registers that I'm lucky he didn't throw me off the edge of the stairs. There's no good end to this.

"You're not *what?*" he snarls, pushing his face in front of mine. By now, all the cords on his neck are taut, like wires, and there are little flecks of spit at the corners of his mouth. "You're not a *faggot*, huh? You're not a *cocksucker*, is that it?"

"No, hey, c'mon man, that's not what I meant—"

"Then why not fucking *say it*, huh? Why even talk to me about all this if you're just going to freak out and gawk at the *queer*? Jesus, most guys don't fucking KISS ME if they're not at least a little interested. What the fuck is wrong with you?"

"That's a really good ques—"

"Save it, shithead!" A gob of saliva wheels off his lower lip and dangles. His eyes are glowing white, surrounded by a road map of creased skin. "I don't want to hear any more of your BULLSHIT. I don't have TIME for people as worthless as you. Wow, no wonder Randall never brought you around. He must be hard-pressed for friends at your fucking school."

In the back of my skull, the venom starts buzzing, vibrating my teeth, my eyes. *Asking for it,* it almost whispers, *he's asking for it. Go ahead. Simple solutions are often the best ones, Locke.* No, no, no. There has to be a painless way out of this.

"Look, I didn't mean that at all," I say pleadingly. "I was just surprised and scared. Please don't—"

"Oh, fuck you, Locke. *Fuck. YOU.* You tell me all this stuff about yourself, and I think, 'Wow, here's someone who's different, who understands!' But you're just like everyone else. You don't know anything. You don't know about the black. I've had to deal with bullshit from people like you for as long as I can remember, and just because you got teased, or your daddy ran away, or life didn't hand you a bouquet of peonies, you think you're fucking Hamlet. Shouldn't you be off cutting yourself somewhere?"

Part of me starts saying that he's drunk and he's got the black in him and he doesn't mean all this (and that peonies are sort of an odd choice), but it's all white noise to the Locke that's standing here. I can feel my pupils dilate and my veins wash over with emotional poison. The muscles flex. The dam breaks.

He understands, my mind pleads, *he cares. He's just in a mood. There's no need to be too hard on him for it. He's confused and hurt. This can't happen.*

You tried, you failed. Fuck off. My turn.

I'm not sure whether his throat feels soft or if my hand feels oddly strong, but soon one's around the other. His face goes from hardened to clueless; he should have considered that maybe, just maybe, I wasn't the guy to piss off. Just like his little outburst took me off guard, he's never met anyone else who's felt the venom before, he's only experienced it firsthand.

Let's see just how fucking well he enjoys a fistful of his own medicine.

"How dare you," I growl, "how fucking dare you, you presumptuous piece of dog shit. Just because I don't want your tongue in my fucking mouth doesn't mean I'm a goddamn bigot, you hear me? DO YOU?"

The twitch his head makes is, I'm pretty sure, a nod. It's worn off for him, so now it's my show.

"I just wanted someone to talk to! I never told you I wanted you to fuck me, now did I? DID I? Now I realize you were only in it for a quick fuck, huh? *You're* just like the rest of 'em, you fucking ASSHOLE. All you want is to get your way and feel good about yourself for it. I don't need to take shit from anyone, but especially not from a poor, lonely *queen* like you."

My hand snaps open, and he thuds to the ground with a gasp. He's so little to look down on. Not even worth the strain of a good kick in the ribs.

"I hope you fucking DIE," I hiss. "And if you ever mention my father again, I'll see to it you DO." There's a swirl of my overcoat, and I'm walking uptown.

By the time I get to 79th Street, the venom has gone out for drinks, and I'm left sobbing. I didn't mean to hurt Casey, but it just happened. Why'd he have to treat me like the enemy? I didn't even know he was gay. It didn't matter. I'd finally met somebody who really, truly understood the way I felt, and it all went to shit. When you're a fucking monster, not even the other monsters will be there for you.

Once I'm home, I walk slowly to my room, hoping to just get there and fall right asleep. No such luck: My mom, waiting up for me as always, sees me and motions for me to sit next to her on the couch. Once I'm up close, it's obvious that things aren't okay. She claps her book shut and sits up attentively.

"Hey," I say, focusing on my hands.

"What's up, honey?" my mom says. Her head ducks to try and make eye contact.

I shrug. "Nothing. We hung out in the park. Played some music."

"Sounds fun."

"Yeah, I had a pretty good night. I dunno, something weird happened, though. I had an . . . angry."

"Are you all right?" Her eyes narrow. "Did you get high?"

"Mom . . . no." Every so often, I forget my mom is A Mom, and then she busts out with a gem like that. "Someone made . . . improper advances toward me." Wow. Just about as stupid as it sounds.

My mom puts on this really sly smile. "Must've been one pushy girl."

I glance back. "Wasn't a girl."

Her smile disappears. We start talking.

THE ALLEYWAYS whipped past me as I flew through the narrow passages between buildings. The creature from the other night had preempted me three more times, but I had finally managed to surprise it as it was finished squeezing the life out of some dirtbag with a gun and an ego. Now I was rushing after it, barely keeping up with its lopes and bounds. All I could tell of its figure was that it was huge, twice the size of a normal man, that it had tentacles of some sort hanging from its body, and that its presence felt . . . familiar. For some reason, the city's song grew in me when I neared it, as if in recognition.

The massive silhouette grunted as it began leaping over a chain-link fence separating two alleyways. I pushed myself, forcing my body to fly faster, putting my fists out in front of me and charging my body with dark energy.

"STOP!" I called as I slammed into its back. The creature bellowed, and we exploded through the fence, crashing among newspapers and other wretched detritus. I was on my feet in a second, shaking the impact from my brain.

The being appeared like a huge octopus, a lump trailing a mass of black, slimy tentacles.

"Can you speak?" I whispered. No answer. Tentatively I reached out my hand to touch the lump—

The thing roared and reared back, showing me its full form. Horror filled my heart.

It was hard to describe what it was. It distinctly had the form of a human—arms, legs, eyes—but its attributes were hideously bestial. From its face, fingers, chest, knees, there came huge twisting masses of black tentacles, pulsating and grappling—a sewer anemone, if you will. Its face was almost like an insect's: Two huge segmented eyes stared vacantly at me from a round head, another wriggling mess of black feelers where its mouth should have been. Its form was muscular, but it bent and turned as though it had millions of joints in every part of its body. There was nothing fluid about its posture or movement; it seemed to twitch its way around things rather than actually walk or crawl. As a being, an existing entity, it was just not right.

"My God . . . ," I whispered.

The monster responded by sending one of its massive claws smashing into my head. I felt my body, limp and helpless, hit a brick wall. Red dust and blinding light filled my vision, and I stumbled, trying to regain my footing. When I looked up, the thing had disappeared into the night.

Whatever the monster was, it was dangerous. And if it could hurt me, *something was wrong. Somehow it had found a way to access the city's negative energy as well. It had powers similar to mine.*

Next time. Next time I would be ready for it.

CHAPTER FOUR

"LOCKE! TELEPHONE!"

Maybe if I push my face hard enough into my pillow, I'll sink into it and disappear forever.

"LOCKE!"

No dice. "For Christ's . . . Who is it?"

"No idea!" my brother yells out.

Yuck. Something happened to my hair last night. It's grosser than normal. What day is it? Sunday? Has to be. I was out last night. My mouth tastes like vomit and my shoulder blade hurts. I wonder—oh. Oh wait. Oh yes, thank you, memory, you bastard. The collage of emotions that was my night whizzes before my mind's eye: first excitement, then joy, then fear, then rage, then disappointment. Jesus, Locke, if this isn't proof that you just shouldn't leave the house, I don't know what is.

My hand scrambles around the floor of my room, among books, magazines, CDs, and socks. Phone . . . phone . . . there. I grab the cordless and put it to my ear, pressing the talk button. "Mrf. Hello?"

"Locke?"

There's something about the voice that I can't put my finger on. "Yes?"

"It's Casey."

I wake up really quickly. He sounds like a different person when he's sober. More timid, maybe. How did he know my number? "How do you know my number?"

"Randall gave it to me." A pause. "Did I wake you?"

I shake my head, then realize he can't see that. Locke Vinetti as the yardstick of human intelligence. "No, my little brother woke me."

He chuckles. "You know what I mean."

"It's no big deal. Really."

"Okay." Another pause. This one's much longer than the last one. I'm *this* close to blurting out, *So, about last night* when Casey cuts in. "You live on Eighty-sixth and Broadway, right?"

"Yeah?"

"Wanna go to Three Star?"

Is this a joke? Getting lunch with this guy is the last thing I want to do. "Um, wow, I'm not sure that's, y'see, my mom needs some help today. I gotta look after Lon, my brother."

"I won't keep you long. C'mon, just get a burger."

"No, I mean, if it were up to me, man—"

"Come on, Locke, give me..." He sighs, then takes a deep breath. "Listen, Locke, I know it's asking a lot, but please, do me this favor, even if you owe me nothing. I'm no good at this, but just . . . five minutes, if that. I promise. You're free to bail at any time, guilt free."

He sounds desperate and confused to the point of tears. Cruelty isn't in my nature (*Locke's* nature). I make plans and hope I won't regret them.

Three Star Coffee Shop is a diner on 86th Street and Columbus. It's a quaint, ratty little place with great coffee and great burgers—and that's it. Everything else there is terrible. Their fries aren't even that good. But seeing as it's already 11:30 by the time I wake up, I think a burger and some coffee might do me good.

As I walk out of the house, I yell out to the house in general, "Mom! I'm going out to lunch!"

"With who?" I hear from somewhere in the apartment.

I brace myself. "Casey!"

The next thing I know, my mom's in front of me, wiping her hands on a rag, one eyebrow almost leaping off her face. "Casey. The boy from last night." I nod slowly.

Her eyes become slits. "So why are you going out to lunch with him?"

"I dunno. He sounded like he wanted to apologize."

"I'm not sure I want you spending time with this creepy little rapist."

"Mom, he's not a rapist."

"No one treats anyone that way, Locke, and especially not my boy."

"Mom, come on. He's, y'know, troubled." The words leave my mouth, and I realize what I'm trying to get at. "Like me."

She shakes her head, but I can see her face soften a little. It clicks. "All right. Just don't let him try anything else, okay? Remember, honey, men are pigs. They're thinking with something other than their minds, something arguably smaller and certainly less important."

"You always wanted a daughter, didn't you?"

She laughs. "Just so I could say that."

"That last part, the 'arguably smaller' bit, that was good. You're funny."

"Don't be a wiseass. No one likes a clever teenager."

Casey's there among the tobacco-tooth yellow interior of Three Star, staring into a cup of coffee as if it was a scattering of animal bones and he was a shaman. My nerves shiver at the very sight of him. Sweat starts forming on my brow and chest.

I'm not used to having lunch with people I hardly know. The only reason I even considered approaching Casey last night was because everyone had seemed so cool and relaxed with me. And here we are, in the most intense conversational situation imaginable. Welcome to my nightmare.

I walk in and sit down across from Casey. He looks up and smiles a little, resting his head on his folded hands. It's all bullshit, though; a vein like a blue tree root throbs under his brow. He's terrified.

I order a cheeseburger with Swiss and a cup of coffee, and we sit in silence.

Finally Casey says those fateful words. "So, um, about last night."

I can't help but laugh a little. He looks up, slightly hurt, a little jumpy. I just shake my head and say, "It sounds like we had unprotected sex."

He grins. "You're right. Sorry. Nerves. Weird position I'm in. Don't quite know . . ."

"Same."

"Well, I've never been choked before, I'll tell you that," he says, sipping his coffee. He tugs back at the collar of his shirt, and I wince: On either side of his throat are perfect little circular bruises, obviously from my fingers. I feel like I'm on *COPS*. "That was new. Definitely helps my street cred."

"Glad I can help," I say. My face begins to burn. I'm such a jerk. Normal people, *healthy* people, don't do things like that. Everything's dramatic and powerful, out of my control, until I have to stare down the ugly purple marks that my "situation" leaves behind.

He reads me with a glance and frowns. "I'm not trying to be glib, man. It was okay that you choked me. I think it was for the best." My shrug doesn't seem like enough for him, so he keeps pushing. "I mean, how do you feel after last night, if you don't mind me asking?"

"How do I feel?" This isn't the question I was expecting.

"Yeah. What're your reactions?"

"How the fuck do you expect me to feel?" I blurt, getting venom-tremors along my fingers and forearms. "When I said all that shit, I kept punctuating it with 'never told anyone this before' for a reason, dammit, and then it all gets spat back at me because I'm not a . . ."

Casey beams as I twitch and sputter. "Oh, man, this is the best part. Watching you search for a term."

My face floods cherry, 'cause he's got me right on the money. "That's not funny. This isn't funny."

"Are you kidding? This is hilarious! This is like the part in a Van Damme movie where they explain the accent!"

"Shut up! I'm not a homophobe!"

"I never said you were," he says, now compassionate. His eyes still have the knowledge they carried last night, an unfamiliar understanding; he knew exactly what buttons he was pushing and how many times he could push them while still being fair. "That's not what I'm trying to do here, Locke. I'm sorry."

"I didn't even know you were gay." I sigh. "You left that part out when we were talking. I didn't *know*."

"You're a guy," he says. "It freaks a lot of guys out. Makes them think I'm just going to hit on 'em nonstop. Plus, Randall's friend and all, you know how it is."

"So what, you *don't* tell me so I won't see it coming? *Thanks*."

"Okay, okay, bad explanation. Forget it, I'm a moron." He holds up his hands in defense, giving me his most humbled, pitiful look. "Last night was my fault, no questions asked. I'm really, really sorry I acted that way, and you have every right to be mad."

The question that's racked my brain all night bubbles up to the surface: *"Why?"*

His eyes go to his coffee, irritated, angry at himself. "Number of reasons, I guess . . . Well, the easy one is that I just broke up with someone. Religious kid, typical self-loather. He got in a fight with me Thursday night, called me a lot of really fucking awful things, and then told me never to call him again. Which is why I was sitting alone, drinking myself into a warm little coma. So there's that. . . ."

He makes eye contact with me again, and it hurts; there's shame there, the kind that I recognize on a daily basis. "But also, y'know . . . You're not the only one who realized they weren't alone last night. The black is something that's been screwing with me, mucking up my whole existence, for as long as I can remember, and soon I convinced myself that it was just me. That my anger, my hate, was unique, because it existed in a way that no one else seemed to understand. Trying to kiss you last night was sort of impulsive and . . . and *drunken*, but a good deal of it was . . . excitement? Rejoicing?" He shakes his head. "That's the best I can do. I'm sorry, Locke. Really, really uncool, I know."

My cheeseburger comes, and I load ketchup onto it, giving myself time to think through this emotional swamp before me. How can I hate him for feeling the same elation I did, knowing there was someone who gets it? The venom growls, aching for action, but I manage to push it down with a bite of burger. Condemning Casey any further for acting the way he did last night wouldn't be warranted; it would be cruel, unnecessary.

"Well, look," I say, "I'm not gay, so please don't try that shit again."

"Yeah, duly noted." He chuckles. "Well, there go my plans for the afternoon."

I laugh despite myself, and he can tell we've slain the monster of this particular conversation, and we're okay again. The laugh feels good, unscripted, real. "You okay from last night? I didn't do any real damage, did I?"

"Nah, after some coughing and sputtering, I was fine. I ended up going to Renée's, spilling my heart out to her about the whole thing."

The venom raises its head, interest piqued. "You told Renée about what happened?"

"Yeah. She likes you, by the way. I can tell. Randall really has talked about you a lot, you know? We've been *mad* excited to—"

"Bullshit, Casey, don't try to make me feel okay. My dad does that voice on Christmas a lot better. You didn't tell her about me, did you? About, y'know. The venom."

"Well . . . yeah," he says, puzzled. "Kind of an important part of the story, that."

Anxiety explodes into my head. "Oh fuck, Casey, why? That was private! I didn't expect you to tell anyone about . . . fuck. *Fuck*."

"Oh, get over yourself." He sneers. "Look, Renée's been one of my best friends since God knows when. She knows all about the black, so it's not like you freaked her out that much or anything. Honestly, the only thing that upset her in the least is that I made a move on you. Relax."

As we finish up the meal and pay, I try to calm myself,

pushing away the idea that any chance I had with Renée is already poisoned and heading toward a slow death. We come out into the glaring autumn sunshine, burning out our retinas from a hundred reflections in a hundred apartment windows. Casey effortlessly throws on a pair of stylish wraparounds, transforming him from angsty teenage gay guy to slick badass villain. Which reminds me.

"Can I ask you a question?"

Casey nods.

"When you're . . . every night, going to sleep, I have a character, or a couple of characters, and I play out situations in my head. They're superheroes, or wizards, and the venom is . . . their power, the source of what drives them. It feels really childish, but I play out these story lines in my head, and it makes me feel safe, like the venom's not my enemy anymore." I gauge his reaction to my ramblings and find it's not wary or weirded-out, but anticipatory. "Do you do that?"

"Not really," he says slowly, his brow furrowed seriously. "It's not characters and superheroes for me, but I sometimes think of the black as a power. Something I can use, tap into if need be. *However*, while we're on the subject of superheroes . . ." He reaches into his tote bag and pulls a book out with sort of a Shakespearean flourish. "Check page forty-five." There's a slap on my shoulder and a warm smile, and then he bounds away uptown in a jovial, charming sort of way.

The book is a graphic novel, a collection of Spider-Man comics. The cover shows Spider-Man leaping out of the path of what looks like his evil twin, a big, bulky Spider-Man dressed all in black with a gaping mouth full of sharp alligator teeth and a long, thick tongue. The character looks familiar, and I try and remember who he is for a few seconds before looking at the book's title.

The cover reads, *Spider-Man versus Venom!*

The world around me goes silent, and everything on Earth becomes this all-too-perfect creature trying to tear Peter Parker a new one on the cover of this book. This is going to be good.

Absentmindedly I flip to page forty-five. Sitting there is a small scrap of paper reading, "Renée," followed by a phone number and an address.

This is going to be very, very good.

The rest of the day is spent in my room, on my bed, with this book open, falling in love with Todd McFarlane, comic-book artist extraordinaire.

Venom's actual name is Eddie Brock. Apparently he was a big-time reporter until Spider-Man exposed him as a fraud and his career got ruined, after which he was forced to write for tabloids and scrape together just enough cash to eat. He blames Spider-Man for the whole ordeal. Then one night, while he's trying to kill himself, he's attacked by the symbiote, this black, drippy alien that Spider-Man used to have as a costume before he realized it would try and bond with him for life—this thing lives inside a person and manifests itself as a suit, pouring out of the host's body like black fluid coating. The symbiote bonds with Brock, and he becomes Venom, who's basically Spider-Man's insane, buff, and utterly hideous doppelgänger. He's a good guy at heart, really. Just homicidal.

How the hell have I not discovered this character before? I have the Internet (Topher Grace played him in the movie? Is that a joke?). I'm kind of a geek, in that I don't have many friends and like reading. But this whole time, there's been a character in comics literature that looks, acts, feels like he was created for no one but me, and I've been clueless to his existence. What the hell, man? Watching him get beaten down every issue is murder. Every sanctimonious speech Spider-Man screams out about innocence and sanity, I want Venom to open his huge caiman mouth and bite that little red head off.

On my way back from grabbing a soda from the kitchen, Lon spies the comic book in my hand. "I didn't know you read Spider-Man," he says excitedly. It's the first time he's really spoken to me since the whole bookstore thing yesterday, so I take what I can get.

"I don't, really," I say, "but a friend gave this to me. It's really good."

"Spider-Man's cool," Lon says, smiling at me.

"Yeah, but Venom's cooler."

He nods thoughtfully, as though I've just stated a universal truth. "Yeah, Venom is really cool. Carnage is cooler, though."

This statement means nothing to me. "Nuh-uh."

"Uh-huh."

"Nuh-uh."

"Uh-huh."

"Nuh-uh times infinity."

Lon looks at me funny and says in a diabolical voice, "You've won this round, boy."

I actually try not to laugh, but it's no use. He's such an amazing kid. He's so witty and smart and prepared for anything; you can see the gears in his head working at all times. If the Rapture came down tomorrow, Lon would have his bags packed. If Godzilla attacked, he'd have his English subtitles organized and spell-checked. Like I said before, he's basically the anti-me, a fact that I am grateful for every day of the week. There's only enough room for one wretched fuckup in this house.

But that's not what's really on my mind right now. Right now, I have something else to deal with.

"Stay off the phone, okay?" I say, and saunter back to my lair.

One ring. Two rings. Calm down. The scrap of paper begins to dampen in my palm from all the sweat. I'm trying to hold the phone steady with the other hand, but it's kind of hard when you're this nervous. The phone vibrates, like an angry fucking ferret.

A click. Some music in the background. "Hello?"

I gulp. "Hi, is Renée there?"

"This is she."

Calm down. "Um, hi, it's me."

Silence.

"That really doesn't help me much. . . ."

I AM A FUCKING IDIOT. "It's Locke. From last night. Sorry. Locke here."

"Locke!" she chirps. "Locke, Locke, Locke. How are you, Locke?"

"I'm fine. Sorry about, y'know, not saying my name when I first called, I was just thinking that maybe—"

"Locke?"

"Mmm-hmm?"

"Breathe."

In. Close. Hold. Out. "Gyah. Sorry."

"Totally cool. ¿*Qué pasa?*"

"How're you?"

"I'm great. I'm playing Scrabble with my cat."

"Are you, now?"

"Word. He's not very good. Lots of 'meow's and a 'hiss' once in a while. So, how was lunch with Casey?"

"You know about that?"

"I am the Hierophant. I hear all."

At some point, someone will be kind enough to tell me what that means. "Right. It went fine. He apologized, and I ate a burger, and it . . . was fine."

"Mmm, burger. Did he give you my comic book?"

"The comic book is yours?"

"Mmm-hmm. Y'know what? This whole phone conversation thing just doesn't really work for me. I don't get to see your eyes widen in terror, and what fun is that? You should come over."

Holy hell, I've never met a girl this forward. "Should I?"

"Definitely. I'm sure you'll be a better Scrabble player than Dupin here."

"Um . . . okay . . . Dupin? Like, 'Murders in the Rue Morgue'?"

"Impressive. Now get your ass over here."

• • •

When I show up at Renée's place, she's wearing a black T-shirt advertising something called BAKER STREET, with a picture of a straight razor on it, and black jeans. There's less of the eye makeup, lipstick, and paler, making her look less Goth, but still considerably vampiric. Her smile, however, suggests anything but darkness and despair. Her apartment is smaller than mine but much better kept and massively better smelling. She leads me to her room, apologizing for the mess, or as she calls it, "the abattoir that is my life." That's a direct quote, by the way.

Her room is just how I imagined it: covered in posters of bands and horror movies, filled with black candles, dripping with teenage pain. Her bed has a black veil around it, making it look like one big funeral shroud. All around the room are blinking Christmas lights in the shape of skulls. Incense burns in the corner. The place smells like a church. Clothes are strewn around the floor; the only white garments are socks.

I've never really gotten the whole Goth thing. Maybe it's just me, but I've always sort of felt that one's dark side is just that: the part of themselves that they keep hidden for a reason. So the idea of purposefully reveling in the things that make you dismal and frightening just seems counterproductive to me, even a little ridiculous. I mean, people should be focused on making themselves better human beings, right? Renée seems different about it, though. She cracks jokes about herself and the gloom-and-doom motif, almost adoring the silliness of the entire Goth lifestyle. It's as though the aesthetic is what drives her, not the feelings of inner pain. Which makes her sort of a poser, I guess. But I'd rather have a happy-go-lucky Goth wannabe than a kid stewing in some inner agony that doesn't actually exist.

In the center of the room sits a Scrabble board with a cat on one side, licking its paw and dragging it across its head.

"That's Dupin."

"I guessed." Glancing down at the board, I notice a "MEOW," a "ROWR," one "HISS," and a "HACK" in a row. The cat is staring with an intent expression, and for a second I wonder if it actually was playing.

I look down at the words closest to me on the board. "TURN AROUND."

I do that, and there she is, standing about two inches away from me. Her breasts are actually *just* touching my chest.

"You're not a very social animal, are you?" she says slowly.

I shake my head. I can barely breathe, much less speak.

She cocks hers to one side. "Why? You're cute enough. You seem nice."

"I'm not as cute and nice as you think," I manage, trying not to sound too melodramatic. "I'm a bit of a bastard, when it comes down to it. Kind of a loser."

"Really? Then why haven't I seen this bastard? Where does he live? What's he into?"

"Why are you asking me these questions?"

"Because you puzzle me," she murmurs. "You're very puzzling."

"You've only known me for, like, a day. Of course I'm puzzling; who wouldn't be?"

She puts her index fingers by the sides of her head and twirls them, the international symbol for *loco en la cabeza*. "But I am the Hierophant, remember?"

I shake my head again and wave her fingers away. "What does that mean, anyway? What's a Hierophant?"

"One of the Major Arcana—"

"No, no, I get that," I interrupt with a sigh, "but what is it?"

By this time, I'm aware of the fact that we're leaning incredibly close to each other. I'm staring into her eyes, can feel her breath on my lips. She smells a little like chocolate.

"The interpreter of inner secrets and arcane knowledge," she whispers.

My voice begins to quaver. "And so you're thinking," I say softly, turning my head just a little to the side, "that you can interpret me."

Time slows and reality fades, and—

Whoosh, she's gone before I can say another word. There's

some masterful darting and leaping around the room, until she's back in her place opposite Dupin and cleaning off the board. Dupin takes the cue that the game is over and hops up onto her bed, circling his place twice, and then hitting the sheets with an audible thud. "Come!" calls Renée. "Let us Scrabble!"

As I sit there trying to figure out a word with both a *Q* and an *X* in it, I jump right into what's been on my mind since I left the house. "Thanks for the comic book."

She keeps her eyes on the board. "Hmm?"

"The comic book," I say. "I really enjoyed it."

"Everyone likes Spider-Man. He's cool."

"Yeah, well, I like Venom more."

"So do I."

I stare hard at her. "Yeah, but I think we like him for different reasons."

A shit-eating grin covers her face. "I bet."

And that's all it takes. There's a thrust of misery with a pinch of infuriation, and the venom fills me like a drug. This time, though, it's the loathing and shame, not the explosive rage: I feel clammy instead of warm, lifeless instead of energized, embarrassed instead of bold. The room grows cold, and I try to burrow into my coat, hoping it'll take me away from this beautiful girl who knows my most horrible secrets.

The venom loves it. *Hope you enjoyed that kiss, buddy,*

it croaks, *'cause it's the last. She knows. Two words: damaged goods.*

"Hey," she says. She leans over the Scrabble board and runs a hand along the side of my face, warm to the touch. Its movement is one of comfort, and it works. As her hand glides along my skin, the worry disappears, and the despair blows away. "Bad moment there?"

I force a nod. "Came on kind of quick. Sorry. Really sorry."

"No apologies," she says, turning back to the game. "I've been friends with Casey since we were ten, and he's had the black for as long as I've known him. I've had some bad run-ins with it too. But that's no reason to be afraid of him. Someone's issues don't have to define them as a person, do they?" She puts down the word "GOTH."

I cross with it, using the *O*: "LOSER."

She glances at me and smirks. "I mean, are you defined by this 'venom'? Does that make you who you are?"

The harder I try to say something, the harder the venom pushes down on me. The room is suffocating, incense and candle smoke choking me. The shadowy decor blurs together into a squirming ocean of black. Eye contact is out of the question. The venom whispers angrily at me, doing everything it can to keep me from divulging its secrets. "It affects everything," I finally say, running my hands through my hair. And sighing. "It *poisons* everything. Every time I think I'm better, it comes back, and it laughs at me. I'm losing track of who running the show these days—me or it."

She cocks an eyebrow. "Well, *that's* not a good sign."

"It's not my choice."

"I didn't say that. Just that it's not okay."

"I know that. God, how could I not know that?"

She puts down a word in front of me, unconnected to the others. I'm about to tell her that she can't do that when I read the word: "UHOH."

"Why'd you—" Before I can finish the sentence, Renée's flung the Scrabble board aside, bent back on her haunches, and sprung forward onto me like a huge house cat. My trench curls around us like seaweed, tangling and binding me until I'm useless. Pretty soon, she has me in a headlock and is giving me a noogie.

"Say 'Uncle Fester'!" she yells.

"Buh! Never!"

"Say it!"

"Make me!"

She swiftly stops noogie-ing me and lets me out of the headlock. I'm sitting up, leaning against the side of her bed, and she leaps onto me, straddling me. I don't know how she moves like that, as though she's been raised in a jungle. Her face is right up in front of mine, moving as if she's trying to get my scent. "I could, you know," she whispers.

"Could what?" I gulp.

"I could make you," she mumbles, and lowers her lips slowly and softly onto mine, the way Casey did last night, only a lot better. She pulls the trench coat around her like wings, and with each kiss, each push together, we sink deeper into it. Finally, snuggled up together like we're in a big black cocoon, she wraps her arms around my shoulders and nuzzles her face into my neck, stopping here and there for a little nibble. I pull my arms inside my coat and wrap them around her waist, which feels liquid, agile, but soft and warm. Whatever I did to get this lucky, I'll never know.

"Mmm," she says. "This is nice."

I am inclined to agree with this.

Cuddling becomes resting, and resting becomes napping, and napping becomes most of the day's activity. Sleep is not an easy thing for me, especially with someone else present, because it means letting my guard down (summer camp sucked). The fact that I can fall asleep with this girl nestled on my chest? Unbelievable. Unheard of. Truly a miracle.

When my eyelids drag their way upward, I notice two things: (a) the clock on the wall says I should be home by now, and (b) there's someone knocking on the door.

I shake her back and forth. "Renée. Renée, wake up."

"Murf," she replies.

I hear the knocking again, louder this time. A woman's voice on the other side calls, "Renée! Renée, you there?"

She squirms in my lap and yells, "Come in!" in an annoyed whine.

Is this girl out of her mind? Delirious with fatigue? She's making no effort to get out of my lap, no effort to unbutton the coat containing both of us. What if her mom freaks out? What if I'm chased out of the house by an angry older brother? Or two? Or seven? I imagine using the hall fire extinguisher to smash open the skull of a burly Goth sibling, but shake the thought off quick. Venom talking. This isn't the time.

The door opens, and in waddles a chubby old lady with curly red hair and itty-bitty spectacles sitting on her huge face. "Oh, I'm sorry to interrupt," she says politely, with a tinge of French in her voice. "Renée, who is this?"

The monster. The pervert. The evil boy trying to defile your precious daughter.

"This is Locke," she mumbles. "Locke, this is my aunt Marie."

"Hiya." I cough.

"It's nice to meet you, Locke," she says warmly. "Locke . . . that name sounds vaguely French, does it not?"

"Maybe. My last name's Vinetti, though."

"That," she says with a chuckle, "sounds not in the least

French. Renée, just remember your brother's staying with a friend tonight, so you have to do the dishes."

"Umf," she says, and nuzzles back into my chest.

"Nice meeting you, Locke," says Aunt Marie, and closes the door.

"Wow," I heave. "I was scared she'd flip out."

"Aunt Marie doesn't care," she murmurs, shifting in my lap. "She trusts me. Besides, she's French. The French are a lot worse than this in public."

"So you have a brother?"

She nods.

"What's his name?" Maybe he and Lon could—

"Andrew. You know him."

Wait. Oh, shit, wait. Andrew. Can't be.

"Older or younger?"

"Older."

"Your last name isn't Tomas, is it?"

She shifts a bit more. She knew this topic of conversation *had* to come up at some point. "Yeah. I told you, you know him. He goes to your school."

He does. That's the problem. The venom writhes on its back, pointing and cackling, sending waves of worry through me. Nothing can be perfect for me. It's just not allowed.

THREE DAYS scouring the city, and no luck. The creature seemed to always be around, but it was rarely visible. A roar would sound and I'd turn left, only to hear claws clattering on the pavement to my right. The beast, while horrid, was incredibly intelligent, and it seemed to possess the hunting powers of a wolf. Even though I couldn't find it, I could feel those glassy eyes boring into me, twitching as it observed my presence.

I glided noiselessly through Central Park, indistinguishable from the shadows. I had been following the lanky junkie in front of me for a few minutes, waiting. Woe came off him in waves; I could smell his guilt, his hatred, from a block away. He was scrambling through the park, clutching a broken bottle, eyes wide, breath ragged, clothes filthy, hair wild. He was dangerous, and I had to be here to stop him.

The junkie came onto a path and approached a hobo lying curled on a bench.

"It was beautiful fabric," said the junkie sternly.

The bum looked back at him, half-awake. He was young, maybe twenty-five, and blond. "Whazuh?"

"IT WAS BEAUTIFUL FABRIC!" yelled the junkie. "YOU DIDN'T TAKE CARE OF IT RIGHT. NOW IT'S RUINED."

"Look, man, I don't know what you're on tonight, but—"

"Don't tell ME what to do," the junkie shrieked. "I MADE that. It was such a good situation before you came, and now we have NOTHING BUT TELEVISION!"

The junkie raised the jagged glass bottle high, an urban Norman Bates.

I raised a hand, and a lash of black lightning hit the glass, which exploded out of the doper's hand. He turned, enraged, but upon seeing me, fear took over, and he scrambled away with a scream.

The young bum sat up on the bench, eyes bright, face gnarled into a grimace.

"You have no need to worry," I said. "I mean you no harm."

The bum opened his mouth to scream, and all that came out was a hideous, blood-soaked roar.

Out of his mouth squirmed the tentacles—huge, meaty, writhing with a sound like wriggling scorpions; clicking mixed with squishing. All over his body, his skin seemed to stretch, bloat, and then split open, revealing the black many-tendriled body of the creature. Finally his eyes seemed to melt, dribbling down his face. Behind them sat two red, segmented orbs, twitching at me curiously, studying my every move.

CHAPTER FIVE

ANDREW TOMAS IS in my grade, but he's a year older than the rest of us because he got held back a year for being a smartass and an asshole. He wears Polo and North Face and Armani Exchange and refers to certain kids as "faggot motherfuckers." He's not a jock, although everything about him would suggest it. He listens to hardcore rap and tries to freestyle in the student lounge over the ghetto kids beatboxing. He has the Tasmanian Devil in bling-bling jewelry tattooed on his calf. He's a sadist, the worst kind of bitter, arrogant bully imaginable, who just wants to take his anger out on anyone who looks weaker than he does. *My* violence is something uncontrollable, a gut response to being treated a certain way; *his* is calculated and plain old mean. And while he makes my academic nightmare a living hell, his beautiful Goth sister holds my heart at her all-girls academy thirty blocks away.

I'm privileged enough to have moved from being a "faggot motherfucker" to being a "freak-ass bitch" in the vast, complicated mind of Andrew Tomas. The only reason I've had this wonderful privilege bestowed on me is because a kid who hangs out with Andrew named Omar once took my glasses off my head and started playing Monkey in the Middle with Andrew. What happened? Well, the venom went off and I tore Omar's eyebrow ring out, and when he tried to fistfight me afterward, I knocked one of his teeth loose. I got my glasses back and was immediately transferred from being a "faggot" to being a "freak" or "schizoid" or whatever the word of the day was, it doesn't fucking matter. It's one of the venom's most prominent traits: If you're someone I like, I'm a violent, twisted bastard. If you're someone I don't, I am the Marquis de fucking Sade. The only reason that Omar didn't report me to the administration was because telling the full story would've involved explaining why two strapping young lads were tormenting such a "sensitive" and "troubled" young boy as Locke Vinetti. Andrew, however, put my name down in his head.

If my life were an Archie comic, Andrew would be Reggie. On crack.

When I get to school Monday morning, I decide to speak privately to Randall about it.

"Did you know Renée is Andrew Tomas's younger sister?" I yell right into his face.

He holds up a finger—he needs to finish the paragraph in his book. *WHAM!* Down come my books on his desk, illustrating the urgency of the matter.

Randall looks up from his copy of *Kerosene* with a frustrated groan. "Jesus, Locke. You didn't know that?"

"No, I didn't fucking know that! She's YOUR friend, not mine! This girl's older brother is the jock asshole in an eighties movie! I'm fucked!"

Randall stares a bit, his face devoid of thought. "I don't see why this is so much of an issue."

The venom roars in anger. I blink hard. "Randall, what the hell are you talking about? There's no way I can be with this girl when her brother tortures me every day at school! I can just see a family dinner—'Hey, Andrew, pass the pork chops!' 'Here you go, you freak-ass bitch!'"

"Since when are you going to Renée's for family dinners?"

"Well, not *yet*," I say, turning crimson, "but perhaps someday I will! Perhaps I meet her mom and dad and all they've heard about is how much of a 'whack spazzoid' I am!"

Randall's face darkens. "I wouldn't worry about that, Locke."

"Why not? What part of this shit SHOULDN'T I worry about?"

He doesn't even look up from his book when he verbally punches me in the heart.

"Renée's parents are dead."

I reach for words and find a big empty space. I speak, and all I get is a thin, reedy noise, like a deflating balloon.

"Yeah," continues Randall. "*That* I didn't expect you to know. But it's something you should."

I suppose so.

"Wow. Randall, that's . . ."

"Explains a lot, doesn't it?"

I manage a slow nod and a gulp. "The Goth thing's not just for show, is it?"

"She's a dark one, man. You okay?"

"Yeah, it's just new, I . . . you know, I've never met an . . . orphan before."

"That's not a very PC word, man. Besides, Oliver Twist was an orphan. Annie was a fucking orphan. Renée's just a girl with no parents. Call her an orphan and she'll probably slug you." A smile crosses his lips, just a little; the idea amuses him.

"How'd they—"

"This line of questioning needs to end right now, Locke," says Randall, looking at his book. I'm about to ask why when I hear my last name shouted from behind me. I turn around and surprise, there's Andrew Tomas standing right in front of me, back hunched slightly so that his six-foot-five frame can lean down to my five-foot-ten size. Scenes from *Jurassic Park* flash before my eyes.

"How was your stay at my place last night, Locke?" he asks, mock sincerity bright in his voice. "Did you have an okay time? Was everything to your liking?"

"Hi, Andrew," I say softly. I need to keep it together. The venom shakes and shouts, tensing my muscles, but I plaster my hands at my sides. This is Renée's older brother, and I have to start dealing with that right goddamn now.

"Answer the question, Locke."

"It was fine."

"Good!" he barks accusingly. "Because that visit to my house was your last. My sister may be a bit of a freak, Vinetti, but not your kind of freak. Not a psycho."

The venom swells in me to the point where I want to cry or scream, I'm not sure which. It's no longer flying off the handle; it's building, storing itself until it takes over. *You're nothing, Tomas*, it cries, preparing to strike. *Give me one more minute of buildup, and then say the wrong thing. I'll rip your face off. I'll make you eat your fucking teeth.*

"What about her house, Andrew?"

He looks at me like I'm an idiot, which just makes *him* look like an idiot. "What does that mean?"

"Well, apparently I'm not allowed in *your* house. What about *her* house? Can I visit there?"

Andrew slaps a big hand on my shoulder. It weighs, eh, seven pounds. "Is that supposed to be funny, Vinetti?"

I could break every single one of your goddamn fingers right now. I could bite a hole in your neck the size of a grapefruit.

"You're making me angry, Andrew," I say. I squint my eyes, squeeze my fists till my fingernails dig into my hands. *You like this girl,* I repeat to myself, *and that means you can't do this.*

"Listen, Lou Ferrigno, I don't give a shit how angry you get. Just keep your grubby hands off my sister, y'dig?"

"Leave me alone, Andrew," I snarl, pulling his hand off my shoulder.

"Or *what?*"

The venom grins and starts going haywire. Oh, fuck, it's too late. I blew it. This is happening. It's—

"Okay, guys, back off," snaps Randall, pushing roughly between us. "Both of you, just chill out. None of us need this bullshit right now. Andrew, go away. Locke, sit the fuck down."

Andrew shakes his head and snorts. He likes Randall—the two of them have partied together in the past, though, as Randall puts it, "we're nowhere *near* friends"—and so he doesn't try and get past him. Instead, he just points at me and says, "You better keep that dog on a leash, Randall, or else I'm gonna have to put it to sleep."

"Whatever, Andrew. Walk away."

You're lucky, Tomas. You owe Randall your nose. Let's do this again sometime, huh?

He backs off slowly, grumbling under his breath. I do the same, sitting back down and letting my aching fists turn back into hands. Sweat begins swelling on my brow as the blood begins its routine of rushing into and draining out of my face. Rage roars through my ears to the point where the classroom is seemingly nonexistent.

"Well, I guess you were right," says Randall, taking his seat. "Who knew Andrew would react like that?"

"I did," I say a little too quickly.

Randall eyes me. "You okay? Bad moment?"

Talking feels clumsy. "I almost . . . your timing was good. Something was about to happen. Venom was getting . . . difficult. Fuck, Randall, *fuck.*"

He puts a hand on my shoulder. "Glad I got here in time, then," he says. "It'll be okay. I mean, come on, if you start dating his sister, he can't keep threatening to beat your ass, can he?"

I hope not. I need to get a carton of chocolate milk and calm down.

The rest of the day is problematic. The venom isn't happy. Which raises questions.

Forget the drama-queen-fictional-reality bullshit. I don't

believe that the venom has opinions of its own or that it's some sort of alien entity, using me as a host or some such nonsense. That's an attractive thought, sure, but it's the stuff of comic books, and reality's my place of residence. The venom is part of me; it was born out of my own twisted, ridiculous mind, and as such, all of its preferences and thoughts come from my own. If I like something, the venom is quicker to like it, and vice versa. Thank God for that—it's the only thing keeping my family and friends safe. I have never had a serious attack of the venom aimed toward my mom or my brother. Maybe in front of them, but never *at* them. Randall's come into contact with it, but he has a good sense of when to cut shit out. Randall's fatal flaw is that, because he's so well-liked, he's prone to cockiness. Every so often, I become the weird kid in the black coat who tags along with him, and the venom responds accordingly. Overall, though, it acts more like a barometer for Randall: When I begin to get abrasive, he takes it as a sign that he's gone a little too far, and tones himself down his self-righteousness. Point is, I've never taken a swing at him or anything.

But things are changing. The venom has its own voice, its own plan. There's more to it than a break in the dam or a short fuse on a big bomb. The venom's taking sides and making sure I know what they are. I feel less in control of it than ever before, because it's not one poisoned personality. It's two minds about everything, two competing viewpoints—or at least, one vying for access to the other.

The venom is not a fan of the Andrew Tomas situation. In fact, it's so displeased by it that it's decided to make this issue the be-all and end-all of its wretched little existence. Maybe if Andrew were just a tiny bit less of a stereotypical asshole, or maybe if I wasn't so utterly enamored of this odd girl who wears too much makeup and plays board games with her cat, or maybe if she and Randall had warned me what I was getting into before I started falling for her, or maybe if she wasn't so incredible and he wasn't so fucking *big*—maybe then the venom could sit back and let me take care of this one. That is not the case. Renée's face passes through my mind and I get goose bumps, but then it's replaced by those squinted eyes and that asshole sneer. The smell of her skin crosses my nostrils, and for a moment I'm lost in romantic bliss, until the rank smell of his blunts-and-forties breath pops right into my brain. The idea of dating her is permanently linked to the idea of getting the shit kicked out of me by the school bully, all thanks to the venom. It won't let me think about the one without reminding me of the other, just to make sure I understand its feelings.

Meanwhile, the dead parents are making the venom anxious. The venom is almost intimidated by the dead parents, which is an understandable reaction—I can't begin to fathom something that horrible happening to me. Having my father leave was bad, but the idea of being truly left alone is a concept beyond anything I can grasp. And for a living, thinking entity based solely on sorrow and rage to be confronted with an idea so bad that it can't truly process it, that's humbling. "Humble" doesn't exist in the venom's dictionary. It's used to holding dominion over all things miserable in my mind, but suddenly it's looking at a trauma so horrid that it has no idea how to confront it.

So, between fighting for its place in the sun and feeling obsolete, the venom broods and stews in my head, fueled by nagging worry and depression. Every minute walking around school, I feel it work its way deeper into my mind, finding any way to make me unhappy. It's taking this to the max. Being all it can be.

You can see where this is going.

I get home from school and Lon's sitting on the couch, reading about sea turtles. He has two piles on the coffee table in front of him, and I'm assuming that one pile is what he's already read and the other one is stuff that he has yet to read. They're huge, the kind of books with little text but lots of glossy pictures with informational captions next to them. The kid never ceases to amaze me. There's nothing more charming than coming home to find a small person who is earnestly eager to spend four hours scribbling notes about sea turtles. When I see Lon, I temporarily feel okay for the future of our species. He represents the people we all hope to one day know and elect into office. He looks up at me and gives me a know-it-all smile that suggests an impending trivia question.

"Hey, Locke, how long d'you think a sea turtle can live?"

I bite. "No idea. How long?"

"Over two hundred years."

"Two hundred years? Damn, that's one wrinkly old sea turtle," I scoff, playing amazed. Lon's ten, so he gets weird taboo pleasure out of hearing the word "damn" said freely in the house (if it's an extra-rowdy day, I throw a "shit" or two in there, maybe a "bitch"; nothing makes a ten year old feel special like the casual use of swear words). "Do they get put in sea-turtle nursing homes? Do their shells begin to smell like old people?"

Lon starts laughing, and for the next ten minutes I pretend to be a sea turtle with a walker, complaining about shell pain and claiming that the hermit crabs rob from my room while I'm asleep. Soon we're both a giggling mess, with me trying to get out final zingers between gasps and Lon spinning on the floor like he's on fire and loves it. I can never do this for anyone else. Randall gets it sometimes, but then my sense of humor is more quiet and dry. With Lon, I can go all out and act like a total idiot. Whatever it takes to hear him laugh. I think I might have to admit to myself that I'm physically addicted to that kid's laugh.

Once I'm in my room, I exhale and allow myself the rare gift of an unhindered grin. Goddamn, Lon. You've made my day. My life, even. You're the reason, plain and simple.

I walk into my room and hear: *Cute kid.*

Whoa. Okay. I stop, feeling cold all of a sudden. My room is silent. The hum of the city outside is all I can hear.

I close my eyes, take a deep breath, and consciously think, each word booming through my mind.

You, I think, *you stay the FUCK away from him. You stay away now, and you stay away in the future. You never, EVER, come near my brother, because I guarantee that if you approach him—and I'm not saying you will, I'm just saying that IF YOU DO ever come near him—I will do whatever it takes to keep you from ever raising your ugly head again. Let's keep in mind here that, as much as it pains me to say it, I am afraid of you. And when the person you live in is AFRAID OF YOU and is giving you an ORDER, you will fear it. I will destroy you. Any. Way. I. Can. And if you try to come anywhere near him, I will set you on fire and shoot you in the fucking ankle, so I can watch you hop around and bleed to death while screaming in pain. I will cut your screaming black head off and send my foot right through the back of your repulsive, rotting skull.*

You will be NOTHING. And once you don't exist, he will be safe, and I will have won. Do I make myself CLEAR?

I wait for a response, a laugh or some kind of cruel little quip, and hear nothing. Behind my door there's the flipping of pages in Lon's book, and out of my window there's the sound of tires and sirens, but here it's quiet.

Did it actually speak in the first place? Was there really any reason to go on that mental rant? An idea strikes me, sending ice through my veins: Did I say that out loud? Was I mentally responding to words that came out of my mouth? Oh, fuck. Oh, fuck, no.

Chocolate milk is of the utmost necessity right now.

My mom finds me in the bathroom with a determined look on my face, downing gulp after gulp of rich, brown emotional anesthesia straight from the carton.

"Good day?"

I take the time to belch before I answer. "It was okay. Got in an argument with Andrew Tomas."

She shakes her head and clucks, "That boy needs to be locked up somewhere, I swear. He's the kind of guy who gets cheerleaders pregnant. What was the argument about?"

"A girl," I say casually, hoping my mom reacts the way I want her to so she can finally assign me the title of Normal Kid.

Her face explodes in joy. "A girl? Have you been seeing someone lately? Oh, wow, is it someone he's interested in too?"

"Yes, a girl; yes, I've been seeing someone; and no, she's his sister."

My mom doesn't say a word, just stands up, snatches the carton from me, and walks into the kitchen. She returns with the chocolate milk in a glass and a single black-and-white cookie, and then drags me by my hand into the living room and onto the couch. I begin to sip, and we talk. Our conversation takes the serious-talk-of-the-day form: She asks, I answer, and vice versa.

"When'd you meet her?"

"Saturday night, while I was out with Randall. She was with us."

"What's she like?"

"She's a Goth. But she's really sweet."

"What's a Goth?"

"It means you dress like Alice Cooper or the people in the Cure. Do you know who the Cure are?"

"Yes, I know who the Cure are, thank you very much. Does she wear all that horrible schmutz on her face?"

"Yeah. She looks good in it."

"Pff, sure she does. Where does she live?"

"On Fifty-third Street in a nice little apartment."

"What do her parents do?"

"Lie in the ground." It sends an electric current through my heart and down my backbone. That's not how I meant it to sound. It's not funny, and it's not cool. It's the most desolate, hopeless thing that can happen to someone, and that someone is mine. I can't control the venom enough for even a little tact.

Mom frowns. "That's terrible. Don't say things like that."

I bow my head a little. "Yeah, sorry. Tough situation to deal with, though, y'know?"

She nods, still put off by my bluntness. "Did she bring it up herself?"

"No, not yet, anyway. Randall told me, and I just don't know what to say to her."

"Then don't. It's not the kind of thing that you ask someone to tell you about. She'll tell you when it's time. Besides, you've only known her a few days."

"She's nice. I think I might date her."

My mother goes back to planning her grandkids. "Really?"

"Yeah."

"You going to ask her about it first? That'd be a good start."

"Am I—Yes, I'm going to ask her about it! Mom!"

"Honey, some guys don't realize that you have to ask before you can move in."

"Was Dad like that?"

She doesn't even flinch, and I love it. "God, no. Your father worked every angle until I couldn't take it anymore and finally degraded myself by accepting his invitation to dinner and a movie."

I smile. "I wonder why he was so cautious."

She winks. "You know it."

I tip back my glass until all I'm getting is the grainy chocolate mix sludge. Mom balls up the dish towel in her hands and throws it at me. It slaps across my unsuspecting face damply.

"Now be a good boy," she says with a chuckle, "and wash that."

"You want me to wash . . . a dish towel?"

"No, the glass. Jesus, we send you to all these nice New York schools and listen to you. . . ."

THERE, ON top of the El Dorado. I could see it. Whatever it was.

I leaped through the air, and soon the wind was rushing past me as the powers of the city's sorrow sent me sailing into the night like a god. Flight—arguably the best part of the job. A moment later I was fourteen stories off the ground, hovering over the left spire of the El Dorado apartment building, where the creature hung apelike from the roof, an oversized gargoyle dressed in a nightmare. My costume shuddered as I hovered closer. This thing was disrupting the flow of its energy. I had my work cut out for me.

"Don't move," I snarled, reaching out to the creature. "I mean you no harm. Your mission seems to be the same as mine. I only wish to know what you are. Can you speak?"

The tentacles at the beast's mouth reared up, and from them, there came a mighty roar, like a soul spewed out of the depths of the pit. It pointed one taloned finger at me, calling me out, and gibbered at me in a language that might have been spoken on the ocean's floor. Every tentacle on its body vibrated in my direction, its whole body targeting me.

And then it froze and quivered. The tentacles at its mouth spread wide, flesh spreading back from it, like water or smoke, and suddenly a human face, the pale, terrified face of the bum from the park, appeared amid the mess of its body.

"Blacklight, Locke, for the love of God, stay back!" screamed an all-too-human voice. "I can't keep it from attacking you! I only have so much power over it!"

I floated closer, the core of my being running cold. "How do you know my name?" I hissed. "What manner of monster are you? Who *are you?"*

"Please, you have to get away! It knows what you are, how it can hurt you! If you don't—oh GOD!" The face wrenched its mouth wide, as though to scream, and then the black fleshy tendrils swallowed it back up. Where the face had appeared, those two eyes, insectoid, cold and dead, focused in on me with clinical resolve.

"Release him!" I said, raising a crackling hand. "I only want to speak to your host! I repeat, I mean you no harm—"

The beast gurgled again, and then sprang through the air and tackled me. The wind left my lungs, and suddenly the city went silent. My suit flickered, sputtered. Lightning exploded from me; my head became a blur of horrible thoughts and sweaty panic. We spiraled downward toward the sidewalk, a collage of emotional electricity and putrid squirming meat.

CHAPTER SIX

A WEEK OR so later, when Casey calls me and tells—not asks, tells—me that we're going shopping, I find myself saying yes before I have time to think about it. It's like instinct. Shopping isn't my thing, but a shopping trip with my first gay friend I've ever met? Too perfect. Hell, I might be able to get some leather pants out of the whole thing (note to self: keep the immature gay jokes at a minimum around new gay buddy).

When I emerge from the Union Square subway station, I see Casey, wearing a large, puffy North Face jacket and talking to a boy dressed to kill with stringy black hair and sunglasses. There's an argument going on, but a jovial one, where no one's worried about what might come of it. Casey throws up his arm a lot and yells out his answers between cackles, while the other kid uses his cigarette as a classroom ruler and growls out his parts of the argument with a clever little smile on his face, which lets me know that he's very nice and not to be trusted.

As I approach, the stringy-haired boy points at me and says something, to which Casey turns around and waves.

"Locke! This is Brent. Brent, Locke."

Brent puts his hand out and I shake it—warm, steely, a businessman's grip. "Ah, Locke, you've been mentioned. Casey tells me you were molested by him." Casey smacks him in the arm and swears laughingly under his breath. My face ignites with blood and timidity, and I pull out a cigarette of my own, which Brent willingly lights. "Nah, just fucking with you. You're Randall's friend, right? He calls you 'Stockenbarrel.'"

"Right. You know Randall?"

"Met him here and there through this fag over here." Another playful arm slap. "Does he call you that 'cause you're named Locke?"

"Uh, yeah."

Brent grimaces. "Randall and I shall have words."

I bet he's told them about me.

He wouldn't dare.

Randall is proving himself surprising. Talk to him or I will.

Sadly, it's got a point. There is something massively discomforting about finding out that there's a body of people out there who you've never met, and that this body knows who you are and what you're like.

"We're heading out," says Casey, giving Brent a pat on the back. "Tell Sam I'll give him a call, okay?"

A knowing nod. "He'll really appreciate that. Have fun, kids."

"I bet. Later." Casey and I start walking slowly toward Broadway, our hands in our pockets, the wind blowing our hair back. "Brent's cool. He's the devil in our tarot deck."

"I'm not surprised."

Casey nods, beaming. "No one is. You probably wouldn't like him. He and his friends can be a bit intense. They party really hard. He's going a little crazy now, though."

"Why?"

"One of our friends just had a nasty breakup. Long story. C'mon."

"Where are we going, anyway?"

"I wanted to go to Leather Man on St. Mark's. They have an adorable pair of chaps that fit me like a goddamn dream. I was thinking about buying a cowboy hat, too."

"Oh, wow. Really?"

"No, of course not. Man, do I *seem* gay enough to pull off leather chaps?"

Have I mentioned I'm a towering rube? I'm a towering rube. And now I seem like an ignorant fool of a towering rube. Splendid. "Sorry. I'm, uh, still a little . . ." What, you moron?

He puts a hand on my shoulder. "Worry not, young Jedi. We'll teach you the ways of the pink lightsaber yet."

Now that was pretty fucking gay.

I swallow the venom and walk.

Shopping is a nonstop blast. We rip through the Virgin Megastore like a swarm of critical locusts. I never knew I could get so invested in a conversation, but our argument about the Strokes proves me wrong—I posit they have drive and energy that sets them apart from most of the other bands in their genre, and Casey thinks they're "utter hogwaste." After that, it's ripping on Emily the Strange clothing and flipping through horribly pornographic manga. It's stuff like this that makes me happy, things that I spend most of my time being paranoid about getting laughed at for. Randall is too straight and *cool* to appreciate things like this: He has somewhere to be, someone to impress, something to uphold. Casey doesn't seem to care in the least about wandering around for the sake of doing so, and instead points out horrific images in the comics we're reading and cracks jokes like, "That girl is having her period of the black" and "Oooh! venom orgy with huge eyes!" And it's nothing more than fun. My eyes don't glance worriedly around at people near me. The room isn't squeezing the air out of my lungs. The burden is, maybe momentarily, lifted. The venom works in mysterious ways.

Halfway through a collection called *Ultra Gash Inferno*, Casey's head turns with a smile and he says, "Sssoooooo, how'd things go with Renéeeee?"

I glare at him. "Shouldn't you know already? You people seem to have this little conspiracy routine going on."

"Okay, point taken, but I want to hear about it from you."

I bite and relay the entire meeting, give or take a juicy detail. When I get to my sudden revelation about Andrew, Casey nods knowingly.

"Oh, Andrew," he says, sighing, "constant proof that caveman still exist. Honestly, don't worry about him, he's basically harmless."

"You don't have to go to school with him every day."

"No," says Casey in a harder voice, "I've just had to deal with that idiot's bullshit every day I'm over there since I came out. Andrew always sort of liked me, but the minute I told Renée and she told him, he's let me know what Middle America thinks of me. But in all honesty, it's a lot of hot air. Just forget him and think of her."

"Well, at least you don't pose a threat. You're her gay guy friend. There's no problem."

"That may be true," he says, "but you'd think that getting

tormented for *who I am* is a lot worse than for *what I could do*."

Times like this remind me how utterly naive I am. Jesus Christ, Locke, wake up, the playing field has changed. Casey's honesty, though, lets me know that he's the person who I have to ask, who'll answer the question that's been eating away at the back of my head.

"How'd Renée's parents die, Casey?"

Casey won't look at me; he just nods and pulls his lips tight and looks up and down the comic-book shelf. "How'd you find that out?"

"Randall told me."

"He shouldn't have. It's not his story to tell. It's Renée's."

"He thought it would be important for me to know, but Andrew was there, and he couldn't . . . Please, man. What happened?"

His mouth flaps open and closed again and again, but eventually he just shakes his head. "Not right now," he grumbles, flipping through more graphic novels. "Now's not the time. I don't really want to dive into that yet."

"*Please*, Casey."

"Locke, this isn't a joke," he snaps. "Let me think about it. She should tell you, 'cause . . ." He trails off, waving his hands.

"It's bad, isn't it?"

"Yes."

There's a flutter of venom. "How bad?"

"Worse than you think."

In the New York Milkshake Company on St. Mark's, I take my mind off this afternoon's craziness by informing Casey that he has no friggin' idea how to drink a root beer float.

"What're you doing?"

He looks up. "What? What do you mean?"

"I mean, what are you doing?" I ask, jabbing at him with my still-dripping spoon.

He glances down at his cup and then back at me. "I'm eating my ice cream. What does it look like?"

I sigh dramatically. "Bad enough you get chocolate ice cream in your float—"

"I hate vanilla, I told you."

"—but you're eating it wrong."

Casey puts up his hands in defense and leans back in his chair, saying, "Elaborate, sensei."

"Well, it's okay if you eat a *bit* of the ice cream and drink a *bit* of the root beer"—I take a sip to illustrate—"but then you have to let it sit awhile, y'know, stir it every few seconds, until some of the ice cream melts."

He looks focused but perplexed. "But then you just get this ice cream–root beer mixture."

"Now you've got it."

He shrugs and starts stirring his float. I watch him and think about what he told me before in the comics section until I feel like my brain is going to burst, so I go for a new subject.

"So, any boys lined up?"

He sighs. "No, not yet. Still a little sore from the last one, y'know, Catholic boy."

"Sorry about that."

"No worries, it was as much my fault as it was his." He stares into the swirling float, zoning out. "Honestly, I'm not going to worry about it too much. Love has never really treated me well."

"How so?"

"I've got a thing for boys I can't have," he says quietly, never moving.

"Straight boys?"

"Yeah, but . . . Well, it doesn't matter." His eyes meet mine, and I realize this conversation is over. "Can I drink the damn thing already?"

"Sure," I say, and we both chug.

Casey licks the last of his drink from the end of his straw and looks up at me with amazement in his eyes. "Damn, Locke," he says in awe, "you're the man."

Even with the float, the thought won't go away. The venom keeps scratching at it like a rash, until I have to ask again. "How'd they die?"

"You ready?" he asks.

"Yes."

"I'm serious, man. This is really bad, and I feel pretty fucked-up being the one to tell you. Are you ready for this?"

Obviously not. "Yeah."

There's a pause, and then he monotones, "Renée's dad stabbed her mother to death, and then he cut his own wrists and died with her. Renée was thirteen."

Oh Christ.

"Renée's dad had all sorts of problems with drugs and started getting violent, seeing things, making up conspiracy theories, the whole nine yards. So one day her mom scooped her and Andrew up and left San Francisco, meth, and her husband behind. For a couple of years, everything was fine; Renée was eight when they left, so they'd had a chance to start a new life, until one day out of the blue, Andrew gets a phone call from his dad, who apparently sounded totally coherent and reformed. He doesn't tell anyone, he just talks to his father, who he hasn't seen in years. And a week later, Renée's mom's boyfriend comes home and finds them there, bled to death."

Oh God, no.

The blood drains out of my face, and the room swirls purple and green. The air seems suffocating, full of dust or smoke to the point where I can't see or breathe. Using every ounce of my willpower, I manage to climb out of my chair and stumble through the glass doors, spilling out into St. Mark's Place. I hold myself up against a wall, trying to catch my breath, to regain my balance, to not throw up. A crew of punks jeers me, but I can barely hear them. It's too big. Oh God, it's way too big. It's unbearable.

Misery magnet, hisses the venom, *I told you. It's not just bad, it's beyond horrible. It's the principle of evil. One girl, hurt beyond anything you can imagine, and* you *found her. Bravo.*

Casey comes out and hands me a bottle of water, which I pound down my throat. Standing back up, wiping my face on my coat sleeve, I stare at him in horror. His eyes reflect back an understanding, a grasp of just how terrible the whole thing is. There's no sense of patronization; neither of us is the bigger or little brother. This is just horrible in the worst possible way, and it happened to someone we both hold dear.

"You gonna be okay?" he says, his voice shaking with worry. "It's a lot to take at once, I know. That's why she doesn't like to talk about it."

"Got it. . . . So Andrew . . ."

"Yeah. Andrew blames himself. Thinks if he'd only just dropped the phone . . . but yeah. Now you see how bad it is."

"How do I . . . What can I do to make this better?"

He shrugs. "You can't. You're in no position to save anyone, Locke. Just be there when you can, do what needs to be done. It's all she's ever needed."

We take a moment to stand and feel beaten before moving back down the street.

I come back home wearing a new shirt from a store called Search & Destroy. It depicts a black-and-white drawing of a man standing at the edge of a rooftop in an overcoat, exhaling a puff of smoke that drifts dramatically from his mouth and surrounds his head in a stringy cloud, as though his hair is on fire. Casey had brought it up to me and declared, which seems to be his way of doing things, that he was buying it for me. This was still taking some getting used to—not just being treated to random gifts and excursions, but the self-assured attitude all of these people have about, well, everything. Casey never asks or wonders—he *declares* or *states*. It's both comforting and unnerving, like at the Milkshake Company today. The garment hanging from my torso felt like a bribe to make up for sometimes treating me like an insect, and I don't like to be bought. The venom despises it. Everything wasn't what it seemed, and that left me feeling caught in the crossfire.

Lon's sitting on the couch watching TV as I walk in. He does a double take after glancing at me. "Wow! I like your shirt."

"Thanks," I say, running my hand over the plastic printing for the millionth time in the past hour.

"Renée called," Lon says, going back to Samurai Jack,

who is tearing art-deco robots to shreds. "She wants you to call her."

I'm in my room with the door shut in five seconds, and I'm punching numbers shakily into the phone in eight. For some reason, hearing about her twisted past has only made me want to talk to her more. This girl may not be normal, she may not be "okay," but she cares for me, and all I want to do is let her know how amazing I think she is.

The venom snorts. *Always the superhero, Locke. Go ahead, try to face something this terrible. I can't wait.* Ignoring its voice is impossible, and I shudder. Blurting something out at the wrong time is not an option here. Don't be toxic, Locke. Careful.

A droplet of sweat forms in the center of my forehead and begins to trickle annoyingly down the bridge of my nose. After two rings, it's hanging on the tip of my nose, and I'm about to wipe it off when someone picks up the phone, at which point the droplet sails down and spatters onto my pants.

"There's no excuse for you calling me so late, you know."

Caller ID. I hope. "Well . . . actually, there is."

"Oh, really? And that is?"

"How've you been?"

"Ha, yeah, *that's* gonna work. Answer my fucking question, Locke, why didn't you call me?"

As my mouth opens, the venom screeches in the back

of my head, louder and louder until it's all I can hear. Even considering her parents up has sent it into a psychotic tantrum. My throat feels closed up, and I have to clench my eyes as hard as I can just to concentrate. No, no, no, not now. Think of something, Locke, something good and reasonable, something that isn't the truth.

"Look . . . Renée, you being Andrew's sister, that's a delicate issue for me. You know?"

"Nope. Keep going. How so?"

Fantastic. "Look, Renée, why didn't you mention that your brother was Andrew Tomas?"

"Hmm, what about him?"

Oh boy. This isn't easy. "Well, I mean, I don't want to sound like a wuss or a jerk, but the kid threatened me with physical violence because I wanted to date you! And I—"

"Waitwaitwait. Stop. You want to date me? You never mentioned this."

"Y'know, my mom actually brought this same thing up—"

"Oh, wow, you discussed me with your mom?" She chuckles. "This is some serious shit. I guess you really *do* want to date me."

"Well, I only curled up with you in my lap and made out with you for about an hour."

"I've done similar with boys who I've had no intention of dating."

Suddenly my head is filled with a picture of me force-feeding these faceless boys glass. Glass mixed with wasps. I tell it to shut up. Venom talking. "So the idea never crossed your mind?"

There's a pause before she says, "The thought *did* cross my mind, yes."

"Well, yes. I really want to date you."

"There it is, out in the open."

"So."

"Go on."

"There's . . . not much to go on about. I'd like to date you."

"Well," she says, sounding somewhere between annoyed and giddy, "if that's the case, maybe you ought to ask me out?"

I remember my mom's words and cringe. "Would it be okay if I dated you?"

"Wow. I don't know."

"WHAT?!"

"Well, that had so little confidence behind it. 'Would it be okay'—I'm not sure I can date someone who—"

My mouth shakes, falters—

And then something new happens.

Renée's comment acts as a challenge, a shove, and I can't help but shove back. The venom fills me, screaming in my ears and blazing through my blood, and takes hold of the words in my mouth. There's no poison, though, just the confidence and grandiosity the venom gives me, the godlike part of the change, as though I'm . . . *tapping into* the dark reservoir in me, taking what is needed, leaving the muck and the pain behind. It's the venom and I speaking as one, communicating as a full being.

"Okay then, fine," I say, fueled by this new sensation. "Renée, I want you to be my girlfriend. I want to be your boyfriend, and I want to be your boyfriend right fucking now. That cool?"

"You see?" she squeals into the phone. "That was perfect! A little harsh, but perfect! So, yes, okay."

"Okay?"

I can almost hear her smile. "Okay. You're my boyfriend now. Perfect."

The words hang on to the strings between my heart and stomach. *You're my boyfriend. Perfect.* I've never been *anyone's* boyfriend. Amazing.

"Hey. You really like me?"

She titters. "Of course I really like you, you buttface. I'd be in a bad place if I didn't like my own boyfriend."

"Call me that again."

"You're my boyfriend," she purrs. "My wonderful, wonderful boyfriend."

Wow.

"And your first action as my boyfriend is to wash my feet!"

Huh?

The door's open when I get to Renée's, and the lights are out in the front room of her apartment, but I can see a faint yellow glow coming from a room off to the side. A jab of cold hits me right in the chest as the venom spits horrid images of her father, straight razor in hand, leaning over her mangled corpse with a terrifying smile on his face. Sweat begins to prickle behind my brow as I stomp in, eyes frantic, hands clenching. I call out her name, scared, desperate. Please, oh please, oh please—

"In here!" she yells. "Lock the door behind you."

When I get to her room, there's no one there, only the window-lit silhouettes of a Goth kid's paradise. I call out her name again, softer this time, and nearly jump out of my skin when the outline of a door right next to me says, "No, in *here*."

I open the door slowly, and I'm hit with a wall of steam. Once it clears, I'm greeted with basic white tile walls, a white sink, a toilet with a fuzzy purple seat cover, and Renée in a bathtub overflowing with suds. She glances up at me and smiles a little at the corners of her mouth. "I've been waiting," she says, and then flicks her lip ring with her tongue.

Mother of God.

Hormones and romance both flood my brain, like the venom's good twin who's charming and horny all at once. My hand copies another part of my body and immediately goes up, shielding my eyes from the one thing I want to keep looking at. "Whoa, hey, Renée, I've only been your boyfriend for about twenty minutes here!"

"Oh, be quiet, you." She laughs. "I've got enough suds on top of my body that Superman couldn't see it right now. Your virgin eyes are protected."

Sadly, she's right: There's a mountain of white fluff over her, everything under her armpits completely opaque out of my line of vision. I walk over to the far wall and sit where I can see her face. As I lower myself onto my haunches, a foot with black toenail polish and a loofah dangling from the big toe rises out of the suds like a very cute shark.

"Scrub," she commands.

Foot fetishes are an absolutely foreign concept to me, maybe because up until now I associate feet with stepping in dog shit or wearing tennis shoes, neither of which are the pinnacle of sexiness. Feet are about utility, not hotness. And yet I'm absolutely, positively enamored of Renée's foot. Each tiny toe seems alien in its shape and size, a sculpted variation on the normal model of the human digit. I can't help but go over every inch and crease and line with the loofah in the greatest detail. The arch of her foot reflects the curves of her body; her toenails, painted black of course, seem too delicate to belong to a human being. There's a little callus on her heel, which I run my finger along and get rewarded with a small sigh in the back of her throat. I can't help it—I take off my glasses, lean forward, and press my lips against the ball of her big toe, soft and cushiony beneath my kiss. Renée lets out a soft "Oh" and then lets her left foot drop slowly back into the water.

I slip my glasses back on and figure out a way to talk again. "Left done. Right, please."

"Just the one will be fine for now, thank you," she says with sincere contentedness. "That was extremely pleasant, Mr. Vinetti."

"Just doing my job as your"—breathe in—"boyfriend, Ms. Tomas."

She chuckles. "I didn't actually think you were going to wash my foot."

"Neither did I." I sigh. "Guess you just bring out the gentleman in me."

Her eyes flutter open, and it hits me like a two-ton sack of wonderful. Makeup or no, she's beautiful. I lean slowly forward on my hands and knees and plant a kiss on her lips as carefully as I can; this boyfriend thing is new, and I want to enjoy it as much as possible. She responds slowly, her breath shaky and hot, the whole kiss a little too tentative for either of us. Our tongues touch, just a little, and I'm stuck, frozen, enraptured by this person I'm somehow allowed to be dating.

We pull back and stare, astounded. "Damn."

"Damn indeed," she murmurs.

Slowly, so as not to faint from sheer head rush, I get to my feet and take a moment to throw my coat into her room. If I didn't walk away right then, I might've jumped into the tub with her.

"So, what's going on with you? You sounded freaked out when you came in. And don't give me any nonsense about Andrew."

I laugh and try to play it off. "Yeah, fearing for my life is nonsense. Besides, your door was open, I don't know . . . something could've happened." There. See? Didn't blow it. Kudos.

"No worries about that," she says, accompanied by splashing. "I'm a big girl. I can take care of myself."

"Well, hey, y'know, big city and all, you're never sure who's going to try and break in—"

But my words flee from me, because in my fervor I've marched right back into the bathroom and discovered what the splashing was all about, 'cause Renée's standing up.

I've never seen a woman completely naked before. I mean, on the Internet and magazines and all that (I'm a teenage male, after all), but a warm, breathing, nude woman is a new sight for me. I always thought that airbrushed beauty was the height of perfection, but I'm wrong, dead wrong. She's wearing only bubbles, water and suds sliding slowly down her curves, her hips. Her nipples stand out pink on her pale skin, and there's a tattoo of two snakes intertwined, like those on the Red Cross logo, right below her navel. She has her legs placed together to form a reverse teardrop shape, and the dark patch of hair where they meet is smaller than I expected, yet still unspeakably inviting. She's leaning against the wall; her body slants slowly downward into a mountain of soapy white. I feel my breath begin to labor in my chest, and I'm pretty sure my glasses are starting to fog up. The look on her face is somewhere between surprise and shy pride; oh God, she's biting her lower lip. The venom twitches giddily, bearing an ear-to-ear grin. *Well, now,* it sneers excitedly, *you want to take this, or should I go ahead*?

"So," she says softly, "are you going to hand me a towel or what?"

"I don't really want to," I manage.

There's a moment, an acknowledgment of the tension in the air, and then we're done. Splash, splash, she's out of the tub and grabbing a towel. She turns away from me, and for a second I stare at the curves of her body from the back before everything between her mid-thighs and armpits is wrapped in fluffy white cotton. I cough as I wipe off my glasses.

She gives me an over-the shoulder glance and says, "Man, let's hope the teacher doesn't call *you* up to the board."

I look down at my pants and swiftly get the point. She struts back into her room, a David Bowie song on her lips. And I'm about to follow her like a slave when, out of the corner of my eye, I catch something that stops me dead in my tracks.

The sink is lined with containers of pills, orange with the chunky white childproof tops. Prozac, Lexapro, Ritalin, Dexedrine, and a myriad of others. Study aids. Antidepressants. Antipsychotics. A laundry list of dosages, intended effects, alcohol warnings.

"Locke? You coming?"

I shove it to the back of my mind, getting it out of my thoughts for now. This girl is hurt, but she's wonderful, she's your *girlfriend*. Be careful, man, for your own sake.

I'm lying on the bed as instructed when she comes back into the room, wearing a H.I.M. T-shirt and her underwear. She bounds onto the bed and snuggles up against me, all warmth and curves. I've never snuggled with a girl before, and so far it's proving pretty great.

"Hey, you," she says, putting a hand over my heart.

"Hey."

"You're my boyfriend." A shot of energy goes through both of us. Our grips on each other tighten.

"So. About Andrew."

"Do we really need to keep talking about Andrew? I, for one, am interested in the boyfriend aspect of this conversation. Here: Andrew is my brother. He is also a bully at your school who regularly torments you and wants you to keep your grubby hands off me." To emphasize the rule I'm breaking, Renée grabs one of my hands and slaps it, firmly, on her ass. My mouth goes dry, and I focus on breathing steadily. "Since this is not going to be the case, he will have to learn to deal with it. You will treat each other with the restrained dislike of in-laws, and all will turn out happily." She looks up into my eyes and smiles. "Though if you cheat on me, he'll break your kneecaps."

"If Randall and Casey don't do that first."

"I'll let them know your kneecaps are on reserve. Just the knees, though."

And with that, the issue is closed. We stay still, listening to each other breathing until our chests rise and fall together, synchronized.

"What's the deal with Casey? Is there some sort of epic heartbreak in his past?"

Renée chuckles. "You could call it that. More love-in-vain than anything else."

"Anyone I know?" Renée doesn't say anything, just laughs, louder and louder. I'm baffled until the answer hits me smack-dab in the face. "Oh my God. Not *Randall.*"

"Shhh," she says, "it's the big secret. Don't even say it out loud."

"Randall, though? The straightest dude in the world? Are you fucking kidding me?"

"He's clueless about it. Honestly, Casey's kept it hidden for so long at this point, it's almost a joke. He's terrified that it would ruin their friendship, that Randall would just start treating him like a queen."

"I can sort of see that, honestly. Randall's very much a *guy.*"

She pecks me on the temple. "Mmm-hmm. It's why I'm glad to have you. You're just enough of a woman for me."

"Oh, *thanks.*"

She giggles and burrows deeper into me.

Wonder what cocktail of meds makes her treat you like this.

I focus on her breathing, her warmth. The weight of her in the bed. Anything else.

No, really, you should get that recipe down, it chuckles. *She gets in a bad mood, you'll know what to give her to make her love you again. Maybe even buy some of those tiny plastic cups.*

A twitch of anger jolts my body. Her hand slides across my chest. "You all right?"

"Yeah," I mumble, "little venom moment. No worries."

"Hey now," she whispers, snuggling even closer to me. Her

kisses move from temple to ear. "None of that today. Let's keep this venomless for now."

"It's not that simple, Renée."

"Sure it is. Just forget about it. Stay here with me instead of inside your mind."

This from Miss Psychopharmacology! From what I saw, your whole personality is a series of chemicals swimming inside your head.

I pull her tighter to me, trying to drown it out. "I know, I know, it's just . . . Sometimes it's out of my hands, you know? I don't get to choose."

"The Hierophant disagrees. The choice is always yours at all times. Be who you want to be."

Oh, yeah, is that how it is? Were you dressing like Morticia before your dad went slasher movie on your mom?

"Look, in this situation, there's no puzzle or game to be played, okay? You really don't know what you're fucking talking about, so just . . . leave it alone."

The words leave my mouth too harsh, too riled up by the venom. There's a pause, and then she sighs and gets up. Shit. My hand is desperately aware that it's no longer resting on ass cheek. I can almost hear the venom laughing; its work is done. GodDAMMIT, Locke.

"I'm sorry," I mumble. "That came out totally wrong."

"I'll say." She folds her arms across her delicious breasts, standing at the side of the bed with a Rosie-the-Riveter jaw.

"No one talks to me like that. No one *orders me* to do anything."

"It wasn't an order—"

"Bullshit, you just *told me to do something,* Locke. Incredibly uncool."

"It's . . ." My mouth goes dry, slack, but I force it into movement. "It's hard to talk about. Even Randall only knows so much about it. Casey's the only person who has any sort of idea what I'm talking about, so . . . I'm sorry. This is new, and I'm doing my best not to fuck it up."

She stares at me for a second, and finally lowers her arms. "Here's the thing," she says. "I won't pry too hard. Sorry if I did. I like you a ton, even though I've only met you, what, twice, so I want to get to know you, understand what I'm dealing with. But from what I've heard, the venom's not my type, so he can go fuck himself. From now on, I will not let some destructive force play a walk-on part in a relationship that I think has a metric buttload of potential."

This piques my interest. News to me. "What kind of potential?"

She shrugs, and that sexy half smile creeps onto her face. "Well, I'm not sure. I guess we'll have to find out, huh?"

I think about every word before I say it. "I'll try to keep the venom out of this relationship entirely. At the same time,

I just need you to know that I'm not totally put-together, and you're the first girl to want to know why. It'll take some time to get used to."

"Time, I can do," she says warmly. "Time is manageable. But I am serious about this."

"Likewise."

A pause. Neither of us know how to respond; there's no answer that either of us can give the other, and it feels too deep too quickly. I open my mouth again, to try and explain what I meant by the whole thing, and finally choose to go with what I feel right then and there rather than fucking myself over with any more venom talk. It's a big risk—might make me sound really creepy—but right now it's all I've got.

"I want you to meet my mom," I say. "She's a total character, and I think she'll really like you."

"That's the most romantic thing anyone's said to me in ages. Kiss me."

I do. For a long time. We run our hands up and down each other's bodies, savoring every touch. She pulls up my new shirt and lets her hand sneak across my stomach, her nails scratching me lightly around my belly button. It's never been like this with a girl. I'm used to light pecking or sloppy, overzealous kissing, but this—it's soft yet slightly aggressive. Subtle yet undeniably explicit. I can't believe I'm allowed this.

If there's another shoe around, it better drop soon, 'cause I'm getting real comfortable here.

We both come up for air, our noses centimeters apart and our breath mixing hotly. She lets a finger stray across my cheek, circling up to my ear.

"Dark boy," she whispers, "with your long black coat and downturned eyes . . . I don't buy it."

"No?"

She shakes her head, smiling. "Nothing poisonous can make me this happy. No way."

I bite my lip and dive back in.

I SAID STAY DOWN!"

BOOM. I let my fist hit its head like a sack of dumbbells. The sidewalk ruptured around the monster's frame, giving it a nice little smoking crater to rest its head.

Silence. It twitched a bit, and then stopped moving all together.

"Okay," I panted, "okay. This needs to stop right—"

A massive claw slammed over my face and pulled me off my feet by my head.

So now this was happening.

For a second, between its fingers, I could see those eyes, bulbous and lifeless, staring into me, and then there was wind with intermittent moments of incredible discomfort. The thing wheeled me around by the skull like a rag doll, slammed me into something hard and rough, and then flailed me around again. Swoosh, BOOM, swoosh, BOOM, swoosh, BOOM, until it flung my limp form across the street and through a shop window.

I dragged myself to my feet, brushed off the broken glass and mannequin anatomy, and surveyed the situation. We were in a narrow shopping street downtown, where I'd managed to chase the grotesque beast. This fight had happened every night for the past couple of days. Every night since the El Dorado, it had been the same: I would find it, question it, fight it, and then lose it among the back alleys of the city. We'd grappled along 121st Street, terrifying pedestrians and sending traffic to a screeching halt before the creature had lurched its way to the rooftops and taken off downtown with huge, agile leaps and bounds. I had lost him for a while around Times Square, but finally caught him again in the West Village and went straight to the task of beating the snot out of him—which was, I admit, proving hard than I'd imagined.

It was changing. This was the problem. With every fight it was leaner, stronger, a little more unpredictable. Every night I lost a little ground with it, and it got a little more eager to see me. . . . In fact, tonight it had gone right where I wanted it to. This thing's human side had told me, screamed out to me, that this creature knew what I am. Whatever this beast was, it wasn't right, *wasn't what I thought it was.*

It hunched down across the street, bigger, more repulsive than ever. God, it was hideous. Trails of sweat and mucus trickled down its anemone-like tentacles. Jumping at it, tackling it again, would just prove even more useless. Face it, if you don't reason with this thing, it'll probably kill you. Take a moment and try again. Take a moment and try again.

"Whoever is inside this monster, please step out," I barked, raising a hand in defense and praying that whoever was behind this mass of twisting fury could hear me. "You are more powerful than this, this thing *that has a hold over you. I know you can break free of its hold. Please."*

The beast lumbered to its feet and tilted its head.

"Please. You have to fight it."

There was a dry sound, like something slowly splitting apart, and then the monster began to disappear, drying up and rotting away. Bit by bit, the decay seemed to climb its way over the beast's figure, every inch of skin drying, cracking, and falling to the ground as nothing more than ash. And when the beast was no longer a monster, just a silhouette in filth, a gust of wind blew away the last of the decayed body to reveal the bum from the park, naked, pale, and wide-eyed. He shook a little, made a soft noise in the back of his throat, and then tumbled to the concrete.

CHAPTER SEVEN

WHEN I COME into school Monday, I'm glowing almost as much as I was Sunday. Randall notices immediately and starts trying to get all the "scrumptious details" out of me. Most of the questions just get a big smile and a chuckle as a response.

"Did you guys hook up? Is that it? Oh my God, you didn't sleep together, did you?"

I smile and chuckle. "No."

"Well, what then? You're about as bright-eyed as Martha Stewart on speed, Stockenbarrel."

Smiling, chuckling. "I saw her naked."

Randall's eyes become like those of Sissy Spacek in the prom scene in *Carrie*. "What? You *what*?"

"I saw her naked for the first time."

"You guys had *sex*? You've only know each other for, like, what, a couple weeks! You're the man! How did I miss what a pimp you were?"

"We didn't have sex. I just saw her naked, y'know?" Wow, that actually sounds a lot more stupid than it seemed at the time.

"But what's the context? Did she put on some sort of show for you? Was food involved? A pasta show, was that it?"

"I don't even know what that is, and you're a terrible person. It was only for a moment, anyway. We just had a really nice time. She's incredible, you know?"

He nods with a look of honest agreement. "Yeah, she is. You lucky bastard." The rest of the walk to class is silent and heartfelt. We're happy, Andrew's nowhere in sight, everything's nice. Until I open my big mouth.

"Renée takes a lot of pills, doesn't she?" I ask, trying not to sound too worried.

Randall nods and glances at the floor. "Yeah. A whole bunch. It's always one cocktail or the next, so the results are . . . inconsistent. It's hard to describe."

Yowch. "Why doesn't she tell me about these things? What're they for?"

He shrugs. "Some are for basic things. Her ADD isn't too bad, but it's bad enough that the meds are a necessity. Most of the rest are for depression, anxiety disorders, the occasional psychotic episode, things surrounding her parents . . . Basically, they keep her from going bugfuck."

The venom gnaws at the back of my head. It's there every minute of every day now, endlessly laughing, growling, biding its time. There seems to be no hurry for it to break free and wreak havoc now; it's content to wait in the background, to brood. The Renée issue isn't helping.

"You ever seen her go 'bugfuck'?"

Randall nods and looks away from me. "I have. You don't want to deal with that, man. The meds might weird you out a bit, but Renée's much better off with them. Trust me on that point at least."

"I want to help her, Randall. I feel so helpless about all of this. The medications, and . . . her parents . . . I dunno."

"Just look after her. Take good care of her." His smile splits open. "Or I'll fucking kill you."

Just wait, hisses the venom, *it's coming. You think things are getting better, you're in for a surprise. You're a part of something now, a cog in the works, which means so am I. This shitstorm isn't going to get any smaller, and I know just how to deal with it. Just you wait. It's gonna be huge.*

When I get home from school, I hear voices in the living room, at least one unfamiliar. I carefully lay down my backpack, hang up my coat, and eavesdrop.

"It's not that he's mean or threatening, Laura, he just gets really emotional when he gets angry." My mom.

"Does he get violent?"

This would be about me then.

"Yes. Sometimes way too violent. I get scared for him, but also scared for his friends . . . and sometimes, I mean . . . he'd *never* hit his brother."

"Are you sure of that?"

Bitch, screams the venom, *bitch, you don't know a single goddamn thing about me, so keep your fucking mouth shut. I'll hit who I want to.*

The silence that follows hangs in the air, like a suicide jumper about to splatter.

"No. No, I'm not. I wish I was, but when he's around his brother and he begins to get agitated, I'm scared that he's . . . I can't even say it. That he's going to take it out on the nearest person available. These outbursts—"

Angries.

"—they're scary because they aren't just him being upset. It's someone else. When I look at him, I see this sweet, caring boy who loves his family and his friends, and then, suddenly, there's this other person in my house where my son once stood. This screaming, seething person who scares the crap out of me and everyone else around him, and honestly is *not welcome here.*" She realizes what she just said and sighs, ashamed.

This again. More therapy, more long talks, like I'm a disorder, like you can be cured. I'm not impotence or alcoholism, I'm rage in its worst form. They'll never take me alive.

"Well, that's unacceptable."

"Laura, what else is there to do? He hated Jim Reiner so much. . . . Any time I bring therapy up, he gets this look on his face, like I'm stabbing him in the back. . . ."

It's a shrink. Must be. No one else is as good at making people spill their guts out. Fucking parasites.

"I'll talk to him, Charlotte, but this is up to him."

That's all I need to hear. I walk out from the front hallway and march over to the fridge, doing everything in my power to keep the venom at bay. The energy of it, the power, is already coursing through my bloodstream. I can barely keep my hand steady as I reach for something to drink. I hear Mom's voice say, "Hey, honey, how was your day?"

I turn around and face her, making sure my voice is good and hard. I am ready to be a bastard. "Fine. Who's she?"

"I actually wanted to talk to you about this. . . ."

My vision starts blurring with anger. It's half me, half venom at this point. "Well, you didn't. So who's she?"

The woman sitting with my mother looks like Ann Coulter. She's blond, not that annoying bleached blond but that warm, natural blond, her hair reaching down past her shoulders. She's wearing a blue turtleneck sweater and wire-rimmed glasses, and she has the biggest breasts I have ever seen in my entire life. The muscles in her back must be insane to carry those things around. Given different circumstances, they'd almost be comical, but now they only serve to make her grotesquely irritating. She's holding a mug of coffee and staring at me with utter neutrality. *Yeah, that's right, bitch, keep looking at me like I'm a specimen. I'm real fucking scared. You have NO IDEA who you're dealing with.*

"Locke, this is Laura Yeski. She's an old friend of mine from college."

I sneer. "Ahhh. Psych major?"

"Locke," my mom says in a voice that lets me know I'm going too far, "Laura's a psychologist. I wanted you to talk to her."

I shrug and glance at my boots. "Why not? Let's rap."

My mom stands up and walks over to me, putting a hand on my shoulder. "Look, honey, I have to go pick Lon up from school. All I ask is that you talk to her until I get back, and see how you feel. Afterward we'll talk about it, okay?"

I calculate the time in my head. It'll take my mom about a half hour, forty-five minutes to pick up my brother. I can go that long without putting my boot through this woman's skull.

A few minutes later, after my mom's thrown her coat on and said her too-cheery good-byes, I sit down across the table from Laura—sorry, *Dr. Yeski*—and slowly sip my soda. She hasn't stopped staring at me, and it's making me a little uncomfortable and a lot pissed, because I can tell that behind her eyes it's all zeroes on the checks my mom will have to write her.

"So, you seem not to like me very much, Locke," she says, bringing her coffee to her lips.

"Nope," I say.

"What's that about? You don't know me, after all."

"Well, *doctor*," I say, emphasizing her purpose, "the last psychologist I dealt with was one of the bigger assholes I've ever met. I'm not sure you'll be any different."

"So you're calling me an asshole?"

"Maybe not calling you one . . . I'm expecting you to *be* an asshole."

"And all you know is that I'm a psychologist."

"That's all I need."

"Well, first off," she says, looking up into my eyes, "Jim Reiner was a psychiatrist, while I'm a psychologist. They're different things."

"How so?"

"One is crazy, the other isn't."

"Which one's the crazy one?"

"I guess you'll decide that for yourself."

Touché. I can't help but laugh a little, a tiny snort of amusement at the comment.

"Second, your mother invited me to talk to you because you yourself seem a little uncomfortable with these problems you're having. These . . . what does she call them?"

"Angries."

"Right. What do you call them? She said you had a name for them."

"I call it the venom."

"Interesting. Anyway, I just want to be someone who you can talk to. You'd come to my office once a week and we'd talk about whatever is on your mind. I'd scribble in a notebook about certain things I notice in your ideas or beliefs, and I'd try to help you work out some of your problems. Pretty painless, and wholly your prerogative."

I sip my soda to show her I'm considering this thing carefully. "And if I refuse?"

"Then I go back to my office and get back to work."

"That's it? I say no, and you leave?"

"Yup," she says. "Locke, I'm not here to be your friend or your confidante. I came here because your mother's a dear friend of mine, and from what she told me, this 'venom' thing of yours is becoming a problem for you and your family."

It's about to become a problem for you in a couple of seconds, you hideous slag.

"You think I need curing, that it?"

"I didn't say that—"

"But you implied it," I snap, rising to my feet. My face flushes white-hot. My hands tighten on the table. The dark parts of my brain twitch. "There's nothing to fix here, okay, doc? I'm my own fucking boss, and I don't give a shit how you know my mother. I've had enough of this psychobabble bullshit."

"Fair enough, but think about this," she says unwaveringly. "You may be content with the person you are, but you're scaring the living hell out of your mother, who seems to care a great deal for you. And while you may not like me, or therapy in general, it might be worth a try if it'll stop you from hurting the people you love."

"The people I love can tell me what they fucking think."

She snorts. "Can they? Then why'd your mother call me?"

The words blow out the rage like a candle, and I feel the burning darkness replaced with the emotional muck. She's right, as frustrating as that is. If my mother had been able to tell me she was scared, if I wasn't such a horrible mess, I wouldn't be in this situation in the first place. Slowly, ashamedly, I sit back into my chair and lower my head, defeated. "Point taken."

She smiles finally, a cool little smile that could be a smirk if it wanted to. "So let's talk. Venom, huh?"

"Yeah. *The* venom."

"Like the comic-book villain or the band?"

I didn't know there was a band named Venom. I hate that. How dare she get the upper hand on me? "Neither. Is that supposed to impress me in some hip kind of way?"

"No. I don't think impressing you is really in the cards. Just a question."

"That's clever. You're *clever*."

"If we're going to do this, you have to be willing. I can't fight you on this, but compromise is always an option. Let's make a deal."

I feel like Faust, but I nod, and we talk.

A couple of nights later, Lon and I are having dinner together alone. It's Mexican takeout, which means we eat it on the couch in front of *The Simpsons*. It's the closest thing to male bonding that we have. I don't do catch, but I'm fine with nachos and Apu.

Lon glances at me midway through his burrito and says softly, "So, was that lady with the huge boobs your new shrink?"

I have no idea how Lon knows any of this. I didn't hide the fact that I'd gone to see Dr. Reiner, but I never really discussed it with Lon, and I didn't think my mom had either. The idea always scared me a little bit: Big brothers are supposed to be protectors, people to look up to. They should be able to beat up bullies for you and make sure you know what terms like "popping her cherry" mean later in your life. The fact that I'm so screwed up, screwed up enough to need therapy anyway, is not okay. I wish Lon didn't have to even consider this shit. Having him ask me about it is almost painful.

I sip my chocolate milk and nod. "Yeah. Her boobs are gargantuan, aren't they?"

He stares at the screen in deep thought, and then nods fiercely. "Do you like her?"

"Y'know, I don't know yet," I say. "Too soon to say. She's analyzing me, and that's weird and all, but she's a lot nicer than the last one. This is about my life, my mind . . . not concepts or whatever."

"Like . . . about the venom?"

The word settles into my blood like a block of ice. "What?"

"The venom . . . right?" he says with a waver. "The venom is the bad thing. Like, your angries."

Either my brother is clairvoyant or someone has loose lips. How the fuck does he know? I've never told him its name, and I've told everyone, *everyone*, to keep it a secret for this one reason. Seeing a therapist is one level of weakness, but this is too much. "Yeah." I sigh, keeping my eyes on Bart. "That's what she's interested in. We're gonna see if we can work on it together."

He nods, and we both return to TV land. I'm stuffing

enchilada in my mouth, thinking this topic is thankfully over, when I notice Lon giving me little glances out of the corner of his eye. Finally I'm quick enough to make contact before he can turn away as though he has no idea what I'm looking at.

"What's up?"

He's quiet for a little bit, and then mumbles, "What's it like, when you get . . ."

"The venom?"

"Yeah."

He's my brother. He has a right to ask, and I have a duty to be honest with him. "It's like I'm . . . really powerful, at first. I feel driven, invincible, but afterward . . . Well, you've seen me, right?" I smile a bit, making him feel like he's "on the inside" with my psychosis. "The shivering, sweating, not being able to talk for a long time, man . . . It's real bad. And it never gets me anywhere, all it does is upset people and make me seem like a total nutcase."

"Really?"

"What—yes, *really*. Why, what's 'really' mean?"

"Promise you won't get mad?"

There's no phrase like it, and I feel like a fink for not being able to say no. "Sure, what's up?"

He looks at his shoes and mutters, "The other day I was looking for that Spider-Man comic, so I went into your room and you weren't around, but I looked for it anyway and I saw your school notebook, and in some of the margins you wrote about the venom and drew some cartoons of it, and it was really cool so I thought . . ."

Somehow I manage to understand Lon's high-speed rant, and I have to take a deep breath to keep down the first pangs of the venom jabbing into the back of my skull. "Okay, well, first off, don't snoop around my room without me there, okay? Next, there's nothing cool about this. Like I said, it gets me nowhere. I just end up being an asshole."

The swearing doesn't delight him this time; he's still really invested in the topic at hand. "But what about the bookstore?" he asks, eyes wide. "You got somewhere then. I wouldn't have any of the books for my project if you hadn't had an angry. That woman was being mean, and you showed her who was boss."

The venom worms through my nerves, sending pure, black rage through me in the form of annoying little pulses. I clench and release my fists as I try to talk. "Right, right, but come on, she was just doing her job, and I didn't need to . . . I mean, remember how you felt afterward? It was embarrassing. You were right, we probably can't go back to that bookstore anymore—"

"I know I said that," he fires out, growing enthused, "but I figured, you were right, she was being stupid, and I *did* end up getting my books, so who cares? You got really strong and really *right* all of a sudden, and you're not always like that. The venom gives you the power to do special things and be really strong. It's cool."

I shut my eyes tight, take a deep breath, mentally count to ten, but it's all bullshit—I'm flipping out. My blood, red-hot, corrosive, throbs in my brain. "Lon, okay, this is a situation where it must seem cool, acting like this, but it's not. This isn't a comic book, it's life, okay? You can't behave however you want. People get hurt."

"But whatever, if these people are going to treat you like this, you shouldn't have to—"

"LON!" I belt, unable to keep my mouth shut. There's the flex, the rush, and the venom spills out, overflowing. "Christ, I get it, 'kay? It looks cool and I seem strong, but you have no fucking idea what you're talking about, so just drop it. You're wrong, I'm fucked-up, and that's all you need to know. Got it?"

"Okay," he whispers.

I put my eyes on the TV and let the venom seethe through me a bit more, then slowly pull back, leaving me with the cold, tired aftereffects. I measure my breath and wipe the beads of new sweat off my forehead before glancing over and seeing—

My brother. My brother, Lon, who's brilliant and funny

and tries so hard all the time to understand his brother. He sits there, burrowed into one corner of the couch, mouth twisted downward, eyes bulging wetly out of his sheet-white face. He's doing everything in his power to keep from crying, digging his fingernails so hard into his knees that it must hurt. And the venom, sinking back into its hole, looks at him and gives a sharp cackle.

Well done.

Jesus.

"Lon, wait," I rasp, all my rage and empowerment replaced with mortified embarrassment. When I say his name, he can't keep holding it and explodes into quiet, scared sobs, mumbling that he's sorry over and over again. And now I'm crying, as there doesn't seem to be anything else to do. I grab him like a rag doll and clutch him to my chest, as if he's going to vanish. I can feel his face, with that blubbering little-kid mouth.

Jesus Christ, I'm a monster. I'm the problem.

Soon we hold each other and make these horrible sobbing noises in the back of our throats. I love him more than anything, but the venom can still find a way into his life. And I just fucking *let it*.

Finally, when we manage to calm ourselves down, I pull him from my chest and look into his face, all puffy and smeared with snot. Before I can try to clean him up, he's talking a mile a minute.

"I'm sorry, Locke, I didn't mean to butt in, and I know you have Randall and Renée and this new lady, but if you ever need to talk to someone, I can listen, y'know, I can help, or I can try, I just want you to be happy, and—"

"Lon." He wheezes and goes silent. "Don't apologize. And if you ever want to talk, that's what I'm here for, okay?" He nods slowly, his mouth still open. "Thank you for talking to me, and thank you for trying to help me. I'm gonna get us some tissues, okay?"

He nods slowly, and I make my way to the kitchen.

As I'm finishing up the dishes, I hear Lon in the next room, talking energetically on the phone. It just seems comical that my brother's chatting it up with his buddies until I hear the phrase "that comic you gave Locke" thrown into the mix. I wipe my hands off, grab the kitchen extension, and eavesdrop.

"Okay," asks Lon, "how about the Silver Surfer?"

"Ugh. No way. Can't stand him." Yup, my brother's getting phone-cozy with my girlfriend. Too cute.

"Me neither! It's all too much cosmic stuff!"

"Exactly! And the deep-seated religious implications! Gag!"

I can hear it taking Lon a bit to work out the religious implications. "Totally."

"Okay, my turn. Ghost Rider?"

"Awesome. Totally awesome. His powers are just too cool."

"Ah, you're a kid after my own heart. Johnny Blaze, though?"

"I dunno. . . . Blaze is cool, but they do that big-bad-biker thing way too much."

"Did you see the miniseries where they fought Venom in the sewers, though?"

"Yeah, *Spirits of Venom*! He was incredible!"

"Hell, yeah! I just loved seeing Venom and Ghost Rider duke it out!"

"I liked Demogoblin."

"He was okay. Hey, your brother back yet?"

"Hey, I'm here. Who's Ghost Rider?"

There's a yelp, and then Lon hangs up like he's scared the phone is going to bite him. Renée tsks me for it. "You scared him off! We were having a great conversation about comic books. It sounds like he really knows his stuff. I really want to meet him."

"He's a great kid," I say. "I'm glad you did that. He kind of needs a little cheering up tonight. I had a venom moment with him." I tell her about my earlier attack, my screaming at Lon, and she clucks through the phone.

"You have to talk to him about these things, hon. Maybe

he didn't know how serious an issue it is for you, but that's because you never really spoke to him about it. Can't blame the kid for being a little confused."

"I just don't want him to start thinking of me, of *this*, as a role model," I say. "I know he's impressionable. I mean, fuck, he's ten, but I didn't think he could ever think of the venom as a good thing."

"Well, it's not like you show him otherwise."

I feel a single pulse rush through the back of my skull. "What do you mean?"

"It doesn't seem like you make it clear that it's a bad thing. Yeah, you embarrass the hell out of him and all, but you still act like a wrathful god while doing it."

Ugh, not you, too. Lady, that Hierophant shit only goes so far here. Besides, in this family, we don't—I furrow my brow, trying to hold in the soot-black storm cloud billowing up inside me. How can this happen? Since when can my mind have two venom attacks within forty minutes? "He's my little brother, Renée. I have to be strong for him."

"Oh, come on, fuck that. You just have to be *there* for him, Locke, you don't have to be some unmovable pillar of male strength. Get over it and talk to him."

"That's NOT what I'm—" I close my eyes as hard as I can and slam a fist down on the kitchen counter. The vein in my forehead is about to pop. I'm seeing nothing but flashing sparks of red and black. Somehow Renée can hear it too.

"Locke? Calm down, okay?"

"I'm calm," I hiss through gritted teeth. Yeah, right, nice try.

"You're not," she says, her voice low and soothing. "I'm sorry, honey, I know he means a lot to you, and it's not my place to tell you how to treat your brother. But you can't flip out every time someone disagrees with you." Without really thinking, I grab a banana from the bowl of fruit next to the fridge and squeeze it over the sink until the soft white goo splits the peel and gushes out between my fingers. Focus on her voice. Focus on her. "Locke? Feeling better?"

Slowly, with every word she says, the venom retreats, until I'm left feeling drained and unsatisfied, the venom equivalent of blue balls. It's frustrating, but it's a start. That, or full-on episode. I slug some chocolate milk and sigh. "I'm okay. Just needed a moment. Sorry. I didn't mean—"

"Shhh. I get it, it's all good," she coos. "Do what you need to do, babe. I'll help any way I can."

"You're fantastic."

"Yeah, I know." She giggles, and the gears in my heart start whirring again.

"So what's up? Or were you just calling to talk comics with Lon?"

"Weimar party. A week from this Thursday. Randall said you don't have school on Friday because of some faculty function. You're gonna get your card, so be there."

"Okay . . . You know, I'm not a big party person, Renée. . . ."

"You will be at this one. Don't worry—Randall, Casey, and I will take care of you."

"Okay . . . my card?"

"Wear a suit—a coat and tails if you can find them. Trust me on this one, hon."

"Wait, a tux?"

"I told you, it's a Weimar party."

"Where am I supposed to get a tux?"

"Well, that's not my problem, is it? Make it a nice one. Look hot. Weimar works best when you look hot."

"Weimar?"

"'Life is a cabaret, old chum,'" she sings, "'come to the cabaret.'"

WAKE UP."

His eyes flickered like those of an acid head. Once the haze seemed to evaporate from his vision, he screamed like a little girl and curled into a ball.

"Please don't hurt me! I haven't done anything! They sent me back!"

"I mean you no harm," I said softly. "I am in debt to you. You stopped that creature."

Slowly his body unfolded, and he gawked at me like I was river-dancing. "You're Blacklight," he panted. "THE Blacklight."

"That I am." I helped him to his feet, and he glanced around the rooftop at the glittering skyline on all sides of us. His eyes stayed wide, nearly bulging out of his skull, his mouth hanging wetly open as he took in the view. I could imagine this was a shock for him, but honestly, I just wanted to get to the bottom of this damn mystery. "How do you know my name?"

"My God," he murmured, "it used to look like this, didn't it? New York. Manhattan. We're in Manhattan, aren't we?"

"Yes, of course. Answer my question."

"Jesus, there's the Chrysler Building. . . . Look at it, like a giant, steel Christmas tree. It's just like I remem—"

I grabbed his shoulder and spun him around to face me. "I don't have time for this," I said, jabbing a blackened finger in his face. "Tell me who you are. Where you're from. What the hell that creature that turned into you was."

He stared into my eyes for a few seconds, dumbfounded, and then nodded slowly. "Who I am isn't important," he said with a sigh, "but when I'm from is."

"I'm sorry—when?"

"I'm here from thirty years in the future, Locke. They sent me back to find you."

The sound of my real name sent vipers through my blood. He really knew. This would not do. "Explain yourself. Immediately."

"I came back in time to find you, to speak to you, to let you know about what horrible things will happen if you don't do away with this little 'gift' of yours."

"What are you?"

"Isn't it obvious?" he said, laughing humorlessly. "The swirling black tendrils, the dead, hateful eyes . . . It's pretty simple."

I knew the answer before he said it. I didn't know how *I knew, but I did. And as he affirmed it, the bottom of my stomach gave way to an endless pit of horror.*

"I'm the new Blacklight," he said. "I'm what you become."

"You're . . . you're ME?"

"Not quite." His eyes glazed over as he took in the city again and mumbled, "That's the problem."

CHAPTER EIGHT

THERE'S ONE PERSON I can think of who I could borrow a tuxedo from (one that fits me, anyway) in time for the party. One problem: He's my father.

Randall drives me, borrowing his mom's car. He's one of the few people I know who can actually drive (it's New York, we have the subway). He'd acted like a suburban kid the day he turned sixteen, talking nonstop about *needing* his license. He drove to school the day he got it (all twelve blocks) just to show off how cool he was, blasting classic rock out of the windows at full volume (or, to quote Randall as he passed us that day, "BAHN! BaNAHN! BAHN-NAHN du nunnah-NUNNAH, getcher mota runnin' . . . !"). It was hilarious in kind of a dorky way, which, I suppose, is Randall's MO.

On the ride up, he takes my silence for an invitation. Which it totally is. "So how *is* Rick? Haven't seen him in a dog's age."

I look at him out of the corner of my eye. "Did you ever meet my dad? I don't remember that."

"It was at that birthday of yours, like, two years ago. Your dad showed up, remember? He gave you that journal, the really nice one with that weird sort of pea-soup-green cover that I could tell you hated. He was awkward and thought he was the shit. Like the really cool kid who's graced the chess club party with his presence."

"Huh, I guess you *were* there. He's good, I guess. I dunno. He's not on my mind much. Hey, why do you keep calling him Rick? Why not just call him, like, 'your dad?'"

He stares ahead for a bit as if he's trying to see his answer on the shoulder of the West Side Highway. "No offense, dude, but he doesn't seem much like a dad. And you never really want to talk to or about him. So to me, he's just this guy named Rick who happened to . . . *sire* you. A father is the man who raises you, not the one who supplies you with genetic material."

For a second the world settles to a halt, and Randall and I are the most important friends in existence.

"And from what I've seen, Rick's not much of a man, and you've been raised by"—he dons a retarded grin—"me."

"Oh, wow, that's one hell of a concept."

"I'll explain it when you're older, son."

We get to my father's house, one of those big multistory suburban deals with a lawn bigger than my whole apartment if you include both the front and back. It looks like the *Addams Family* house designed by Donny and Marie. As Randall parks in the driveway next to two incredibly nice cars (an SUV and an Acura . . . his and hers, or hers and his, or whatever, I don't fucking care), he looks over at me and says, "Hey, do you want me to come in with you? I could take out the wife while you get the tuxedo, tie up your pops, cut up some magazines, and make a note for the police—"

"I'll be fine, thanks."

"Gotcha."

The five-second walk between the car and the massive front door takes approximately twelve forevers. I feel myself begin to sweat nervously, and cocoon my coat around me, which only makes me sweat more. *This will be fine,* I say in my head. *You called ahead. They know you're coming. Just get in, get the tux, and get out. No problem.*

Yeah. Just go in there, smile, and let that son of a bitch believe that he's a good fucking father. Let him know that he can still provide you with something, although it may not be, I dunno, compassion, or kindness, or the time of fucking day. No big deal. Here's a suit, kid.

"Shut up, shut up, now's not the time, please, for five fucking minutes, shut up."

I finally look up to face the door, reaching my hand out steadily for the big gold-plated knocker screwed to the front of it.

Before I even touch it, the door opens, and any remaining stoicism in me becomes sweat. There stands a girl with long blonde hair, dressed in a school-girl uniform, presumably Bethany, my—gyah—*half-sister*. She looks to be about five, clinging to the strap of her backpack like I'm about to steal it. My instinct is to bend down and smile innocently, but something in her eyes creeps me out way too much, so I just say, "Hi, I'm Locke."

Her eyes light up, and she rushes down the hallway, squealing, "MOM!" With nothing else to do, I reluctantly follow her inside.

Millie, my dad's silver medal, is sitting at a small table surrounded by huge front windows, glowing in the afternoon sun. Once she catches sight of me, all other sound is drowned out by a deafening "HIIII!"

"Hey."

"God, good to *see* you!" she says, rushing over and pulling me into a huge hug. I'm not sure how to respond to this whole thing. Something in the back of my head suggests I knock her out, get Randall to go ahead with the kidnapping plan, and maybe snatch a few twenties from her pocket. Venom talking. So I just pat her back lightly with my hand. A nice, neutral gesture. She smells nice, I guess.

Okay . . . OKAY. Fuck. The dinosaurs could've ruled the Earth and died during this hug. Let go of me.

Let go of me, you plastic-ass little—

She pulls back, and the venom eyes blunt objects throughout the room. After doing the arm's-length "good look at you" routine, she pulls me toward the kitchen table. I was afraid of this. If this were Dad, there'd be a handshake, maybe he'd even offer me a drink if it had been a good day. There'd be guy stuff—sports and school and the future—and we'd leave feeling a little better about ourselves. But no, no drink, no football, just this woman pretending I'm family.

"Wow! I haven't seen you in ages! What are you, a senior now?"

"Junior."

"Wow, a junior, gosh! And so handsome in that coat, too. So many people can't pull off the long coat, but you, you do it well!"

"Thanks."

"Wow. Sorry I didn't get the door, the baby was having a moment and I had to get her binky." The baby. I can't even find the words. "Would you like some tea? Coffee? Soda?"

"Got any chocolate milk?"

She gives me a sly smile and says, "A sweet tooth. Just like your father."

I didn't think hell would be this well decorated.

Next thing I know, I'm sipping Nesquik next to Millie around the glass table I'd found her at, wishing she wasn't so fucking *nice*. If she were cold and uncaring, I could at least walk away from this experience feeling vindicated. Since this isn't the case, I'm answering her questions about high school and New York City life. My ego is melting and turning into a pool of boiling bitterness. The venom is like a heartbeat, persistent, grinding into my mind at high speeds. I can't drink the chocolate milk fast enough; every sip cancels out a pulse of unfiltered hate.

After a while, I can't take the suspense any longer, so I finally decide to ask. "Is, um, my dad around?"

She gets an almost hurt look in her eyes. "No, I'm sorry, honey. He's at work. He wanted to be here, but it was one of those days." I let her think that this is a big bummer for me and look at my shoes. "But he did leave what you needed out for you after you called this afternoon. Hold on. . . ." She gets up and exits the room, leaving me to finish my chocolate milk and look around. It's nice. I remember them having a nice home, but nothing like this. The more I stare, the more comes back to me, and the more disgusted and outraged I feel. Christmases in itchy sweaters. Helping Lon with his tie the day of our great-aunt's funeral.

How much do you think this place set him back?

Please not now.

You can "not do this." Me, I'm pissed.

I'm begging you. The room closes in, and my head swims in contempt. *Please, not now.*

You never wonder why your family had to be the test run?

I don't know. I don't want to talk about it. Fuck off.

It's *because I'm* right, *huh?*

Maybe.

"Hi."

I turn around to face the little voice and see a girl who let me in. She stands half-hidden by a decorative umbrella stand, her eyes fixated on me with rapt fascination. This time I summon the stones to smile at her and be at least somewhat welcoming and brotherlike.

"Hi," I coo. "Bethany, right? I'm Locke."

"Oh."

There's a moment of staring at each other, the awkwardness obviously not exclusive to me.

"How's having a baby brother?"

She stares for a second and then whispers, "Okay. Brian's nice. Sorta."

I bite my lip to keep from laughing. Brian. Bethany and Brian. Brian and Bethany. I always forget about it until it slaps me back in the face. Ten dollars says the next one's name is Bridgette or Bonnie or Blake or something. Dad with his stupid fucking letter hang-ups. If he'd had another kid with Mom, their name would definitely start with an *L*. Is there some process to choosing what letter? Why'd we get *L* and they get *B*? Is there a woman out there, waiting for my dad to stuff her womb full of *A* children? I wonder whether he'll keep leaving wives and taking new ones till he has an entire alphabet, but then I tell myself to shut up, because that's venom talking; talking and talking and kicking and screaming—

"Is he?" is the only thing I can think of.

"You're one of Dad's other kids, right?"

I snap back to reality and try being polite. "Right. We've met before, you're just too young to remember. I came for Easter."

Bethany squirms a bit and finally says, "Why're you here?"

"I'm borrowing a suit from my—from Dad."

"Oh."

"Yup. For a party."

"A fancy party?"

"Sssssort of."

"Does Dad know?"

"Yup."

"Okay." She cocks her head to the side and frowns a bit. "I like your hair."

"Uh . . . thanks."

"My mom says you're in therapy."

Oh, DOES she?

"Yup."

"Me too."

"Really?"

She nods a bit, smiling. "I talk to myself a lot, and sometimes I talk about things that aren't nice. Mom heard me."

Just as the venom can't take it anymore and is about to suggest that my half sister is one of the Children of the Damned, Millie comes striding back into the room with a complete coat and tails, all wrapped up and ready to go. She sees Bethany and smiles. "Hey, sweetie. Did you say hello to Locke?"

Bethany nods her head slightly. "I like his hair."

"Isn't that nice?" Looking back to me, she hands me the tux. "There you go. It should fit you well enough. Rick wore it to a costume party once or something, I mean, no one really has a coat and tails anymore. Well. Anyway. All yours."

I smile and take it and, making the excuse that my friend is waiting for me, slowly back toward the door. Millie keeps smiling and says a good-bye and that she hopes to see more of me soon, while Bethany trots over to her and hugs her around the waist as if her mother is a life preserver in the ocean. The whole place seems irritating, jagged. I feel dizzy. The venom sends shocks and strains down the cords of my neck, through my shoulders, down into my fingers. I'm somewhere between enraged and ashamed.

Fucking bitch, with her big, stupid smile and her long hug, fucking athletic blond-haired rugrat, fucking McMansion—

As I'm almost out of the kitchen, Millie says, "I'll tell your dad you said hi."

I nod, and then wave to Bethany. "Later, kid," I say, a little too desperate to get out the door.

Have a good one, kid. Hope you don't grow up to be Ophelia.

I exit the front door, and the fresh air hits me, washing away rage, nerves, and the nonstop buzzing in my head. I let it wash through my coat, my T-shirt, under my armpits and into my hair. Thank God I got out of there when I did; I was beginning to sweat and shake a bit between Millie's niceness and Bethany's therapy talk. Whatever you want to call it. I just felt like I walked onto the set of some weird TV show about the darkness that lives within the typical American family. Or something. God, it's nice out.

Wonder if Dad knows crazy comes from his side. Wonder how it'd make him feel to know that you—and thus I—were spawned from his genes.

As I get into the car, Randall hands me a cigarette, and I spark up. He glances at the suit and smiles. "Shit, a full coat and tails. You'll be the life of the party. Go, Rick."

"Yeah, lucky me."

"The visit wasn't a memory you want to cherish, I take it?"

I shrug. "Millie was too nice, their little girl is in therapy, and both the kids have names that begin with *B*."

Randall raises a hand to cover his smile. "Sorry."

"It's not funny."

"I know." He chuckles. "I know, I'm sorry, it's not funny."

"Just drive."

"Okay. Sorry."

He starts the car, and then, the minute we pull out of the driveway, we nearly die.

Our car and the one barreling toward us both screech to a sudden halt. Randall hits the brake, and we both lean forward painfully, the seat belts cutting into our shoulders. The other car honks at us as it backs slowly up, and I stare blankly at the man behind the steering wheel.

Again the venom fills me, swells up in me, and like on the phone with Renée, *guides* me. There's no dam about to burst, just a quick, clean shot of wit and rage balled into one. Maybe I am in control or maybe it's controlling me; either way, it feels wonderful and right. Destiny.

"Stop for a second. Roll down your window." Randall glances at me funny and does as he's told—my voice has the urgency of a police officer's. Once the window's down, I lean forward and grin politely at the dapper man with the shaggy blond-gray hair, his face curled into a sneer of contempt. "Sorry 'bout that, Dad, us kids all hopped up on goofballs, you never know what we're doing. Thanks for the tux. I'll bring 'er back nice and clean. Nice seeing ya!"

I take just enough time to catch his stunned, stupid expression before I tell Randall to drive.

Five minutes after I get to the waiting room, Dr. Yeski walks out with Shelby Waters, a girl who hangs out with a lot of guys from my school. She's in my grade and runs with a crowd that loves Randall but cringes when I stop by (Randall calls them "vintage T-shirt kids," which I think refers to their tight garments with badly screened images of crappy old cartoons on them). She's obviously been crying furiously: Her eyes are bright red, her nose is running, and there are twin rivers of eyeliner coursing down her cheeks. She sniffles a little and mumbles a thank-you to Dr. Yeski, who just smiles and says, "That's what I'm here for, Shel. Take care until next week. Call me whenever you want to if something comes up, okay?"

The older woman next to me clutches her cakelike cap to her head as if it might fly off, and leaps to her feet. Just as they're about to leave, Shelby spies me and turns pale in recognition. In a soft and terrifying voice, she mutters, "Don't tell anyone about this." And then the old woman is pulling her away, her arm wrapped around her in an ominous fashion.

Dr. Yeski beckons for me, smiling. I trudge into her office, trying to ignore the fact that the last person who walked out of here was crying like a baby. It's a typical shrink's office: desk with a PC, leather couch, chair, potted plants, lots of books, and of course, five, count 'em, five boxes of tissues strategically placed throughout. What surprises me the most is a huge Clash poster on her wall with a scrawled signature reading, "For Laura—Death or glory!—JS." In the lower left-hand corner, there's a doodle of a trout nailed to a cross. I point at it and ask what it's doing up there.

She doesn't smile. "I got it signed by Joe Strummer back when I was about your age."

"What's with the aqua-crucifixion?"

"I asked him to draw a Jesus fish. He'd been drinking."

"I have to tell you, the crying girl and the drunken punk rocker doodles? Hell of a first impression."

"Understandable." Then she plants herself in her swivel chair and picks up a yellow legal pad, and we start talking. Or she starts talking, and I get distracted. . . .

"How're you doing? How's your week been?"

I snap to attention and move my eyes upward, to her face. "Sorry? It's been okay. I dunno. Large. I mean, strange."

She doesn't seem to notice my piggish snafu. "How so?"

"I had to go to my dad's to borrow a tux for a party. It was kind of surreal, being in his house and with his family. We're not very . . . We don't really spend a lot of time together, so it . . . threw me off, I guess."

"Why don't you spend more time together?"

I shift in my seat, feeling warmer than I should. Easy. "I think my mom could tell I hated being there, around his new family, and my dad just . . ." Deep breath, one step at a time. "He kind of considers me a bummer, I guess. Always unhappy, a little crazy, and so on and so forth. Every so often I'd start having a venom moment and would just go out and sit in the car."

She nods. There's sympathy there, although impartial. It feels strangely okay—I'm not being humored. "I bet that's hard. What happened when you went there this week?"

"Well . . . I dunno. My dad's new wife . . . Well, hold on. Is she my stepmom?"

"Not if you don't want her to be."

"I mean, yeah, sure, that's deep as shit and all, but really. Technically."

"Technically, yes. She's your stepmother."

I grimace. "That's what I thought. Anyway, my stepmom was really nice, which was off-putting. She was all huggy and talkative."

"That's a bad thing?"

"It's just a weird thing. I like to vilify them a bit, my dad and Millie and their family. But instead, she was just really amiable and kind to me, and it was a bit of a weird experience."

"Do you expect her to dislike you?"

Okay, here we go. I feel venom whirl around in my heart, ready for the fight. "She's my fucking stepmother. I feel that I have sort of an inherent right to dislike her, and vice versa."

"Why do you feel that way?"

I raise an eyebrow. "Well, that's your job, right? To figure that out?"

She folds her arms in front of her. "If that's how you feel."

"Now we're just going in circles."

"Okay, then let's move forward. What about your stepmom upsets you?"

"I mean, they haven't . . . It's not like she did anything, it's what she sort of left out." I try to hold ground, but I'm losing it fast. She's good. "It's fine that they went off and had their own family. But there weren't two Christmases or group gatherings. He . . ." Deep breath. Drop your shoulders. Calm. "He *left*, and all they knew about it was that he left *us* for *them*. There was always that underlying feeling, like we were something that happened once, y'know? You can hear, in those little kids' voices, that we're people they *have* to see sometimes."

I'm expecting her to hit me with another tough one, but instead she nods and looks at me. "Did you see your dad?"

"Just as we left. He nearly ran into me and Randall, and I was a bit of a jerk to him. I just smiled and thanked him for the suit, and then had Randall drive off."

She smiles, finally. "Like a thief in the night, right? Keep the mystery and all that around you."

I hadn't thought of that. That was it exactly. "Well, yeah. I didn't have much to say to him, anyway . . . y'know?"

She nods and leans back a bit. "What's the tuxedo for?"

"Um, what do you know about 'Weimar'?"

She laughs, and I feel okay, which makes no sense.

HOW DID it happen?"

The time traveler (he refused to give his name) looked thoughtful. "What? Your death, or becoming Tyrant?"

"Both, I guess."

"Well, you became Tyrant about five years or so before your death," he says, as though he's recounting a story from his past. "It was around Halloween or so, a little after, in 2015. November. Yeah, definitely November; I remember it was broadcast during the marathon. You'd been around—you were a fucking superhero, for God's sake, so everyone knew about you—for a while before that. But still, you were a legend, so no big deal, right? And then, one night, you killed the mayor."

"I WHAT?!"

"You killed Mayor Rothchild on national television, as well as the guards, the security, the cameramen . . . pretty much everyone who could've posed a threat to you. And then you got in front of the camera and declared yourself Tyrant of New York City, and said that if anyone thought otherwise, they could happily take it up with you."

I sat down on the cold concrete of the rooftop and rolled a pebble between my fingers. This was madness. I was a protector. "Why? Why did I declare myself Tyrant?"

"The venom," he said. "It took control. You realized that things

would never change, no matter how much you fought, and you let the venom take control. You performed all these acts, yeah, but you weren't really the one driving the bus, if you know what I mean. Don't get me wrong, the city was still safe, but in a Machiavellian sort of way. An iron fist, ruling through fear. You let down your morals, and it took advantage of the opportunity."

"So how did . . ." I pointed at him. This was an awkward transition.

"You were killed five years after you declared yourself Tyrant, but the venom left your system before they got to it. You hadn't really been part of the show for a while, so they just put a bullet in you and continued hunting for the venom."

Icy fingers caressed the back of my skull and sent chills through my blood. "And the venom found you."

"Not quite," he whispered. "First it found Renée."

CHAPTER NINE

BEFORE THIS NIGHT, "Weimar" was eternally linked in my mind to one image—a swastika. Knowing my friends, I assumed that I was in for a history lesson.

I show up at the apartment building and am immediately given a cavity search by a massive doorman with a name tag reading BRAWN. I swear to God, his name is actually Brawn (silently, I pray the tired-looking guy behind him, staring at a stack of security screens, is wearing a tag reading BRAINS, but sadly, his name is Colin). The entire time I'm there, Brawn, good ol' Brawn, gives me a look that lets me know that he's the type of guy who will be necessarily polite to me right up until I step out of line and he tears out my larynx with his bare hands. You'd think that if enough kids show up in tuxes, he'd assume all of them are going to the same place.

The whole thing makes the venom sneer and pant and pound its fist on the table of my mind, livid with contempt. However, seeing as Brawn makes Andrew Tomas look like a mosquito, the venom seethes, letting the rage rush through me without breaking open like a boil. It knows this isn't a battle worth getting into. It's wicked and arrogant by nature, yeah, but the venom isn't stupid.

Finally, after checking out his clipboard, Brawn consents to let me upstairs, noting that he doesn't want "any craziness or such" (*Too bad, too—I LOVE craziness or such!*). I choke down big mouthfuls of verbal razors and let the elevator door shut behind me.

The door opens again, and my hatred takes a backseat to awe. Whoever the host is, he's rich. Like, buying-your-kids-out-of-any-trouble-they-might-someday-get-into rich; Trump money. Because the elevator door does not open to a hallway like a normal person's would. It opens to the apartment itself, to a massive white foyer full of girls in flapper dresses and boys in tuxes. I recognize a lot of them from the party in the park, but not enough. Immediately my coat and shirt become itchy, stuffy, way too uncomfortable.

Oh, for fuck's sake, first Brawn, now this. Let's just go home.

This is important. Casey and Renée are counting on me. We need this.

We?

A man in a tux grabs me by the collars and giggles maniacally in my face. *"Guten abend, mein kleiner Schnurrbart*! May I take your coat?"

Staring hard at him, I realize it's Casey and start laughing. "You crazy bastard! This place is utterly amazing! Whose is it?"

"One of zese beyutiful people," he says, his accent somewhere between German, Russian, and Rastafarian. He sweeps his arms across the room. "Look at zem! All such beyutiful people! Even ze orchestra es beyutiful."

"Casey, you've been drinking."

"No, YOU'VE been drinking!"

"No, I haven't!"

"Why the hell NOT?!"

"Good question. Better go remedy that."

"You better believe it." And with a shriek, he disappears into the crowd.

I filter through the mass of people, in awe of pretty much everything. The clothes, the makeup, the house, fill me with utter amazement. It's a loft apartment, obviously, but it's been divided up into different rooms using curtains hung from the ceiling. Normally a house like this would just piss me off something terrible—Manhattan decadence at its worst—but considering how the party's set up and the type of people in attendance, the whole place just seems magical and hilarious.

One room is the bar, where boys in tuxes and suits are yelling loudly while drinking beer, another a ballroom full of kids dancing to music that sounds somewhere between hardcore punk and big-band swing. There are some others, too, but the bar is really all I care about right now. And lo and behold, standing behind the bar is Tollevin the Tower, shooting me the biggest shit-eating grin I've ever seen. I smile back at him, resting myself on the bar and taking my handkerchief from my breast pocket (I figured since I get sweaty when I'm nervous, it was the ideal accessory) to wipe my brow.

"What'll it be, Locke?" he yells above the din.

"What's good?" I ask, glancing at the rainbow of bottles behind him. If there's a time to learn about liquor, it's now.

Tollevin grabs a bottle reading GLENLIVET and pours some into a tumbler glass for me. "You seem like a Scotch kind of guy. Try this."

I take a sip and feel the fluid in my mouth. It's tough, I suppose. Reminds me of the whiskey Casey gave me, only with an attitude problem. I swallow it and it burns all the way down. I open my mouth and could swear I'm breathing fire. The warmth burns down in my stomach into ball of slow heat that seems to resonate throughout my insides.

I cough. "Christ, that's harsh."

Tollevin laughs slightly. He pushes the Glenlivet to the side of the bar and pours me a shot of what looks like melted licorice from a green bottle. He hands it to me and smiles. "Jägermeister. The Devil's Cough Syrup."

"Am I about to die?"

"A little. It's for the best."

This one isn't tough. It's just a slap in the face, sugary-sweet syrup with an acidic aftertaste. Once it's all down, I let out a gag that makes Tollevin crack up.

"That was awful! People actually drink that?"

Tollevin laughs a little more. Finally he pours me a glass of black fluid with a rising white head and pushes it slowly toward me.

"This is Guinness, right?"

"Right. Think coffee mixed with beer. And bacon. I'm not giving you any more than that; when that Scotch and Jäger kick in, you'll be feeling pretty damn good."

I can't help but smile. "That's sweet of you. Taking care of me and all."

He shrugs modestly. "Renée would kill me if I got you drunk before you got your card." Again with the card. Before I can ask what all this nonsense is about, I hear a familiar voice behind me squeal, "*Dah*ling!" Speak of the she-devil.

I turn around and swell with pride, lust, and adoration. Renée is dressed in a white flapper's dress with intense makeup, black fishnets, heels, and one of those sequiny yarmulke-type things on her head with little strings of sparkles trailing down.

While the dress is tight enough to fit a waifish flapper, Renée is built with curves, making her utterly seductive. Her nails are bright green. It hits me for a second that I've never seen her in white up until now.

I throw my arms up in a greeting gesture, expecting a hug. Instead, she leaps into the air, making me catch and hold her. She stares into my eyes, and her smile and smell tell me that I'm exactly where I should be. The next thing I know, her lips are firmly attached to mine, her tongue snaking swiftly through my mouth, which I mimic in turn. The extraordinary din around us dies in my ears, and I am living for this kiss and only this kiss.

She leans her head back and smacks her ruby red lips, now slightly smudged at the sides. "Mmm," she whispers, "you taste Irish."

I laugh. Already I'm beginning to feel that light numbness slip through me. The booze makes me feel warm and comfortable, but still edgy—it's similar to the moments of controlled, confident venom I've had lately. "I have a taste for Guinness, apparently. Tollevin's been finding out what suits me best."

Renée leaps down from my arms and eyes Tollevin. "Tower, what have you been putting in my boy?" Before he can answer, she's pulling me through the crowd. "I want you to meet people. There are so many here tonight."

"Yes, there are lots of people here tonight . . . but honestly, you have people to see and shit, don't sidetrack your evening of fun just 'cause of me. . . ."

She stops, kisses me, and gives me a good, hard look. "You *are* my evening of fun."

The next hour or so is a blur of names, faces, and hands. Renée yanks me through every room, introducing me to about fifty million indie rockers and crust punks. I get three "So this is Locke"s, seven "nice to finally meets you"s, and even about six "Renée's told me a lot about you"s. Anyone else dragging me around a party and I'd feel kind of ill at ease. Not with Renée, though. Every time she presents me, there's this laser-beam look in her eyes, as though, more than anything, she wants them to adore me as much as she does. And it works—the strange, booze-fueled, easygoing venom stays with me all night, and somehow I'm actually *charming.* At one point I make a comment about seeing Renée in white for the first time, and a whole circle of kids bursts into laughter, including Renée, who pulls me closer to her and snuggles her head into my neck. Locke Vinetti, life of the party—who knew?

We take a break from the schmoozing and sit at a table in the bar, Renée ordering a gin and tonic, and me downing a glass of ice water. All that walking around and trying to appear cool can work up a thirst. As we imbibe, Renée beams at me. "You okay? I hope I haven't been making too much of a spectacle of you. . . ."

"No, it's fine," I say. "I'm really quite down with it. It's incredibly sweet, hearing these people mention what good things you've been saying about me."

"Are there any *bad* things to say about you, darling?"

"Well, I mean . . . you know, I'm, the venom is kind of . . ." I trail off.

"Hey." She puts her green-tipped index finger to my mouth and gets a very serious look on her face. Not angry or upset, just *serious*. "Not tonight. Okay?"

"I'm sorry."

"Don't say that. I'm just telling you." Her expression softens. "Tonight you're Locke Vinetti. Nothing else."

The venom responds to the order strangely. Usually there's a raised fist, a feeling in my gut as though the world is ending and I'm on the pale horse. But tonight it changes its tune.

It shrugs, shifts, and goes to sleep.

We'll discuss this later.

Thank you.

Oh, I wouldn't go thanking me just yet.

I smile broadly. "Okay," I say softly, reaching out and squeezing her hand. "Not tonight."

Her eyes go shiny, and we kiss.

"My dark boy," she sighs. "My hero in black."

"I'm the Vampire James Dean, baby," I whisper back. "It's all in the Marlboros."

"Dean smoked Chesterfields."

I love this woman.

A few minutes later, a boy wearing only tux pants and suspenders walks into the room and announces loudly that the presentation is being made in the main room. Renée lifts me onto my feet, and we walk side by side, arm in arm, into a massive ballroom with a stage occupying most of one wall. Casey's standing onstage behind a microphone stand, next to a huge, veiled picture, smiling like a schoolboy. He lights a cigarette and takes a long, full drag.

As he leans forward and speaks into the mic, the room quiets.

"Good evening, children of the night," he says, holding his arms out in greeting. "Has anyone seen the worst-dressed gay kid in the city around here?"

"THERE HE IS!" responds the crowd as one, pointing.

Casey paws his tux and sighs. "Oh, Christ, good. I was worried there for a second." Requisite chortling ensues. "As you all know," he continues, "tonight is a celebration of the Weimar, the scene to end all scenes, a time of freedom, beauty, and love."

The crowd roars back. Casey mock-stumbles at the pitch of the noise, and then, laughing, always laughing, continues.

"The Weimar was many things. A performance movement, a historical era, and an escape for so many whose ways weren't tolerated by the powers that be. We, though, celebrate the Weimar as a state of mind, an understanding of the need for personal freedom and release. Weimar, for us, is the experience of fun without limits, joy without rules, and life without those foolish boundaries set by little men with stupid ideas. After all," he says, taking on a queeny lisp and standing in a pose that smacks of Prince, "I think we all have our little *differentheth,* don't we, darlingth?"

Again, the room's filled with mirthful noise. I giggle through the childish lump in my throat. Casey. We would go to war for him now, all of us. Our buddy, the gay Henry V.

"However, those little men have gained great power in this world," he continues. "They feed on good things, pervert them, buy them up, and sell them back to the morons out there who didn't think of them in the first place." The black rings in Casey's voice. The air crackles with anger. Something's up. "And in the case of the Weimar, one little, monotesticular parasite decided to poison our expression of love, making the very word 'Weimar' synonymous with his campaign of hatred and cruelty." Ooooh. "And so, *frauleins* and *leiberherrs*, I present to you: our guest of honor!"

Casey yanks back the sheet over the stand to reveal a massive portrait of Adolf Hitler, throwing the heil.

My hand tightens around Renée's. Nazis. Nazi punk rockers. I've somehow fallen in with a crew of Nazis obsessed with tarot cards, and tonight they're going to induct me into their white brotherhood. Tollevin's just a red herring. It all makes sense. I need to leave, to get—

Casey takes one last drag and flicks his cigarette.

There's a whiff of lighter fluid, and then the picture goes up in a ball of flames to the tune of everyone in the room cheering, screaming, celebrating the death of ignorance and rigidity and all things old and evil. After a few seconds, Casey produces a bucket of water, puts out the fire, knocks the picture over, and stomps the ashes until Hitler is nothing more than a slimy black stain on the stage. Once finished, he wipes his brow and steps back up to the microphone.

"Glad we could clear that up. Now, on to other business," he says, suddenly appearing solemn. "Shall we talk tarot?"

Approval booms around us.

"I thought so. As you know, the tarot and its meanings have become an important part of what we stand for. And as you know, we occasionally bring folks we've taken a liking to into the Major Arcana."

Oh my God. My card. I get it.

"We have the Tower manning the bar, a Fool playing a guitar recital uptown, a Hierophant in a beautiful white dress, an Emperor running the show, and a Hermit as our wonderful host. If you ask around, I'm sure the Devil will teach you some fun drinking games, and the Hanged Man will sell you some, ahem, party favors later. But tonight we initiate a new individual into the Major Arcana, a newcomer to our little group, who I, personally, am rather enamored of."

Renée's hand tightens on mine.

"If Renée, Randall, or myself have not yet introduced you to this wonderful boy, we will eventually. Ladies and gentlemen, boys and girls, we present to you: Locke Vinetti, the Strength."

The crowd reaches a frenzy. Applause and exaltation fill the ballroom, and a hundred hands rise into the air, throwing fists in celebration to my acceptance. I'm totally dumbstruck by the reactions. A feeling rushes through me unlike any other, and I almost start to choke up. There is no gnawing anxiousness, no seething displeasure—just joy.

Renée kisses my cheek softly, and then gives me a sharp slap on the ass. "Get up there, you silly boy."

I make my way slowly to the stage, hands patting my back and shoving me forward, almost carrying me to the stage. When I finally reach the edge, Casey pulls me up. And when at last I stare out into the crowd, I see an ocean of pierced faces and colored hair gathered together to honor me, only me, Locke. Pushed into my hand is a tarot card, a depiction of a woman in a white gown, wrenching open the jaw of a fierce lion, her face twisted in a spasm of determination. Casey, at my ear, says, "Welcome to the tarot, ya big hottie."

The venom is gone tonight, but for the first time that I can remember, I am not alone.

A few hours and a couple more drinks later, I'm making out with Renée in the hallway of her building.

The rest of the party was a whirlwind of celebration. We tore the ballroom to pieces once the music started again, a punk-rock symphony of biblical proportions. At some point they played the *Cabaret* soundtrack, which absolutely destroyed any sanity left in the crowd. People appeared to be having sex up against a few of the columns while a couple of Goths dueled with jagged bottlenecks. Pandemonium, pure and unfiltered. Then Renée introduced me to the wonders of tequila body shots; the salt, lemon, skin, and tongue making the liquor somewhat palatable. Randall even called her cell just to send his blessings to me. "Welcome to our fucked-up world, Stockenbarrel!" he shouted. "My work is done!"

And so now I have Renée pressed hard up against the wall across from the door to her apartment, with one of her hands cradling the back of my head and the other one kneading one of my butt cheeks. We've gone from kissing to making out to no-holds-barred dry-humping in less than an hour. I'm not drunk, just tipsy enough to forget everything but this girl. Our tongues are dueling in each other's mouths. Sweat and makeup's just being ground into my face, and I couldn't care less. I've never been so consumed with lust in my entire life. All I want, all I need, is her touch and her taste.

Abruptly she ducks out from between me and the wall and giggles as she unlocks and opens her apartment door. I try to recover my senses and mumble, "Well, um, guess I should get out of here—"

"Oh no, you shouldn't," she says, twirling on one of her heels.

"What . . . I mean, it's late, and I don't want your aunt—"

She reaches behind herself, and I hear the distinct sound of a zipper.

"Aunt Marie is gone for the night," she says, biting her lip. "Andrew is over at a friend's house. The apartment is mine."

The dress hits the ground with a soft *whoosh.* She stands there, clad only in a white satin corset covered in buckles, a garter belt, her stockings and her heels.

"And I'm yours."

A million reasons why I shouldn't do this swim through my head. My mom's expecting me. We haven't been dating for long enough. I'm drunk, or drunk enough to know I'm a little drunk, which means that I'm perhaps too drunk, and she's a little drunk too, and there's nothing wrong with just a quiet evening, which this evening certainly hasn't been so far, but—but—

"Renée, maybe we should think—"

"I'll tell you what," she says to cut me off, "I'm going to go to my room and light some candles and some incense. You stand out here and think. Think all you want for as long as you want. I'll wait in my room. And when you've thought good and hard about everything, you come inside and I'll make love to you real slow." She blows me a kiss and walks slowly into the blackness of her apartment, giving me a shot of her rounded ass bobbing slowly after her before darkness engulfs her.

I think for about twelve seconds, then make sure to lock the door behind me.

HOW?" I said, snatching him by the collar and shoving my face into his. "What happens to Renée?"

"My God, your eyes . . ."

"HOW?!"

"She—she becomes the second Blacklight," he stuttered, scared. "When it escaped you, the venom looked for the nearest possible person who your darkness rubbed off on, who you left a—an impression on, and it was her." His face twists in both terror and grief. "She's the one who does the most damage, who destroys half of the city. With a fresh host, it was unstoppable. God, if you could've only seen her, she was magnificent, this mass of black lightning and burning dark light, like some sort of fallen angel from Hell. . . ." His eyes glazed over, and I could almost hear him imagining Renée, a spirit in black wiping out half of New York. "I remember how she laughed when she killed most of the people in Times Square, it was this huge pile of bodies—"

"And you?" I managed. "How'd you become this . . . thing?"

"Locke."

"Tell me."

His eyes squeezed hard shut. "I killed her," he whispered, "and the venom moved on to me."

That was all I needed to hear.

"How do we stop it?" I blurted out. My costume rippled, crackled,

swirled with my agitation. "We need to stop it. I need to know how the venom can be stopped. There can't be another Blacklight, do you hear me?"

"I know, I came back here to—"

"SPEAK UP, DAMMIT!"

"TO MEET YOU!" he screamed. "I just wanted to meet you! To see you face-to-face, to tell you what was going to happen, and maybe you could stop it. . . . They—they wanted me to—to try and make you, convince you to kill yourself, you know, or try and kill you, so the world wouldn't—"

"THEN WHY DIDN'T YOU!"

"Please stop, I can't—oh no. Oh God, no."

His pores turned deep black, and then begin growing into nubs; shapes; long, reaching appendages. The first of the tendrils began to form around his neck and arms, stretching hungrily out and twitching with anxiousness and rage.

"Get away," he gurgled in a voice only slightly his own. "Get away. It knows who you are, and it won't stop. . . ." And then his voice became garbled, because out of his mouth grew a mass of slippery, wriggling black tentacles, whipping fiercely. I watched as his legs formed huge, backward-facing spindles, like those of a dog or a goat. For a second there was still the silhouette of a man, hanging in the air, and then it was the creature, this horrible Blacklight from the future, my hideous reflection.

It made a noise, sort of like metal being crushed in a scrapyard, and took its first careful step toward me.

CHAPTER TEN

IS THERE ANYTHING more satisfying than taking a shower in the bathroom of the girl who you just had a whole lot of noisy sex with? Unfamiliar showers are a pet peeve of mine, so this moment of bliss is less common. I never know how to operate the shower, what knobs to turn where, and what buttons to push this way or that. The water pressure always sucks, the floor feels strange and slippery, and, of course, there's the pressing ethical question of whether or not you're allowed to pee on the floor. The shower is one of those private, personal spaces that, through constant daily routine and observant familiarity, you know as your own. Cleaning yourself in someone else's shower is like being the Jewish friend who was brought along to Sunday mass. This morning, however, was different. Walk in, turn on the water, and do my thing.

Midway through washing my hair, the curtain gets pulled back and I jump. It's probably Renée, right, but it could be Andrew or Aunt Marie—no glasses means constant paranoia (think Velma from *Scooby-Doo*). Fortunately it is Renée, naked and giving me a smile that I'm pretty sure is reserved just for my lanky ass. Without a word, our bodies mesh together, her breasts slippery against my chest, her lips hot and full and pillowy. As if on cue, everything besides Renée Tomas is gone. Nothing could make me happier than her and here and this.

After we, ahem, wash up for a while, our arms curl around each other and just stand there in the steam, her head cradled under my chin.

"Hey, you," she says.

"Mmm."

"So, last night . . . That was your first time, I take it."

"Mmm."

She giggles and runs her index finger back and forth along my skin. God in heaven, yes. "Is that an affirming or denying mumble?"

"Affirming."

"Right."

After some silence, I have to ask Stupid Guy Question Number One. "How'd you know?"

She makes a noise in her throat that means that she was expecting this. "There was just that little amount of . . . unfamiliarity with the procedure, I guess. Don't worry. You're a bit of a natural in the first place, and I had fun teaching you new things in the second." She chuckles. "Corrupting you is kick*ass*."

And Number Two, of course: "How was I?"

"Good," she says. "Really good. For your first time, stellar."

"Really?"

"You just learned as you went along, y'know, placement and such. You were drunk, too . . . but man. You're just on the ball when it comes to the little things."

"Hrm?"

"You were good to my ears. Things like that."

"Just . . . reciprocating."

"You'll be reciprocating a whole lot if I get my say from now on."

We take some more silence, occasionally rocking back and forth in each other's arms. I feel her head twitch, and she stares straight up at me with a reluctant, miserable look.

"Anyone told you about my folks yet?"

The question catches me off guard, and I can't be clever. "Yeah. I heard about it at school."

She nods. "I figured." A pause, then: "It's okay, you know. We can talk about it, or not, but I just want you to know it's okay if we do. It's not forbidden."

"Okay."

She keeps her eyes locked into mine. "I don't sleep with a lot of boys."

I nod. "Okay."

"I mean, I have slept with some boys," she says way too fast. "And some girls. And some of them were for fun, but most of them were only if I really, really cared about them."

All this is doing is making me think about my girlfriend with other guys, which is the most uncomfortable thing I can imagine, and girls, which is embarrassingly much less so. The venom stirs, mumbling low in its throat. She can feel the change in my body too and holds me out at arm's length.

"Look, this has a point."

"What's that?"

She puts her hand under my chin and guides my eyes to hers.

"That I know last night was a little sudden," she whispers, and then laughs. "And a little drunken, yeah. But I want you to know . . . that this isn't just . . . I'm not . . ."

The venom retreats like a wounded animal, and my heart feels like it's going to burst. I lean forward and kiss her. It's a *Dawson's Creek* kiss, an interrupting kiss that lets the other person know that you understand what they're going to say before you do. Her response is frantic; her hand finds the back of my head and presses. We kiss as if I'm going off to war.

When we come up for air, she looks at me hard. "I'm going to be a bitch now."

"How so?"

"Are you in love with me, Locke?"

"Oh, you fucking bitch."

"I'm serious."

No matter what I answer, I'll think it's the wrong thing. Either I take the clingy, emotional path or the totally superficial path. So I go with what I feel. Which is something I rarely do, seeing as going with what I feel usually results in me standing over someone, cackling and sobbing in the same breath, while they rethink why they were fucking with me in the first place. This time, I feel something random and unprovoked and strange and utterly fantastic lying in the depths of my heart. The Great Truth, the Engine of Survival, the Fifth Element.

"Yeah," I whisper, "I'm pretty sure I am, Renée."

She looks at me for a bit more and then says, "Yeah, me too."

We grab each other tight, fearless.

Renée has made it readily apparent that she's not so adept in the cooking department, and I can make a mean batch of cream-cheese scrambled eggs (hey, you have a little brother, you learn to cook some fabulous platters that Mom wouldn't tolerate if she was around). But as I come through the hallway into the glaring daylight of the kitchen, I realize that I'm in trouble.

Because Andrew's sitting there reading the funnies. The thin newspaper is bunched in his clenched-white hands. He looks like a big, mean, stupid, and thoroughly pissed-off gorilla who likes the Wu-Tang Clan. He looks like someone who's just found the guy who fucks his sister in their kitchen.

I freeze and let cold wash over me and come to rest in the pit of my stomach. A voice in the back of my mind reminds me of something I heard on the Discovery Channel: If a bear attacks, make yourself as big and loud as possible to chase it off. But before I can lift my arms and yell, "GO! AWAY!" Andrew takes a sip of his orange juice and mumbles, "Siddown, Vinetti."

FIGHT! FIGHT! FIGHT! FIGHT!

This is really, REALLY not the time.

Say "make me"! That'd be awesome! Just try it. "Make me, Andrew." It'd be like you're in a Robert Rodriguez movie!

I sit slowly, clasping my hands in front of me and regulating my breathing. The venom crouches calmly on its haunches, preparing to launch if necessary. There's a good chance I'm going to bleed furiously at the end of the conversation, and I have to be ready for that. In the meantime, I can just pray that Renée stays in her room—or is wearing headphones.

Andrew dramatically folds the paper in front of him and gives me a good, long exhale. "You spent the night here, I see."

I nod. Well, glad we got that out of the way.

"You know about my parents, don't you? Someone must've told you, if not Renée."

Change of direction much? I look up into his eyes, which are still hard, but now with prepared stoniness rather than anger or pride. There's no right way to go about this, is there? How the fuck can I answer that? Why does this big fucking monkey have to bring that shit up to me? The venom spins inside me, like a top, frustrated, backed into a corner. After last night, after that shower just now, I can't fight Andrew.

"Yeah," I croak through a mouthful of the venom. "I'm really sorry."

"I don't want to hear it." His eyes flitter like those of a trapped animal, like he can't focus on anything for too long or else it becomes his parents. "I'm incredibly territorial about my sister, Locke. Don't know what you heard, but my parents died 'cause of me, so I tend to think of myself as her protector."

"They . . . It wasn't your fault, Andrew."

"You SHUT UP!" he screams. There's no drama or facade to this statement; it's a primal scream, an uncontrolled blast. I've never seen someone get angry and go pale at the same time. The screaming stops as abruptly as it began. "Shut up.

You don't know what the fuck you're talking about, Vinetti, so I'd appreciate it if you didn't try to have an opinion on the matter. I made a mistake and they died because of it, simple as that. Have you ever lost a parent, Locke?"

"My dad left us, and I . . . think it's 'cause I'm such a spaz." Jesus. I've never said that out loud before. "But it's not the same thing."

"Damn right it isn't," he snaps. "You don't know *shit*. You don't have any fucking *idea*. My dad left a long time ago, and it wasn't because of a choice, it was because he was addicted to crystal, and we couldn't get him to stop pawning off about seventy percent of everything we owned. You can't—you can't comprehend what the fuck this family has been through just 'cause your dad left. . . . It's not even the same species."

I shut my eyes tight as the venom brays for blood. Before I can stop myself, the heat behind my eyes gets too high and I blurt out, "Well, what *I* went through was pretty fucking bad, so how about you watch your mouth, okay?"

He sneers for a second and then says, "Fair enough. My apologies."

The venom is shifting like an eel in a coffee can. Andrew's still being an asshole, and the urge to smash his face in is incredible, but something's off here. He's articulate. He's giving me an inch, for once. What's the fucking deal?

"I am very *territorial* of my sister," he repeats, "no matter what kind of psycho shit she's into. She's my *family*. And she . . ." I can see the words arranging themselves in his head. "Renée hasn't done too good since it happened. She's not happy a lot. She's full of fucking pills most of the time, but they keep her pretty cohesive and carefree, so I don't say nothing about it, but I'll tell you that I don't like it, and I hate these freaks she surrounds herself with. I hate that mincing queer buddy of yours, I hate the tall Mohawked black kid, but most of all, I'm *beside myself* that she's ended up with *you*."

"Tough shit, she's my girlfriend." Again, the venom seems to speak for me, standing up when I don't have the spine to.

"Watch yourself, Vinetti."

"Thanks for the advice, Andrew. There a fucking point to this?"

His eyes harden on me, and I can feel his anger in the air between us. "The pills keep her okay," he seethes, ignoring my statement. "And so do you. Apparently."

Something catches in my throat. The venom stops in its tracks, somewhere between infuriated and confused. "Go on."

"She talks about you quite a bit. She's had little pep talks about you with me, which is why I don't destroy your ass regularly for touching her, though I will say, the desire to kill you has been somewhat overwhelming." He sneers, disgusted. "And it pisses me off that you get your spastic little hands on her whenever you feel like it. It . . . *incenses* me. Fancy word, you like that? I didn't get into our school 'cause of Mommy and Daddy or basketball or any corner-cutting bullshit—I studied my ass off and got the grades I deserve. You think you're King Shit because you're all fucking tragic, but you're no smarter or classier than me." I feel his eyes skim me up and down. Planning on where he could break me. "But you keep her okay. She's happy a lot. She sings fucking Joy Division in the shower again and can get out of bed on her own. And if that's the case, maybe she'll be okay . . . y'know, finally. So I want to make a deal with you. Set some things straight."

He stares, waiting for me to reply, but all I'm doing is focusing on not going on a rampage. Think of Renée. He's doing this for her, and so are you.

"Keep her happy," he rasps out. "Don't hurt her, don't treat her like a piece of meat, and we'll be okay. I don't *like you*, Vinetti, but if you make her happy enough to forget what happened, then I can stand you. And I think that's all we both want."

"So basically, you're telling me that if I act like an asshole, you're going to kill me."

"Yeah. But if you keep yourself in check, I'll leave you alone. And . . ." He sighs, resigned. "She asked me to do this part a week or two ago—I'll start calling you Locke now." He stares for a bit longer, and then says, "You have a little brother, right? So you get where I'm at."

I want to be angry. I want to go on a rampage of pure hatred. But the last words kill me, and all the hot, rebellious anger behind the venom deflates, leaving me with just the horrible black depression. He's right. I think of Lon and I know exactly where he's at. As much as I want to hate, empathy wins this round.

"Yeah," I say. "Yeah, okay."

Before I can sputter out more brilliant insight, Renée walks into the room singing, "I don't hear eggs cooking!" and then halts at the doorway with her eyes wide and her mouth hanging open. Andrew looks up at her with a mixture of pride and fear and whispers, "Hey."

"Hey," she says back, her eyes darting to my downturned face and back to Andrew's. "Should I leave?"

"No, but I should," he grunts as he rises. "I'm meeting George to smoke out in about half an hour. I gotta get dressed." As he walks past, he takes the time to stop and put his hand on her shoulder and squeeze. Her hand shoots up to his and squeezes it back, and her eyes and mouth go tight.

"Wanna go see Mom this weekend? I got some time free."

She nods. "I'd like that," she says.

"All right, well . . . just let me know when. I'll get someone to give us a ride."

"Okay."

And then he's gone, his door slamming shut and his music blasting.

Renée runs a hand through my hair. "You okay, hon?"

I sigh, trying to breathe out my anger. "Got any chocolate milk?"

As I'm sliding my key into the lock of my apartment, it dawns on me that I forgot to call my mom. Between consummating my relationship and breaking bread with a heartbroken behemoth, I totally forgot to call home.

I open the door *just* enough that I can slip through it by turning sideways. Every board in the house creaks and moans as I tiptoe my way to my bedroom. The plan is simple: get undressed, get under the covers, and pretend like she just didn't hear me get in.

As I'm reaching the door to my room, I take one last momentary glance around the house. No sign of Mom. Maybe she's out. Booyah. I slide the door open and slither into my room without so much as a click.

"You're in deep shit," says my mom as she folds my underpants.

"Hi!" God hates me. At least, more than usual.

"First off, I don't pay a cell phone bill for you to turn the thing off." Her folding grows more and more frantic. Socks are being balled at sound-barrier speeds. "And second, with how you've been acting the last couple of months, I would hope you understand that I'm a little concerned about you."

"I'm sorry," I say, putting my hands up in defense. "That was totally my bad."

She finally stops folding and looks at me. "I know you have new friends, and I'm really happy for you, but you can't leave me in the dark like this, okay? I spent most of the night thinking you were dead in a ditch. I almost called the cops."

The venom shivers, but I ignore it. She's right. "Again, sorry. I'll call next time."

"Okay," she says, even though it's obviously not. "So how was the party?"

"It was great. We danced and partied, and I got a tarot card from the group, which, like, makes me one of them now."

"Sounds sort of like *Lord of the Flies*."

The venom flickers out into my speech. "Yeah, we chased some fat kid around and chanted for his blood. It was killer."

"Well, I'm glad you had a good time. So whose house did you sleep at?"

I've had this answer primed on my lips from the moment I walked into this apartment. "Randall's."

"Oh, did he meet up with you? He called here pretty late, looking for you."

GodDAMMIT. Come on, Locke, recovery. "Yeah, we found each other."

"Good. Don't forget you have Dr. Yeski later today."

"I had sex last night."

FUCK. How'd that come out? All during my way here, I'd told myself that I wouldn't bring this up in my session, that this was for Renée and me, no one else. And then it's the first thing I say after I sit down. It's been hard—I've wanted to scream it from the rooftops and sing it into the breeze.

Dr. Yeski nods thoughtfully, as if analyzing the concept of the idea of the notion of me getting busy. It's like talking carnal pleasures with Professor X. "With whom?"

"With my girlfriend. Who else?"

"I don't know. It doesn't have to be your girlfriend who you slept with."

"But then I'd just be a scumbag."

"No, you wouldn't, you'd be imperfect. There's a big difference, Locke."

"I'd like to think that sleeping with someone else when you have a girlfriend makes you a scumbag as well as imperfect."

"Well, that's your opinion."

"Yeah, it really is." I start to pick at the arm of the couch, not quite sure what to say to that. Is this supposed to be a form of progressive new therapy, being okay with asshole behavior? It's like a lack of warmth is a job requirement.

"Well. Anyway. There. I had sex with my girlfriend."

"Was this your first time having sex?"

"Oh. Yeah. That's sort of the point."

"Uh-huh. How'd it make you feel?"

"Amazing."

"What does that mean?"

How else is *sex* supposed to make you feel? "It means that orgasms create a pleasurable feeling that I'm sure is biological encouragement for reproduction—"

She laughs out loud, and I feel victorious. "Emotionally. Are you glad it happened? Was it what you had envisioned?"

This question I actually threw around in my head a few times. I mean, I love Renée and last night was incredible, but did it live up to my expectations? Sex had always been this looming, crucial thing in the background. Now that it was over, where do I stand?

Finally I look at her and smile. "Y'know what? I regret nothing about last night. It was perfect. It wasn't *at all* how I envisioned it, but it was even better because of that. I feel like a million bucks."

She smiles. "Good for you. But back to what you just said—how had you envisioned it?"

Tender area, that. "I mean . . . honestly? I had sort of

envisioned it being really awkward and bad," I say softly, throwing a little laugh in there to try and prove that this didn't make me *really fucking uncomfortable.* "I thought that I'd be too nervous, and she'd get tired of me, and I wouldn't be able to find . . . it, and—"

"The clitoris."

GYAH. Come on, lady. ". . . yeah. And also, I always was afraid . . ." The tension builds, and it's as though my jaw won't work.

"I'm listening."

I squeeze and shove until it pops like a mental zit. "I was afraid something would happen with the venom. That things wouldn't work, and I'd get frustrated, and maybe even violent. I think it's why I've always been kind of freaked out by sex, because I was scared it would open up some sort of gateway into the worst part of the venom, and someone would get hurt, and my pride would . . . well, you get the picture."

"And what happened to it?"

"It disappeared the minute she touched me." As I say it, it registers as real, true. "And when we were alone, it ceased to exist. Not just the feeling of it, but any memory of it. The venom didn't matter."

"Very good. I think we're making progress," she says softly.

"What, because the venom doesn't show up during sex?"

"Well, sure."

"What if it does?"

"We'll cross that bridge when we come to it." She scribbles something on her notepad. "And how's the venom now? How has it been lately?"

"I'm . . . it's changing," I say, trying to assign words to the whirlwind of emotions I've dealt with the past couple of weeks. "Recently, it's been there constantly, this pestering voice in the back of my head, at all times. Like it's becoming less and less localized. I don't feel like I'm having as many attacks, but the poisonous side, the hurtful side, seems to have come up to the surface."

"Mmm-hmm. How has that affected you?"

"Actually, it's been sort of helpful. At times. It's as though, when I get a *little* angry, instead of blowing up or just taking it and swallowing the anger, the venom takes over and makes me sort of . . . dangerous, you know? I feel risky and tough, but confident. Sharp. Does that make sense?"

She nods, cradling her chin. "The venom is, if I may, your Mr. Hyde. It can do things you can't, go places you're too scared to."

"Not the analogy I'd use, but sure. Just, now it's less of an explosion. Like it's in my hands."

"You sure about that?"

I eye her nervously. "Wow, what does that mean?"

"From what I've seen, you're coming to terms with your anger," she says, scribbling another note. "Whether or not you're in control of it is an entirely different issue all together."

"You make it sound really terrifying."

"No," she says in her stupid fucking shrink voice. "I'm expressing my opinion. If it's terrifying, then you're the one who's making it so."

Dr. Yeski's full of shit. The next couple of weeks are a blur of happiness.

School is wonderful. Andrew leaves me alone and Randall seems like an even better friend than before, now that I'm part of the tarot (which is a little fucked-up, but I'm too ecstatic to care). Occasionally, when we go walking or go downtown, someone recognizes me as the new member and talks to me, makes me feel magical and important. Randall just acts as if it's all old, if pleasant, news. He's used to this kind of reception almost wherever he goes. For me, this is Shangri-la and Hollywood rolled into one. I feel like Madonna.

I am, as it turns out, a love machine. Renée and I spend more time having sex than we do eating. Whenever I see her for the first time that day and kiss, we both get a look in our eyes of pure hunger. She starts wearing clothes when I come over that I know are put on for the sole purpose of making me hot under the boxers—fishnet shirts, bondage skirts, low-cut pants, bras with studded straps. New concepts and practices enter my mental library, positions and sweet spots and condom brands. The best part is the reciprocation: I don't just want her, we want each other. There's energy in the air when we're together—fiery, passionate, horny energy. It's incredible to be in love with this girl, but it's even more incredible to know that she wants me, wants my smell and my skin, wants my sweat and my hair and my butt. That's a weird concept: a girl liking my butt. How the fuck does this *happen*?

And on top of all that, the venom only makes its entrances charmingly now. Occasionally I get those flashes, like the one time with Renée on the phone, when the venom seems to lace my comments and attitude with wit and power. Rage seems to melt on contact with me; I brush it off my shoulders and look on the bright side. For the first time in as long as I can remember, I feel totally in control. Every moment is like that first shower with Renée—I feel my venom alarms begin to light up, and then the sight and sound of her just make them go dead quiet before they even really start sounding off. No one is poisoned, including myself, and every day seems to push it farther and farther. Who knew that after all the soul-searching and despair, she was what I needed to fend the venom off?

Love was the cure all along. It'd be disgustingly predictable if it wasn't so great.

• • •

Then there's the party.

The door booms open, and the city skyline glows around me. My coat flutters in the rooftop breeze, but I barely notice.

"Where'd this . . . what is . . ."

Casey slaps me on the back. "Told you this'd be worth your while."

The rooftop, lit by the harsh fluorescent glow of nearby Times Square, is covered with artists. Kids dressed like redneck circus performers scamper across the concrete, spraying tags and slathering canvases. Great swaths of poster paper have been laid out and thoroughly marked. Every place I look, someone is creating, illustrating, building. The whole process moves at a steady rhythm. No one takes a break; they just move from one strange emotional expression to another. The whole thing makes me think of an ant colony.

Off to the side stands a table covered with bottles. I ask Renée and Casey about it. When Casey informs me it's the bar, Renée and I decide that we have our work cut out for us.

As we're mixing up White Russians, Randall appears beside us and mumbles, "What's up, guys?"

Renée gives him a huge bear hug. "Where have you been? I haven't seen you in ages!"

Randall shrugs and says something about it only being a few weeks, which isn't that long. There's something wrong with him tonight, I can tell. He's not in his normal master-of-ceremonies mode, but instead looks like I normally do at parties, shifting his weight constantly and glancing around with a severe look on his face. After a little small talk, Renée kisses me and excuses herself to hug and chatter with a massive raver-looking guy who has glowsticks somehow braided into his dreadlocks (classy). I turn to Randall and smile.

"Are you okay, man?"

He shakes himself off a bit and shrugs. "I'll be fine."

"That statement right there doesn't make me think you're okay."

"Just a little—" Before he can finish, Casey shoves his way between us, grabs the bottle of Jim Beam on the table, and slugs down about two shots before disappearing into the crowd with a whoop.

"That why you're worried?" I whisper, throwing a thumb at Casey.

"Yup." He sighs and stares down into his drink.

There are a million things I want to do to help, but I have no clue what they might be. Randall's the one who's supposed to be on top of things, taking charge, keeping all his insane friends in check. Me, I can barely tie my shoes, much less control a herd of emotionally unstable teenagers with my very presence.

I open my mouth to say something, but then Renée is at my side. "SPRAY! PAINT! THE WALLS!"

Randall waves his hand in the air at me. "Go make art. I don't want to ruin your night, anyway."

"Randall, you're not—"

Renée tugs at my arm. "IT FEELS GOOD TO SAY WHAT I WANT! IT FEELS GOOD TO KNOCK THINGS DOWN! SPRAY! PAINT! THE WALLS!"

Randall shoots me a vicious look. "Go have fun." It's an order. I'll trust him tonight. I follow Renée, who keeps screaming "Black Flag" like it's her fucking job.

The can feels heavy but satisfying in my hand. Every shake gives me the clak-*clak* back-and-forth of the propellant-widget, and a mere touch of the head sends an invisible jet that shines black against the gray stone. I curve my arm, and a curve appears; I pull back, and the black breaks up, gets fuzzy. Renée and I dance with our spray cans, hooting and hollering as our hands shoot magical markings on the wall before us. Our nostrils burn with the deathly exhaust and our ears seem to vibrate with the thing, the *KRRSSSH*! of the art leaving the can, until the whole rooftop and skyline seem to be leaning in and watching us, mesmerized. From nothing it builds, growing larger, more intricate; it begins to have a point, a destined design. Finally our cans give their last pathetic aerosol whisper and fall from our hands with a metallic rattle.

We step back and observe, beaming. It's a reaperlike figure, cloaked and hooded, rising from an ocean of black and red swirls. He hangs in a Christ pose, claws extended, with his heart glowing red, sending wisps of crimson out of his chest and like an aura, the bright red wheeling out of the blackness in his cold, dark center.

I'm the only one who knows his name. Blacklight.

"Whoa! Dudes, come here and look at this!"

The crowd takes me by surprise. Ten, fifteen kids, all beaming in awe at our spray-can creation. Renée and I lock eyes and share a smile. We rock.

"What'd you fucking say to me?"

The shout yanks the whole group out of our dumbstruck creative love and back to the party. Casey stands across the rooftop, swaying drunk, pointing at a couple of kids and laughing like a madman. I register the kids: Terry and Omar, friends of both Andrew and Randall, staring down at my friend as though he were an insect.

"It's just that by the way you two're whispering and talking," slurs Casey, "you'd think that you're playing on *my* team."

Renée bursts through our onlookers and jumps between Casey and Terry. "Listen, guys," she says, "there's no reason—"

"Out of my way," yells Terry, and—

—shoves her.

Knocks her on her ass with a good, hard shove.

Something familiar opens its eyes, and then rockets through my system.

Two minutes later, Randall is pulling me off Terry by my elbows as I wrench and pull. The noises coming out of my throat are primal, a mix between the shriek of some jungle bird, the snarl of a wolf, and the cackle of a hyena. Blood is everywhere, on my fists, on my shirt, all around Terry's face that he's now clutching as he rolls back and forth. There's blood on my glasses. Spit runs off my lower lip, and tears course down my cheeks. Renée stands on the sidelines, her hands to her mouth, looking aghast. Omar is crouched by Terry, suddenly wishing he weren't as drunk and stoned as he looks. From the wet sounds spurting out of Terry's face, he owes Randall a thank-you before he heads home. The motherfucker's still breathing.

By the time Randall gets me over to the one secluded corner of the roof, all eyes are on me. Not in artistic appreciation like before. Now it's horror. My hand crosses my eyes, and the grainy touch reminds me that I'm covered in someone else's blood.

Randall stands over me, eyes accusing. "I thought you were getting better."

"It's never . . ." I try to get the words out between quiet sobs, but my throat keeps spasming. Focus on each word before you say it. "It's never happened like that before. I've never done anything that bad before. I've never wanted to hurt anyone like that before. It's always been me losing control."

His laugh is like the rattle of bones. "Oh yeah, and you weren't losing control back there. Fuck, Locke, FUCK. What the fuck do you want us to do?"

"It—it was like—like I had a direction. I channeled it. As if the venom latched onto him like a grappling hook and pulled me in. It was all intentional. There was no regret or care or worry."

"It was pure," says Randall.

"Exactly."

"Fantastic," he spits. "A record low. I'm so proud, buddy, I'm—"

"Locke?"

My eyes come up on Renée. She's holding her purse with both hands in front of her, her entire body turned into one rigid line. Her eye makeup is running down her face in inky black rivers, making her look even more Goth than usual, which breaks my heart and makes the venom laugh. The old familiar discomfort and guilt, the knowledge that anything bad about tonight came out of me, it's all right there in front of me, staring at me like I'm a fearsome animal.

Randall shakes his head and makes his way past her, back across the roof. I immediately hear people inquiring about what happened, and his awkward responses. It's of no concern, though. I've got my problems right in front of me.

"Hi," I rasp.

"What . . . Why did you do that?"

"It was seeing him . . . he—"

"I KNOW what he did, Locke!" she bawls. "But WHY? Everything has been so nice lately, *we've* been doing so well, and then you did THIS!"

"Renée, you don't understand, he—"

"He what? Shoved me, knocked me over? I can HANDLE THAT, Locke! And yeah, yeah, it's really nice to know you're protective of me, but for Christ's sake, there's a limit! A FUCKING LIMIT!" Black tears are spattering off her face, onto her hands and the roof. They remind me of blood. "You can't pulp someone's face every time they do something obnoxious to me! I KNOW Terry, Locke; he's a pig and an asshole, but he's not a bad person! What he did was stupid, but it's a party and he was wasted and provoked, and there was no reason to DO THAT!"

"He deserved it." I try to say something else, something to make her happy, but the venom speaks for me, and I have to agree with it. It was Terry's own damn fault.

"He deserved a TALKING-TO!" she screams. "Not a beating! Andrew would've talked to him, and the whole thing would've been settled! He would've apologized to me and that would be that!"

The idea that Andrew can take care of her in a way I can't burns, and the venom rears up again. There's no exhaustion, no limited supply, it's just there, and it's pissed. "You want me to just sit back like a dick and let that happen? Let some bastard—"

"I want you to GROW UP! That didn't solve anything! Now all that's going to happen is that Andrew's going to find out that my boyfriend, the one he ALREADY DISAPPROVES OF, is not just a 'spaz' or whatever but a fucking *monster*! Did you SEE that kid's face by the time you were done with it? What were you thinking? God, how can you do that, how can you rationalize hurting another person like that? What makes it possible that you can beat someone until they're just BLOOD? You're worse than Casey, you, you—" But then she can't speak anymore, because she's crying too hard, her voice dying in her throat as she puts her hands to her face and wipes violently at her eyes, and soon she's just silent, racked with tears and making me wonder if I've just fought my way out of my one true saving grace.

"Do you hate me?"

"Never," she whispers. "I could never hate you. Sometimes I want to so badly, and I just can't. I love you more than *anything* in the world. It won't change."

I look up into her face, and she's closer to me now, her one hand held out toward me, shivering slightly. I reach up and take it, pressing it against my face. I hear her breath come in sharply.

"I'm sorry. I'm so sorry."

She moves suddenly, wrapping herself around me, her arms locked on my waist and her head on my shoulder. We shake and rock with weeping, as if every so often the venom gives off an electric shock that slams into our bodies. She feels it, absorbs it, swallows my pain when it's too much for me to handle.

"I don't know what's happening," I moan. "I'm fine for so long and then this happens, and it's like I can never be free of it, like every time I start to feel normal or cured, it rears its head and laughs at me and lets me know that I'll always be poisonous, and that anything I touch will just die . . ."

She tightens her grip on me, and I stop and wipe my nose. I want her to say something, to tell me I'm okay, but she stays quiet. We hold each other like that until she gets the phone call telling her to come home. She steps out of my arms too fast, and doesn't even kiss me good-bye.

The roof clears off shortly afterward (surprise, surprise). There are comments, whistles, a couple of encouraging statements telling me to stay cool and wishing me a good night. Omar curses Randall out; Casey moans apologies through his hideous drunk, but soon they all leave. From my corner, I hear Randall talk to Alan, the gathering's host, who tells him to let me stay up here as long as I need, we're all tarot here.

It's harder this time. It won't speak or move or communicate with me, just sits there feeling pleased with itself and drumming its fingers. It isn't asleep or drained, it's just bored for now.

After a while, Randall comes over and joins me. His walks implies that he's been drinking down the tension. With a slump, he's next to me, back propped against the roof's lip, and we stare out at the New York skyline in the growing morning light.

"God, that's pretty," he sighs, lighting a couple of smokes and handing me one.

I nod, and then look over at him, a lump rising in my throat again. "Thank you, Randall. Thank you so much for looking after me tonight."

He shrugs and takes a drag. "Fuck you, Locke."

The words land in my ears like a cold, heavy rock. He's never said something that blatantly heartless to me before. Tonight was worse than I thought. "I'm sorry, Randall."

"'I'm sorry, Randall,'" he imitates in a plaintive little voice. "'Didn't mean it. It was the venom. You wouldn't understand.'"

My sympathy begins to do combat with rage. "Hey, man, that's a little unfair, isn't it? Come on."

"FUCK YOU, man!" he yells, leaning forward with the effort of the words. "Look at you, man! You're sitting on a rooftop, caked in blood. I'm sick of having to pick up after you every time you get pissed off."

You preppy little shit.

"It's not like I'm TRYING to do this, Randall!"

"Are you sure of that?" he snaps. "Is there really ANY effort on your part not to go ballistic? Does the venom take over or do you LET IT FREE? Part of me wonders if you just enjoy this, Locke. Getting to be the dark hero and all—and don't bullshit me, man, I can see that. Huh, I wonder who the guy with the spread arms and the bleeding heart's supposed to represent. I wonder. Then again, you don't *tell me* anything, because my puny mind couldn't *possibly* grasp your unhappiness."

The venom begins to take over. "What, you just decided to be a dick tonight? You've been acting pissy all evening, and now this. Grow up."

"Oh, look who's telling me to grow up." He chortles. "Y'know, it's not fucking fair, man. Renée falls for you. And Casey finds someone who understands the black. And all these people have gotten into this little tarot card club because I've brought 'em in and I've orchestrated it all . . .

and Randall Elliot gets FUCKED. I'm just the Fool, y'know? You're the Strength, and Casey's the Emperor, and I'm the fucking jester who plays guitar and smiles. No one's ever going to fall in love with me or worship me or even FIGHT me. No one's ever going to think, 'Wow, Randall, he was really something. I remember that kid.' I'm your *training wheels*, Locke. I'm your fucking *driver's test*, your *gateway drug.* Why? Because I'm not fucked-up? Because I try to be a nice, normal guy?"

Cry me a river. Consider this role reversal, asshole.

"It's not like that, and you know it."

"Yeah, well, you're my best friend, of course you say that," he murmurs. Something inspires him then, and he laughs. "But if I did what you do, it wouldn't mean shit. You're so charming in your rage, so broken and fragile and poetic about it all, and people see it as a part of who you are. But me, they see nothing special. You're special in your dark little world, but me? Nah. I don't have some deep, unexplainable thing inside me. I don't beat people into blood pudding at parties. So I guess I don't really matter, do I? Well, I'm sorry. I'm sorry that I'm not bent and twisted to the point where violence is second nature to me. I'm sorry that, overall, I'm well-fucking-adjusted. It's just in my nature, huh. . . . I guess when the end of the day comes, I'm there alone. You're with Renée and the venom, and I'm alone."

"Casey thinks you're—"

"HA. Casey? Everything that happened tonight, even that stupid little atrocity of yours, was his doing. Every time we hang out, he finds some way to ruin it. There's always a fight to be had or inappropriate comments to be made for him. Man, he's worse than you. At least you're trying, or *claiming* you're trying. Fuck both of you. Man, maybe you two should've gotten together in the first place. You're made for each other."

And I bite my cheek, because Randall's my best friend in the world, and telling him this is going to destroy him, and maybe even ruin every good thing that's happened to me recently, but the venom is pissed, the venom is bitter, and *the venom doesn't care.*

"That's cute," I say stonily, "seeing as you're the one he's in love with."

Randall shoots me an evil glare until he realizes I'm not joking.

"YOU DON'T want to do this!" I yelled while leaping away from another lunge by the monster as it tried to attack me. "This isn't who you are! Fight it! I know you can!"

It raised its head and let loose such a deafening roar that I felt a spark of fear spread through my body. Whatever was standing before me now was cold and ruthless, a creature born from an exponential growth in the song of the city, the energy of darkness. It was huge, angry, and unspeakably heartless: Its insectoid eyes rolled grotesquely in its head as its mouth-tentacles twisted wormlike at me. This thing had all the ethics and morals of a scorpion.

"We just spoke! You're not Blacklight! I'll change who I am, rid myself of this poisonous power that lies inside me! There's no need for us to fight! We—"

One clawed hand swung errantly outward and slammed me hard in the jaw. A flash of white, silence, air. I flew backward a couple of yards and skidded worryingly close to the rooftop's edge. This thing was strong. Stronger than before. Better stick to the air.

As I rose to my feet and hovered calmly, my eyes narrowed. "Very well. You leave me no choice."

The creature made a noise, like laughter, and lowered itself back on its haunches.

And then we were airborne, colliding, my cloak swooped out around me like great black wings, its huge body squirming and squishing in response. I reared back my hands, prayed this would work, and then thrust them both into the great black mass of mouth-tendrils that was splayed wide before me and rent it in opposite directions.

Deep within the mass of black gunk, his face lay, pale, stony, eyes filmed over with darkness.

"FIGHT IT!" I bellowed. "MAKE IT STOP! YOU NEED TO MAKE IT STOP!"

"Too late," he spoke in someone else's voice. Someone familiar. "Come too far. We must complete the mission."

"WHAT MISSION? WHO ARE YOU?"

He coughed out a word—it sounded like "cover," but I wasn't sure—and then the fluid darkness's power was too strong. Suddenly it was closing over his face, and the harder I tried to pull back, the tighter it grew. Slithering black tentacles pulled me inward, pulled me deep within the monster itself, while I struggled desperately to free my hands. The beast, unmoved, kept pulling.

CHAPTER ELEVEN

"YOU *WHAT?*"

I'm with Renée in her room, and she's staring at me like I just made a joke about her parents. Which, I know, is an uncool thing to say, but the lines that separated the venom and I are getting blurrier by the day. We are separate but equal at this point, and while it used to be helpful, it's started to get a little intimidating.

I keep my head bowed, trying to keep my focus. "You should've heard him, Renée. He's so bitter and hateful, and at the same time, he's so alone."

"This is a joke. Locke, tell me this is a joke."

"I'm sorry."

"Please, *please*, Locke, this is not funny."

"It's not meant to be."

Her hand floats slowly up to her mouth. "You really did. You told him. Oh my God." Her face goes from dead and stunned to creased and bunched. She shoves me, and I have to remember that I'm angry at the situation, not at her. "*Why*, Locke? *Why* in the world would you ever do that?"

"Renée, wait, listen, you still don't understand—"

"No, Locke, *you* don't understand!" She jabs me in the chest with the other hand. "We've been keeping this a secret from Randall *for years*. This thing predates *me*. Jesus, Locke. How *could* you? After everything that happened last night, he was probably left in an emotional state, but you can't . . . JESUS, I can't believe you did that."

The venom speaks up, pissed. "Well, maybe you guys should start, I don't know, *being honest with your friend*? It's not my fault that you've lied to him for as long as you've known him, and it's not my fault that Casey acts like a shithead nine times out of ten. Last night was a wake-up call for me. Besides, you mentioned Casey's crush so casually in passing, I didn't think it was such a huge fuckin' deal."

"Yeah, but I also told you NEVER TO MENTION IT. GODDAMMIT." Renée starts pacing, shaking her head. "You don't know what you've done."

"Screw you." My face goes flushed, my head's buzzing, but there's no shame or depression, just pure righteous indignation. "Randall's one of our best friends, and apparently he's pretty upset with all of us. Why *not* tell him that one of the few people he respects, worships the ground that he walks on?"

"Okay, fine, let's say you're right, and Randall deserves to know about this. Fine. I'll agree with you there. But take a second to remember that there's someone else on this earth who is as short-tempered, melodramatic, and fucking enraged at the world as you are. Think about *Casey*, Locke, and think about what'll happen to the black when he finds out that his cover's blown. Telling Randall about Casey was the only way you could respond, huh? Well, think about what Casey's about to go through."

It suddenly all makes sense. If Randall revealed that he'd been in love with me for a while, I don't know how the venom would take it, and Casey and he have been friends for years upon years. Casey's black might just explode if he finds out that his cover's blown. This is a lose-lose situation. There's nothing about this that can turn out well.

Renée sighs. "This can't turn out well."

"I was just thinking that."

"Glad we're on the same page. What're we going to do now, Locke?"

The phone rings. Renée stares at me with a horror-movie look, as if we'd just unplugged the damn thing, but it's still ringing anyway. Slowly she walks to the phone and glances at her caller ID. She sighs again and looks at me. "It's Randall."

"Shit."

"I'm putting him on speakerphone."

"What? Why would you do that?"

She doesn't even look at me, her face oozing contempt. "You've helped start this mess, and you're going to help clean it up." She presses a button on the phone's cradle, and then we hear the buzz of the other end. "Hey, hon, what's going—"

"Let's skip that shit, okay?"

His voice makes me flinch. He sounds emotionless, cold, dead to the world. There's nothing in his voice that suggests he's talking to people he even remotely cares about.

"Honey, look, Locke told me—"

"Shut up, Renée," he barks. "How long has he felt like this?"

HE JUST TOLD HER TO SHUT UP.

I'm in enough trouble already.

YOU'RE GOING TO TAKE THAT?

"I don't know."

"That's a lie." His disembodied voice crackles. "How long have you been *lying* to me?"

The venom drives into my nerves, like a dentist's drill. "Randall," I say, "it's Locke. Listen, man, there's no reason to act—"

"Don't try to pull that shit with me, Stockenbarrel," he snickers bitterly. "I'm no idiot, I see right fucking through you. You didn't tell me about this because you thought I had a right to know. You told me this because you knew it would hurt me. Well, it worked. I'm hurt. Fuck off and die, you selfish bastard."

"Watch your fucking mouth, Randall."

"Or what? Pray tell, what'll you do, pal? What more can you do to me at this point, Locke? Poison me, beat me up, kill me. I fucking dare you." He clears his throat. "Now, Renée. How long?"

"Calm down. Let's talk about this, okay?"

"Last chance."

"Randall, it's not that simple."

"Cool," he snaps. "I'll just ask him, then."

Click.

Renée dives for the phone, screaming "No!" and slapping Randall's number onto the buttons so fast and hard that I'm sure she's going to break it. She holds the receiver to her ear with both hands. "It's busy. Locke, he's calling Casey."

My head is shrinking while the buzzing chaos inside it swells and pushes. The venom reaches back and tightens the screws in the nape of my neck. Everything is chaos, like flipping emotional channels, rocketing through my head one after another. I squeeze my eyes shut, clench my fists till they shake, and nothing changes. The venom is barely a voice anymore—it's like a tone, a low-pitched whine behind my face, splitting my brain in two.

"Hey!" She's in front of my face, staring at me with tired eyes. "You with me?"

I manage a nod.

"This isn't unfixable," she says in the same sharp, clear monotone, "but it's pretty fucking bad. And I need you for this, okay? You have a lot of fixing to do today, and I need you here, now, not in your head."

"I got it, okay?"

She puts a hand on the side of my face, and her palm quiets the roar a bit, a familiar sensation calling me back to reality. "Calm down," she whispers. Her voice is like a gust of cool air. "Think clearly. The venom isn't going to help here, it's only going to cause more trouble. Stay with me, kid."

The phone goes off again, and both Renée and I jump. She breathes deep, leans over, and hits the speakerphone button. "Hello."

There is only white noise, the endless buzz of background noise at the other end of the phone.

And then the voice comes out. Like a bunny caught in a trap, bleeding to death. Like a child after his first day in hell.

"Renée . . ."

"Casey," she says softly. "Casey, honey, you there?"

"Oh God, Renée . . . ," he moans, hoarser and louder.

"Shhh, it's okay," she whispers, "it's okay, I know. Where are you?"

"RenÉEE*EEEE*!"

This is like the experiment scene in *A Clockwork Orange*, like I've been strapped down and forced to watch pain. His voice is painful, emotionally damning to listen to. This is torture. Any serenity Renée had given me was running out fast. Casey's every word set my heart on fire.

She bites her lip and puts a hand over her eyes, hissing, "Fuck."

"Renée, oh God, he said . . . he just told me someone told him!" Casey moans again, his voice increasing steadily in pitch and volume. "He knows, and he called me a liar, and he hates me, I know he hates me now, and I'm so fucking sca*AAAARED*!" Screaming gives way to heavy, racking sobs. I can picture him in a ball in the corner, his eyes wide, staring at the wall in a new shade as the black creeps through him. I can tell what stage he's in right now, seeing as I'm in it so much myself. And I'm terrified. Jesus doesn't live here anymore. We're all gonna die.

"Casey," she coos, "relax. Deep breaths. Pull yourself together. Randall doesn't hate you, he could never hate you. Just don't get too out of control—"

There's a thud, deep and resonating, on Casey's side of the

connection. My own behavior in the past springs to mind—he's punching walls. "OUT OF CONTROL? RENÉE, ARE YOU FUCKING LISTENING TO ME? He said, fuck, he wouldn't let me get a word in edgewise, he knows and he hates me, he said so. He told me . . ." Casey chokes a bit, spits. "He told me that it explained my behavior over the past couple of years, it all made sense now. Oh *GOD*, RENÉEE . . ."

"Case. Shhh. It's going to be fine, and we'll work together on this. But you *need* to calm down. You can't deal with any of this if you're acting like a maniac, all right, babe? Forget the black. Talk to me, dude."

"Do you know who told him? Who was it? Who told him?" His voice goes quick and feral. "Was it one of the tarot kids? Do you know when? Jesus fucking Christ, Renée, I need to find out who told him."

The question hangs in the room like a mist, heavy and ugly, clammy to the touch. Renée stares into my eyes with a look of utter fucking hatred, waiting for me to be the brave one, to step up and tell Casey it was me, and I just can't do it. My head is a blur of crushing noise, but it seems to be keeping my mouth shut.

Renée finally picks up the slack. "Casey, look, does it matter? Would it make a difference if you knew who told him?"

A pause. "Oh. It was Locke, wasn't it?"

"Case, c'mon—"

"Why else would you be so defensive?" he snarls, and then softens. "Was it Locke? For the love of God, Renée, don't tell me it was Locke."

Under my breath, I hiss, "Fuck."

Shoulda been quieter, though. 'Cause the phone goes silent. There's still the background noise, letting us know that he's on the other end, but everything else, even his breathing, stops immediately. Renée turns to me, wide-eyed and pursed-mouthed, while I feel the blood drain out of my face.

Casey's voice, careful and measured: "Am I on speaker-phone?"

Renée puts her face in her hands.

Now or never, buddy. "Casey, please, you have to listen to me."

"Oh. My. God," he whispers, voice dripping with hatred. "Oh my God, you're a dead man, Locke Vinetti. I'm going to beat the fucking sinews out of you, you angsty little shit. How *dare* you. I'm gonna . . ." Then there's a smash on his end, like breaking plates, and his voice becomes a furious howl. "YOU TOO, YOU BETRAYING FUCK-ING *CUNT*. DO YOU TWO HEAR ME? I'M COM-ING FOR BOTH OF YOU. HERE COMES THE PAIN, YOU MISERABLE FUCKS. HERE COMES *THE BLACK*. YOU'RE BOTH DEAD WHERE YOU FUCKING STAND." He starts cackling like a madman, his voice louder and louder until it's a static electronic whine, until there's another crash and the call cuts out.

Renée decides that her place "isn't safe," as though Casey is a team of highly trained mercenaries. We walk to my place, a couple of New York City vampires—black coats, dark shades, skin with an obvious lack of sunlight. There's a tension between us that gets worse and worse as the walk continues. We barely speak, our mouths occupied with cigarettes, our minds taut with anxiety. By the time we get to my apartment, I'm almost wishing she would go away and leave me alone with the venom, let me ride its course, but I know her presence is the only thing keeping me from going utterly batshit. The venom's not abating in the least.

Thank the maker, my mom and brother are nowhere to be found. We get to my room and immediately curl up on my bed, still silent. It seems like the only option available at this point—to clutch each other for dear life.

After about twenty minutes of silent cuddling, when the noise in my head has quieted just enough for me to form a coherent sentence, I ask, "So, do you hate me now?"

"Cut that shit out," she mumbles into my chest. "It's as if you want me to hate you at this point. I'm sick of it."

"Why would I want you to hate me?"

"Because it would justify your poisonousness," she says in

an academic monotone. "You would feel justified in thinking of yourself as a blight on my life."

"You agree with Randall then," I snap. Suddenly her touch feels repulsive. "I'm just a melodramatic victim."

"No," she says. "I think Randall was over the line in talking to you like that. You're his friend, and he owes you more than that. But this is a big deal, and I *am* pissed at you, and he *has* a point."

"Is it really, though?" I spit out, speaking before thinking. "So Casey has a crush on him? Does that warrant all the crying and the breaking shit?"

"Look who's talking, Mr. Takes Me Two Minutes to Cripple Someone," she says. "This isn't just a crush, hon. This is years of friendship and embarrassment on Casey's part. You dealt with the venom your own way, but part of Casey is wanting what he can't have, and you just yanked the support out from under *years* of propped-up baggage. What if that happened to you? What if a portion of this *crazy-ass* life you've built around yourself just got smashed?" She shakes her head against me. "There's no right answer here, it's everyone's fault, but it's not the end of the world. There."

You don't know a thing about me, lady.

"I'm sorry. I love you."

"I know," she says, and then as an afterthought, "and I think your mom's home."

The door clicks and opens to the sounds of my mom and Lon carrying groceries into the kitchen. My eyelids clamp together, and I take a deep breath. The siesta was nice, but we have to get out of here. Considering the state I'm in, I can't deal with my family, especially if they're meeting my girlfriend for the first time.

"Locke?" calls my mom. "You here, honey? We got chocolate milk."

There's no way of exiting without running into them. Make this quick. "In my room. Be out in a second."

We straighten ourselves up and get our coats back on. Before I open the door, Renée grabs my face and kisses me, hard, as if we're on our way to a quick demise. I open the door, and we shuffle into the kitchen.

My mom looks up from a paper bag and smiles. "Hey, babe, chocolate milk's in the fridge—Oh, I'm sorry, I didn't realize you had someone over."

"It's cool. Mom, this is Renée. Renée, Mom."

"Renée? *The* Renée?" My mom squeals in delight and, in traditional Mom response, sidles over to us and gives Renée a huge bear hug, pulling my girlfriend into her maternal bosom. Renée's eyes are just visible between my mom's grasping arms, a look of panic lining her face. It'd be cute if I didn't want to leave this place as soon as possible.

The person who gave birth to me pulls Renée back at

arm's length and beams into her face, but her smile suddenly wanes a bit, and then she decides to mortify the crap out of me.

"Honey," she says, inspecting my girlfriend, "do you really need all that mess on your face? You're so *pretty*!"

"*Jesus*, Mom," I say a little too loudly. "Come on, don't do this."

My mom suddenly looks hurt and embarrassed, and I hate myself for it. "I'm sorry, kidlet, I don't mean to be . . . It's just, she's got this beautiful *figure*, and this lovely hair, and then *BAM!* Captain Howdy!" For the first time in my life, I contemplate matricide. Like lightning, I pour myself a glass of chocolate milk and throw it down my throat. It helps. A little. Mostly I just feel nauseated.

Renée stays charming, picking up my slack. "Locke makes me wear it. He doesn't want any competition, and it scares the other boys away."

"Well, good. At least he knows a worthy investment when he sees one."

"Yeah, he's a pretty perfect kid."

My mom glances sidelong at me and stage-whispers, "I like this girl," which sends her and Renée into fits of well-choreographed laughter. I try to force a chuckle, but it dies in my throat. "So can you kids stay for dinner? I was thinking spaghetti, but if we have company, I could do something a little bigger, maybe make some chicken parmigiana—"

"Actually, we have to get going," Renée interrupts before I can act like an even bigger dick to my mother. "We're meeting Casey and Randall for dinner in a little bit, and we've already ditched 'em a couple of times in the past. You know how it is."

"Sure, sure, no problem, have a good time," she says, waving us away. I can hear it in her voice—*I don't mean to cramp your style, you kids go ahead*. I feel terrible, like I'm hurting her, but I'm also enraged. Sorry I have my own fucking life to deal with now. If she had any idea what I'm going to have to deal with today—

"Honey? Come on, we have to run." Renée's hand is on my shoulder, pulling me away. I wave good-bye to my mom, and we move toward the door, thinking only about the fresh air, the sun, all things outside my fucking apartment.

Suddenly a blond blur darts in front of us, and Renée and I are confronted with ten years of overachieving young man smiling up at us.

"Are you Renée?" asks Lon peppily.

"I so am," she says with a smile. "Lon, right? How're those comics treating you?"

"They're *great*," he says, elated to be in front of my comics-savvy girlfriend. "I really liked 'em. Too bad you guys can't stay for dinner. Locke, we're having spaghetti tonight. And you can see some of the drawings I did at school today! Here, stay for dinner, I can show you, I did this one of Iron Man. And his armor's really hard to draw. But I think I got it down. It's just the chest plate, it's a real pain, so I don't think he looks perfect—"

"Lon. We've got to *go*. Back off."

Lon's mile-a-minute speech stops dead with a frightened wheeze. Renée looks over her shoulder at me, equally taken aback—the voice that just spoke was commanding, cold, and impatient, exactly *not* how I should be talking to the best little brother ever.

I clear my throat. "Sorry, man. Rough day, okay? We'll talk about it later. We need to go."

"Yeah," he says, looking down at his feet, ashamed to be shut down in front of company. "Sorry. I understand. Nice meeting you, Renée."

As we tromp down the stairs of my building, Renée shakes her head. "That wasn't cool, Locke. You don't do that to a little kid in front of company. All he wanted to do was impress me, you realize."

I don't. Fucking. Care.

The cool New York air hits me, lowering my insane body temperature a few degrees. Every remedy for the venom—chocolate milk, cooling down, Renée—is frighteningly temporary. Every movement of my body is charged with fire.

Every thought is murderous, persistent. This day could not get any worse.

And, as if on cue, Renée's phone rings.

"Hello? Brent, hey, yeah—What . . . Oh, fuck. Yeah. Locke told him. No, no, we should get to him first . . . Right, exactly. Where is he? Okay. Yeah, sure, it's cool. Yeah, I know where that is. Thanks a bunch, man. Bye." She clicks her phone shut. "He's at a bar on Seventy-third. Apparently, he's called all the Major Arcana to try and put out some sort of hit on us or something. They were less than receptive, so Brent called me."

"So what do we do?"

"We meet him at the fucking bar." She sighs. "What else do friends do?"

The P&G Café is apparently a dive in the truest sense—it is neither large nor well-lit nor clean nor in any way cool. There's a bar, some bottles, and a couple of tiny booths surrounding a broken-down jukebox. While its outside is lined with flashing neon depicting martinis and signs for steaks, it's really only good for holing up and drinking yourself to death. It looks, honestly, like the kind of place I'd normally love to go and drink, probably with Casey. Today it's the house of Dracula.

"Put on your game face," says Renée, staring at the bar with the same dread. "You've seen Casey bad before, but nothing like this. Fuck, this might even be a learning experience for *me*."

"How do we want to do this?"

"I'm gonna go in there and sit down with him and try to talk him down. After that, I'm going to tell him that you're outside, and if he's down, we should go somewhere and work this through. I figure we give *him* the choice, that way he doesn't feel cornered." She gives me a wary eye. "The most important thing is that *everyone keeps their temper*. You need to basically throw your pride away and apologize fully. Remember, in a situation like this, anger never solves any—"

The door to the bar flies open and there he is, standing in the doorway, hunched over and panting. Each time he breathes, a throaty, grating noise comes ripping through his mouth. His hair is mussed, in his face, and even though I know he's only known about what happened since this afternoon, his clothes look like they've been slept in for a week. A line of spittle hangs lazily from the corner of his massive smile, and twitches every time he lets out a breath. His eyes are as big as dinner plates, but for a moment I almost think I can't see any white in them, that they've glazed over with the deepest, darkest black.

"Holy shit," he says, advancing on me. "I'm going to kill the shit out of you."

"Casey, wait."

UP TO my elbows, then my shoulders, in this monster's mouth. Its huge, shiny eyes were only inches from my face, and the whirling tentacles at its maw seemed to be gibbering at me in hideous, hellish laughter. There was no doubt in this creature's mind: I was lunch, a hatred-fueled snack.

Fine. If it was going to pull, then I was going to push.

I closed my eyes and felt the dark energies of the city, the fuel for our fires. Like a ham radio, my mind found the core frequency, the seething black heart of the city's hate-flow, and tuned into it. Be a conduit, Locke. Use it. Your powers are the same as his, just a different form. Attach one to the other.

There. The pain, the evil. Every drop of innocent blood, every life shattered.

Focus it. Move it through your heart and into his.

My costume flared, grew, twisted. With one great push, I used every ounce of darkness I had and fired it into this beast's obsidian heart with one concentrated blast.

And then, fireworks.

My hands exploded in shadows, sending crackling energy and burnt sludgelike tentacle flesh firing into the sky. The bolts of obsidian light rippled through the future-Blacklight's system, burning away and absorbing every ounce of power he was deriving from the city's black core. There was the sound of a thousand people screaming in anguish, and then the monster flew away, its flesh cracking and blowing away with the river breeze as ash, nothing more. I reeled back, taking a deep breath—I'd never released such a concentrated amount of energy before, and I'd never absorbed so much at one time.

My costume rippled and shook. So much darkness. So much avarice and guilt and hatred, pulsing throughout me. I was a god—no, God, the one, the only. I was power and strength, pure and unfiltered. It was incredible.

I stood, watching his slumped form, and remembered the three words he had spoken. The ones that mattered the most.

"I killed her."

The costume twitched. I knew what I had to do.

CHAPTER TWELVE

THERE'S THE SATISFYING tension of my knuckles hitting meat and bone, followed by the stiffening pain down my arm of the pressure from the punch, and then it's dynamite, explosive, out of sight and into the stands.

Casey reels and falls to the sidewalk, but rolls on his back and scrambles to his feet just as I begin to shake off the pain in my arm. I feel my throat already begin to bruise at the points where his fingers gripped it, and the back of my head throbs from being slammed into a wall. My balance feels fucked-up. I'm pretty sure my face is bleeding. Wooo. Party.

"Stop it!" shrieks Renée, looking angrily between the two of us. "Stop it right now!"

Doesn't matter what she says. The words enter my ears, but they're indistinguishable and meaningless, like a bird or a rodent. From the moment that first swing was thrown, this was no longer about talking or having a good cry. This was about pain and anguish, violence and tears and hatred. Casey is completely absorbed by the black, and as hard as I've tried to contain it, the venom has taken over completely. We aren't two friends arguing—we're Frankenstein and the Wolf Man, two monsters ready to tear each other apart for the simple reason that the one doesn't deserve to be alive in the presence of the other.

The point is, me and Casey are overdue to mindlessly beat the shit out of each other. It was the way we'd met, and the only thing we knew.

Casey charges me and throws me to the ground. I throw my arm around his head as we hit the concrete, and start punching him in the back and kidneys, but it's no use, because he knocks the wind out of me with one strong fist to the stomach. The world swims. I will *not* pass out. As I try to regain my breath, he lets out a scream and punches me hard in the temple. I stumble headfirst into a wall and then hit the ground again, the concrete cheese-grating my face. White again. Fuzzy.

GET UP.

The venom grabs my limbs, twisting them into movements of precise violence. As he's bent over me, savoring my pain, I lean back on my tailbone and send the toe of my boot arching right across his chin. His head snaps around as blood starts drooling down his lower lip, but that's time enough for me to get back on my feet.

My mind is a cacophony of barked orders. *Do as much damage as possible. Make him hurt. Make him bleed. Don't do so until he stops saying "please." Go for the eyes. The throat. Knees.*

I throw a right hook at Casey's jaw, and he takes it like a bitch, an arch of blood whipping widely out of his mouth. As he staggers backward, I throw all my weight into my shoulder and send it firing into his solar plexus. I manage to take him off his feet, give him a few seconds of air before he slams loudly into the side of a parked car. The alarm goes off, a high-pitched rhythmic wail. It's incredibly appropriate.

I suddenly realize that, disgustingly, I'm yelling, "MOTHERFUCKER! TAKE IT, MOTHERFUCKER! TAKE IT!" which is about the least dignified thing anyone could do in a fight, but whatever, this is the venom talking, not me. I change it to just guttural throat-noises, things that sound like I'm scraping my own windpipe with a violin string. I feel my fist swing out and collide with his mouth, his lips and teeth becoming a squishy mishmash with hard edges; I actually feel blood drip off my knuckles as I pull my hand back. I make a note of it and get ready to swing again—

Pain. The worst kind of pain.

Casey's knee hits my groin and doesn't move, just keeps

pushing harder and harder. I yelp, feeling my testes lunge up into my intestines, and curl over on my side, clutching my aching manhood.

Heh, aching manhood. It's like a line out of a romance nov—

He's up on his feet and kicks me in the stomach before I can reach out and grab his leg. I feel my gut cave in on two sides now, from between my legs and from its front, and something in the back of my mind prepares itself for the loss of my stomach contents. I lean my head back, grit my teeth, put out my hands, and wait for a second kick.

"*STOP IT RIGHT NOW!*" screams Renée, launching herself onto Casey's back. He sways and stumbles like a lush, caught in midkick and now trying to regain his balance while a harpy bites his shoulder, screams into his ear, drags her nails across his scalp. A crowd has gathered around us, watching with something between horror and amusement on their faces. For the first time in a while, clarity explodes into my mind—Jesus, what are we doing?

Casey reaches around his shoulder, grabs Renée by her shirt, and in a single swift, brutal motion, whips her around his front and tosses her onto the ground. She lands with a thud and a small cry.

Clarity vanishes. The venom is everything. The pain in my groin and face slowly, piece by piece, flows out of the rest of my body and nestles itself in my heart.

I'm on my feet. Casey growls obscenities at me. I don't listen. I send the back of my hand booming right into his cheek, smashing his face to the side with a small shower of blood and spit. He stumbles back a few steps, wipes off his eyes, lets out a bestial war cry, and then charges me.

And for once, everything slows down. Normally, the venom doesn't act this way. There's none of the car-crash-slow-motion fear that one gets when something goes horribly wrong before your eyes. But this time, things change. This time, I watch intently, knowing just what will happen.

Casey charges me. I sidestep as he pulls back his fist. His knuckles nearly graze my cheek, but just miss it. And with Casey swinging at air, I take one step forward and send my fist arching up into where his stomach and chest meet.

Right on target.

The world just stops.

My life freezes. It's like someone hit the pause button on my existence. I step back and take it in. My face is a malicious grin with reddened eyes. Every muscle in my body looks taut beneath my clothing, pulled tight in both rage and anguish. Casey is actually lifted off the ground by my punch, his cheeks puffing out, his feet hanging about a foot or so above the floor. His body is hunched over my fist, crumpled, like a badly raised circus tent.

I feel powerful. I feel immortal and dark and stark raving mad. I feel like every fantasy character I'd concocted for myself at bedtime, every grand villain or hideous monster I'd used to make my poisonous core into a weapon or a shield against everything else. This is how Vlad the Impaler must have felt, Alexander the Great, Charles Manson—invincible, powered by something beyond their control and feeling deliciously wonderful about it. This is how Blacklight feels. It's fantastic. It's better than every fantasy I've ever dreamed of, every fight I've ever walked away from. Better than sex, than love. Paradise in ebony.

This is nice, I think.

Isn't it, though?

BAM, I'm in the fight again, and after a second of floating, Casey hits the ground. He tries to push away from me, coughing, sobbing, but I grab the collar of his shirt and pull. One of his bloody, drooly hands reaches out and does the same to me. For a second I see his face, my friend's face, pained, hurt—

—and then he smiles, and I know that no matter how powerful or dark I just felt, he understands.

He yanks, and uses the force of me pulling up to head-butt me right in the face. The world shatters, and all is silent for a second, but consciousness spins back into view.

We're both on our feet, but just barely. My head is still swimming from the head butt, and Casey's still choking from the uppercut, and the people circling us are looking more worried than excited now. We're heaving, stumbling, trying to gather our wits, ready for the next move, the next punch. Our eyes meet, and although bloody and bruised, I can tell he's still ready to fight.

"Stop."

Somehow, through the car alarms and the whispering audience and all the city's noise, we both hear Randall and look up at him. He stands at the front of the crowd, arms folded, Tollevin flanks him, aghast. Randall's expression is one of mixed contempt and grief—he's disgusted by us, but it's obvious he didn't expect anything less. There's a smudge of blood on his shirt. I then take the time to look at our battlegrounds and see lots of it, spattering the sidewalk, my clothes, my fists . . . *JESUS.* Now that I look at it, there's blood everywhere, even smeared on the walls and the car we hit. This place looks like a food fight at Hannibal Lecter's place. I had no idea there was this much blood in a person. Or that I could shed it.

After this pause, there's no more momentum. I feel numb, obliterated. I can't even cry. There's nothing left in me, like the venom has passed out from exhaustion and left a big empty room behind. I open my mouth and feel my lips sting as the blood and mucus coating them stretches and then cracks.

I turn to face Randall. "Brent call you?" I manage to hiss out. He nods, slowly. "How do I look?"

"You'll be okay."

Greeeeat. "You okay?"

He opens his mouth to say something, and then his eyes widen. "Locke—"

A hand grabs my hair and yanks, accompanied by the most gut-wrenching scream I've ever heard. Casey sweeps me off my feet and slams my head into the car's hood. Everything swirls purple before going straight to black.

"Locke? LOCKE?"

A hand slaps my face awake, and I sit up on the pavement. Tollevin crouches in front of me with a glass of water, which he shoves into my mouth, and I gulp greedily. The side of my forehead cries agony.

"Oh fuck," I mumble. "How long was I out for?"

"Only about twenty seconds," he says, shaking his head in disbelief. "Long enough to make us worried, though. Jesus, I'm beginning to wonder if it's possible to kill you. Man, you need to see a mirror."

The details of the situation rush back into my head. "Where're Randall 'n' Casey?"

"Over there."

I follow his finger to a couple of yards away, where Casey

sits with his back up against a wall, head between his knees. Randall crouches in front of him, face pained and exhausted. A small trail of blood runs from Casey, dribbling down the pavement and into the street.

Okay, friends accounted for. Next problem. "Where's Renée?"

Tollevin hisses, "She's inside the bar, man. Now might not be the best time."

"Help me up."

"Locke . . . fuck."

Tollevin yanks me to my feet and hands me my glasses, surprisingly intact. I hobble into the bar, dark and ratty, and find Renée on the stool, picking her nails to pieces. Great black gobs of makeup drip down from her animal eyes, darting every which way in case of predators. One knee moves pistonlike; her foot beats out a double-bass rhythm. The bartender, a cute girl in her midtwenties, has a hand on Renée's shoulder. As I enter, she takes just enough time to return my glance and turn away in horror. The more I walk, the more I feel the blood move down my face.

"Renée?"

She shrieks and goes a foot in the air. Instead of going to my face to help me, like they should, her hands go straight to and into her mouth, her fingers shoved between her teeth. Her eyes well up with tears, and her shoulders go up in a defensive posture. Jesus, how bad *did* Casey beat me? We didn't get that out of hand, did we?

"Renée."

"Look at you," she gurgles. "Look at yourself."

She stands up and marches out of the bar, crying quietly. I follow her into the street, as fast as I can.

"Renée."

She turns the corner, trying to outwalk me. What the fuck? I grab her shoulder and spin her, *make* her look at me.

"Renée!"

Before I can say anything else, she's screaming and hitting me, pounding her fists at my shoulders and neck and making these horrible leathery noises in the back of her throat again. My wounds scream out in soreness, so I just put my arms up and back off. I take the hint and don't touch her again, just follow her.

"Renée."

Past the remaining members of the audience, disgusted, whispering. I start switching sides to make sure both ears can hear me.

"Renée."

She walks to the curb and throws one hand up, the other one clutching at the back of her neck. I pray that our appearances will make every cab driver in a three-mile radius turn their OFF DUTY lights on.

"Renée."

A cab pulls up in seconds, and she's inside it, barking her address. I grab hold on the door handle and try to keep her from closing the door.

"Renée."

She screams and yanks with all her might before crawling into the far corner of the taxi and hiding her face. The cab, whose driver probably thinks I'm a budding Ike Turner, disappears with a screech and a cloud. I memorize the plate: EVH5604. Soon, though, it blends in with the New York City mob of yellow cabs, and it's lost, taking my repulsed girlfriend with it.

"Renée."

The wounds on my face and the bruises on my arms sting as my sweat and blood roll into them, as if someone had dripped poison into my open gashes and aching muscles. Somewhere in the distance, there's a high-pitched wail, growing louder and louder.

Tollevin runs up to my side. "Dude, that's the cops. You need to get the fuck out of here, pronto."

And even though it makes no sense, a word forms in my mouth, the only word I think I can say other than her name.

My lips curl, teeth press, tongue wavers, and:

"Venom."

ARE YOU alive?"

He sputtered out another gurgling response. The monster that had nearly killed me was no more, leaving this charred little . . . man. A man, an engine of blood and ligament, nothing more. Weak, easy, shallow, murderous.

There was another spasm in the energies of my costume, and I crouched, preparing to do what I knew had to be done.

"I understand your intentions," I whispered, "but you killed her. Terrible future or not, you killed her, my friend, and I . . . can't let that be forgotten."

"S'posed ta . . . kill you," he spat. "Send me bacckkh to kkill you . . ."

"I can't allow that, either. What I am, what I can do . . . It's all too important, you see. Too important to let one little pissant put it in jeopardy." I grabbed his collar and flipped him over, his face finally facing me. I raised my fist, begging for the impact of blood and bone. "I'm sorry. Understand, this is for your own good."

He sputtered out a mouthful of blood, and then he smiled. A sly smirk up in one corner of his face. "I'm glad I got"—he managed to croak out—"got to meet you . . . helped me remember what . . . you were like . . ."

My hand froze, the energy still raging through it but the motivation lost. Again, the overwhelming feeling that something was not right *with this man washed across me. "I don't understand."*

"You were—" Another cough, another spray of gore. He caught his breath. "You were a better brother than you were a tyrant."

Pow.

No.

My fist dropped. My face dropped. My entire body let out a collective heave of sorrow, and my hands clutched the broken man before me.

"Lon."

"Hey, mmannuh . . . I'm schorry about Renée. . . .

"My God, Lon. I'm . . . oh God, LON, WHAT THE FUCK WHAT THE FUCK NO, NO, NO . . ."

"The venom remembered me and thought—" And then his body shook, bent in the middle, twisted up in weird, insectoid ways that no human should be able to move. "Found me, found the well inside of me when I killed herrrr—" More gurgling. Another twitch.

"LON!" I clutched his body to me, trying to shake some life back into it. I heard him cough, and then I grasped his face, staring straight into his eyes, blue and fading quick. "LON, HOW WAS I SUPPOSED TO KNOW?" I screamed. "WHY DIDN'T YOU TELL ME IT WAS YOU! YOU'RE OLDER, AND I COULDN'T RECOGNIZE . . . YOU CAN'T EXPECT ME . . . OH GOD, OHGODOHGODOHFUCKING CHRIST, *I'M SORRY, I'M SORRY!"*

Static hiss seemed to fill the air, and his body went rubbery, unreal in my hands. "Going back." He moaned. "When you die, they bring you back. . . . Don't forget what . . . what you are . . ." His eyes, floating Cheshire cat–like in the darkness, focused on mine. "It's not you."

And then my hands clapped together, because he was gone, sucked into time and away from me.

I stood on the rooftop, feeling the city's sorrows whirling around and through me.

Somewhere, off in the distance of my mind, I heard an echoing laugh.

"Admit it," said a voice that wasn't mine, "I'm starting to get to you."

CHAPTER THIRTEEN

IT IS MY firm belief that if I ever smoked crack, my mother would sniff the air, glare at me, and ask me why I was smoking crack. The Mom Sense gives all mothers an internal gauge that reads what kind of trouble their child has been up to, and how badly said child is gonna get it. So it's no surprise to me that the minute I get home, even though I've been trying to be quiet and discreet, my mother calls out my name and walks into the living room to see me, bloodied and broken, slumped against the door frame.

"Oh my God! What happened to you?"

No talk. Face hurty. Maybe later. Her hands grab at my shirt, but I keep moving, brushing them off as I go.

"Honey, what happened? Are you all right? Let me see,

let me see, oh my *God*, sweetie, tell me who did this to you and I—"

I put up my hand to signal that this conversation is not meant to happen yet. Once I make it to my room, I slam the door behind me and gimp over to my dresser so I can see my face in my mirror.

Well, holy fucking shit.

I'm all fucked-up. Like, *Rambo* fucked-up. Girl-who-survives-the-entire-horror-movie fucked-up. My lower lip is split in two different places. My left eye is a swollen mass of swirling blacks and blues, accentuated by a small scratch that had decided to bleed profusely down the side of my face. Small brownish bruises line my neck, each one a marking from where Casey's fingertips had dug into my throat. There's blood, snot, sweat, and tears all over every part of my face, some even clumping my hair together, turning its usual mangy blond to coppery and festering (man, I love using *those* two adjectives as a self-description). One lens in my glasses frames is slightly cracked but still usable, and has managed to stay in its frame, which counts for something, I'm sure, in some fucking ridiculous karmic way. It's like a bus hit my face.

I heave a sigh through my bloodied mouth, and the air rattles through my lungs and rasps out dry. A shell, a husk, a shed snake's skin. I just feel sagging flesh on aching bone. An out-of-service machine.

In the bathroom, I dampen a washcloth and get to work. The minute it touches my face, stinging nettles stab my entire head. The pain registers in the back of my brain, but just barely, not enough to make me care. The cloth and my face trade colors: My skin is revealed as pale and sickly, while the cloth turns a dark, chunky brown. It reminds me of chum.

When I finish wiping down my mug, my wounds don't look half as bad as they did before I cleaned myself up, but they're still bad enough. The eye still looks hideously ballooned, but the cut above it isn't visible in the least. One split in my lip seems gone already, but the other is ragged and swollen enough to present a problem. The bruises on my neck, though, stand out like a forest fire. I wouldn't give me a quarter if I saw me on the street.

My mother, arms crossed and face tight, greets me as I crack the bathroom door. I try to force a smile to let her know that I'm okay, but my entire face screams in pain, so I just sort of grimace like a moron.

"I want to know what's going on, dammit," she says. "You don't just come home looking like that, slam the fucking door in my face, and not explain to me what's going on. JEsus-MaryandJOseph, Locke, look at you."

My brain's pilot light comes on, and I think of an

appropriate response. "It's nothing, really. I'm all right." Good one.

"Get out here this instant and tell me exactly what happened to you. It's like . . ."

"Do I have to?"

"Do you—" Her face softens suddenly, and my heart shatters. "Locke, honey, please. Look at you. I'm so scared. What *happened*? Who *did this* to you? You don't have to be afraid, you can talk to me about this."

"Got in a fight. Look, let me get a few hours of sleep. Please. And then I'll tell you all about it. Every last detail. Just . . . I'm exhausted."

Finally she shakes her head and turns back toward the living room. "Fine. Go to sleep. We'll discuss this when you wake up." Her voice lets me know that I'm in deep, deep trouble. Big surprise.

The sheets feel cool and soft on my body, compared to the roughness of everything else. I wrap and tuck until the whole bed is a cocoon, a comfort burrito with a scrumptious Locke core.

As my head sinks into my waiting pillow, I reach out for the venom, the constant presence that's been my companion for too long now. The venom sighs and waves me away, as though exhausted.

Long day. Good work. Kudos, buddy.

Everything's poisoned, I think. *You ruined it all. My friends, my family, it's all been tainted, turned to shit. This is your magnum opus, isn't it?*

I told you not to thank me. Not to get too comfortable. All I needed was an even playing ground, an amount of equality. And all that took was a little hope. Once you were lifted up, it was just a matter of waiting for the downfall.

Always poisonous, I think, yawning. *Nothing changed, it just looked different. Fuck you.*

You probably have a concussion, you know. If you go to sleep, you might not wake up.

Maybe that's for the best.

I let my eyes, heavy and irritated, close softly.

Sadly, it's not my time, and after a few hours of dreamless black sleep, my eyes click open again. My wounds, now rested, have been given time to be sore and uncomfortable. I roll over and feel everything from my scalp to my toes scream bloody murder. I lift my arm to scratch at the cut above my ear, and everything from my fingertips to my shoulder blade becomes a bag of rusty nails and shattered glass. Well, at least I can feel real pain again. Good to know. Christ, this SUCKS. Every movement is torture. I want to fucking die.

Lon sits at the kitchen table when I enter. He's reading a comic book, and he does a double take when I come into the room: looks at Batman, looks up at me, looks back down to Batman, and then gapes at me like I'm a circus freak.

"Holy crap!"

"Language," calls my mother from the other room.

"Hey," I mumble as I sit down at the table with the speed of an octogenarian.

"What happened?"

"Got in a fight."

He laughs like it's not really that funny. "With what, a bear?" My mom snorts approving laughter toward my little brother. Being the subject of ridicule is, in this case, tolerable. "Are you okay? I can get you some ice. . . ."

"I'm fine. Just a little sore."

He tilts his head sideways, fascinated by my face. "Wow . . . I've never seen a real black eye before"

I lean forward. "Wanna touch it? Softly, though."

Just as he reaches out to feel my swollen face, my mother enters the room and slaps his hand out of the air. "Leonardo, honey, will you excuse us for a second? I need to talk to your brother."

Your brother. Oh man . . .

Lon nods to us, and then in a blur he's in his room. My mother goes about tidying some things up in the kitchen before she slowly takes Lon's seat and lights a smoke. When she doesn't offer me one, I take it upon myself to spark up.

I haven't had a cigarette in way too long, and my throat has finally stopped aching from being choked. A minor blessing.

"So," she snaps, "want to explain yourself?"

"It's a long story."

"I have time," she says, taking a deep drag from her smoke. "And so do you."

"This is gonna be unpleasant, you realize."

"I'd have *never guessed*." She shoots a smoke ring in my face. "Talk."

I spew, starting with Renée telling me about Casey's love for Randall and ending with me chasing my girlfriend to a taxi, with all the drama and bloodshed in between. No emotion crosses her face the whole time; she just nods every so often to show me she's listening. I leave out certain parts of the whole ordeal—the night spent at Renée's place, the fight with Terry, things like that. By the time I wrap the story up, we've motored through three cigarettes each, with no finish line in sight.

"Okay," she says, little ghosts of smoke escaping her mouth with every new syllable. "So you and your friend beat each other half to death because you revealed something about your friend. All this while your girlfriend was there. That nice girl I met *earlier today*."

"Mmm-hmm."

After a moment of contemplation, she looks at me with

death-ray eyes. "Christ, Locke, I don't even know what to think anymore."

Thank God for my bout of apathetic emptiness, 'cause otherwise I'd be cursing out my mother right now. "Wow, no Mom sympathy? Can I at least get a bowl of Chicken and Stars out of this, maybe a glass of choco—"

"I mean, he's your *friend*," she says, shaking her head. "He's someone you care about. I mean, Jesus, I don't blame you for telling Randall about how Casey feels—he's your friend too, I know, and he was upset—but even if your friend who . . . who has angries like yours is the first person to throw a punch, you hold back. You don't beat up your friends. You turn the other cheek and forgive them for being stupid or selfish or *wrong*. Being in someone's life means overlooking their faults sometimes and being the bigger man, not retaliating against them."

"That's very Christian of you."

"It's very HUMAN of me!" she bellows, and jabs the lit end of smoke at my face. She's close to tears. "This isn't about philosophy or faith, it's about basic human treatment! You don't *DO* this! To *anyone*. Have you seen yourself in the mirror?"

She's got a point. "Okay, yeah. I look pretty . . ."

"Hideous? Gruesome?"

"Oh, thanks, Mom, you're a *peach*."

"LOOK at you! This is the face of what these spasms of anger are gonna lead to if they keep going on! You look in the mirror one day and you see this stranger with a busted-up lip and a dazed look in his eyes, and you want to know who he is and how he got there! Don't, honey; Locke, you're so much better than that. Come on."

She pulls hard on her cigarette and then, with a flourish, jams it into the ashtray. Her mouth opens as if to say something, but then she just goes quiet and shakes her head again. Finally, with nothing else to say, she stands and starts getting dinner ready.

"So, that's it?" I say. "What do I do, Mom? There's no way to fix this. The venom's ruined everything. I don't know how to go back."

"No, you know what, enough of this," she says, waving me aside. "I officially divorce myself from this issue. Until you're ready to get yourself together, I'm not listening to any of this venom bullshit. I love you to death, Locke, and I always will, no matter what, but enough is enough. You want to be a thug, go for it. You want to get better, work on it and then talk to me."

"Mom, please," I say. Now I'm the one close to tears. "I don't know what to do."

"That makes two of us," she snaps, and turns to leave the room. "Start thinking."

• • •

The next day is Sunday, thank God, so I hole up in my room and recuperate. It's not as bad as it sounds. I get most of my homework done and manage to replace my Band-Aids every couple of hours without making my wounds reopen (lucky me). My mother doesn't try to baby me either, just announces when food's ready and reminds me that I have a meeting with Dr. Yeski the next day. The military vibe goes on all day, with my mother playing the general and Lon playing the spy who peers at me over chairs and couches to get a good look at someone who's taken a decent beating. And all I can do is laugh and think, *Man, I wonder how Casey looks.*

Somewhere in the evening, out of both loneliness and worry, I call Randall. When he hears my voice in response to his greeting, he sighs.

"How are you? How's Casey?" I ask.

"Casey is, thankfully, not in the hospital," he says, his voice heavy with the fatigue of having to tell this story over and over again. "Things were shaky for a little bit, 'cause he kept coughing up blood, but we think it's just blood he swallowed over the course of the fight. I imagine you did the same thing. You knocked one of his teeth loose, though. I talked to his mom and dad, and they've decided not to press charges. You're lucky for that."

"You two have talked?"

"Yeah."

"Are you . . . I mean, did you . . . was, uh . . ."

"Spit it out."

"Are you *with* him?" I spit out.

"No, of course not. Don't be stupid. Just because he's in love with me and I'm taking care of him doesn't mean that I'm going to fall for him. That's hideously offensive to both me and Casey."

"My mom called me hideous last night."

"What can I tell you? Small world."

I wait for him to answer my other question, but there's only silence. "So, how are you?"

"Do you actually care?"

"Of course."

"I'm tired and I'm hurt," he says. "I'm sick of everyone overlooking their own feelings in favor of appearances or other people's feelings. This thing was so blatantly indicative of how fucked-up we all are that there's no point in trying to move on right now. This boil has been coming to a head for a while, and now that it's been opened up, we need to let the infection run dry. Until then, you're all on friendship probation. Don't come to me for advice or instructions, because I'm all out of ideas.

"How's Renée doing?"

"I don't know, she hasn't been answering my calls."

"Do you think she's okay?"

"No." The response makes me feel cold and stupid. "I'm not her fucking boyfriend, Locke," he spits. "None of this is my doing, and it's not my job. If I were you, though, I would prepare for the worst. Beats me why, but *carnage* is one of her turnoffs."

"I'm really scared, Randall. I don't know what to do."

"Good."

"You think she's gonna dump me?"

"I would." A pause. "I have to go. Take care of yourself, Locke, because at this point, I don't think you have anyone coming to your aid."

I decide to give Renée a call. I owe her that much. Randall's wrong: I am her boyfriend, and I fucked up royally, but no matter what's happened, I love her, and I know she loves me. I have faith in her. In us.

"Hello?"

"Renée?"

Click.

Okay. Let's try that again.

I prepare myself for the shots of fire in my veins contrasting with the blood rising to my face, but the venom seems like a background presence now. It's definitely still there, but the actual attacks seem to have ceased.

There's crying in the background when the other end picks up. "Who is this?" says Andrew.

"Andrew, it's Locke. Is Renée there?"

"Holy shit, Vinetti, I am going to fucking kill you tomorrow."

"Andrew, please—"

"I asked for one thing, Vinetti. One thing. Keep her happy. Your ass is mine."

"Andrew, there's more going on here than you—"

"See you tomorrow, kid. Gonna bite off your fucking head."

Click.

That was productive. Guess I'll give her a night to think about things.

When I see Andrew outside school, I decide that my give-Renée-a-night-to-think idea was about as ineffective as my tell-Randall one. His friends hang back around him, waiting to see what his first move will be. They all look nervous. And stupid. It's a sea of huge pants and stocking caps, huge jackets and attitude. Terry stands off to one side, shooting me a look that's supposed to say that he's not afraid of me, only his face looks like it was run through the dryer one too many times, and I know why.

I reach Andrew and stare up into his stony expression. We're inches away. The air seems to vibrate around us.

"Should we go to a courtyard or park or something?"

Andrew raises an eyebrow. "Pardon?"

I shrug. "I've never been in, like, an official school-yard fight. I figured, y'know, they'd form a circle around us"—I motion to his fan club—"and we'd pace around for a while until you smacked the shit out of me."

He examines my face and sneers. "Looks like the queer beat me to it, though, huh?"

"Yeah, the queer did a number on me. You wanna go talk?"

"Yeah," he says, waving his friends away. "I'll talk to you guys later. Me and Locke are gonna have a chat. Omar, tell Doc Raymond that I had a family thing to deal with and all that." Terry snorts and makes a comment, which I'm pretty sure includes "motherfucker." Andrew and I trudge toward Broadway. I light a cigarette and offer one to Andrew, but he turns it down.

"I thought you smoked."

"I blaze mad trees, man, but don't smoke the bogie."

"Oh. Right."

"I smoke weed," he enunciates for my benefit, "but I do not smoke cigarettes. Jesus, watch some MTV, it's like you were raised in a fridge."

"Sorry. Guess I'm not as 'stupid fresh' as you are. Maybe I should hang out with ghetto idiots." There's silence, so it's apparent that I'm doing the pursuing in this interaction. "How is she?"

"She's not good," he says, peering pensively into the distance like a Calvin Klein model. "It's like something just broke in her, and everything in her head just sort of went disordered, right? Like it got all stirred up together."

"Has she talked to you a lot about it?"

"Nah. Most of the time, it's like she can't even think of the words. She opens her mouth and says one or two things, and then starts crying." He looks at his hands and rubs them together. "Not taking her meds no more either. It scares the shit out of me. I mean, she needs to take her medication or else she just . . . ahhhh. I worry, Vinetti. I worry." He looks everywhere but at me. I don't blame him.

"I'm really sorry, Andrew."

"Ah, y'know . . . I'm not happy with you, kid. Blood has a lot of impact on my sister, and from what I heard . . . Fuck, look at you, it was obviously a bloody match. I think seeing two people she loved and trusted drawing so much blood from each other was just an overload. I think she's scared that if she puts her faith into anyone, they'll only end up hurting each other because of her. And it all results in big ol' pools of blood, every time."

Andrew was so much more comfortable in my mind as an idiot bully. His eloquence only makes him scarier. Still, I find myself walking steadily beside him, a cold numbness spreading through my arms, legs, face, and chest. It feels good, I suppose, in that I'm really beginning to consistently feel things again, but it also feels hideous in a way that the venom never did, all the guilt and pain without any of the fiery hatred that sent me zooming fist-first into the fray. I do realize, though, that it isn't a truly-numb numbness like I've been feeling recently, just a chilling numbness. Which, I suppose, counts for something.

"Wow."

"Yeah."

"I'm so sorry, Andrew."

"I told you, it happens."

I light another cigarette with the butt of the one I was just smoking. If there was ever a time to chain-smoke straight through a pack, it's now. Andrew looks at me disapprovingly and says, "Son, that shit's gonna kill your ass so quickly." Then he smiles like a goon and adds, "Though probably not before the faggot or myself do, apparently. I have to tell you, the urge to destroy you is so fucking intense, but seeing you only fills me with pity."

I can't help but chuckle. Again I make a mental note: just felt something. It's strange, keeping my emotions logged, but after a period of pure nothing, it's nice to be able to recognize an active feeling. "Yeah, well, you should see him."

"Yeah?" He seems genuinely interested. "Did you kick Casey's ass?"

I shrug. A surge of weird macho pride hits me. "Well, yeah. He knocked me unconscious, though."

He chortles. "Man, if I'd done that to either of you, I woulda been put down for a hate crime, but just 'cause you're both psycho little freak kids, you get off scot-free. I'm surprised. That kids looks jacked."

"Hey, now. I still have your sister to deal with."

His face darkens. "Okay, well, maybe not scot-free. But you know."

"I didn't know I was allowed to smoke in here," I say, lighting my cigarette.

"Only patients are, and even then, only certain patients." She puts an ashtray in front of me and stares with a look of slight concern. It's a refreshing change from her usual blank face. "I suppose I should see the other guy?"

"What?"

"Must've been a nasty fight."

I hiss as the lungful of smoke enters and exits my mouth. "My friend Casey," I say softly. "You remember him?"

"The gay kid? With the . . ." She glances at her notepad. "The black, right? The other venomlike impulse?"

"Right." I rehash the story in complete, blood-soaked detail.

Dr. Yeski nods slowly. "Wow," she says.

"Yeah," I say.

"It's been a rough couple of days for you, I take it."

"You have no fucking idea."

"You talked to . . . Randall, right? Have you talked to him about this?"

"A little bit. He's taking a step back from the situation, says he's sick of being our friend if we're going to behave like this."

"Sounds reasonable. How are you feeling about how this all played out?"

I shrug. "It all makes sense."

"How so?"

"Well, the venom acts both as a current for rage and as a poisonous entity," I explain. "Everyone I come in contact with gets hurt, poisoned. But things were beginning to go well, and I was starting to realize how great life could be if I somehow quieted the venom, or learned to control it, but I just played into its plan. I thought I had gotten a grip, but instead I just learned to make the venom part of my personality. Once it was on equal footing with me, it could take every good thing I've gathered in my life away from me in one fell swoop."

She stares at me for a bit, silent. "You don't think that circumstance was a part of it? This can't have all been the venom's doing."

"Why not? That's the power of the venom. It's my Mr. Hyde. It's clinical and evil."

"But it's also a part of you. Maybe you let the venom come to the surface and get 'equal footing' with you because it needed to come out in the open."

"Everyone thinks that," I say. "Randall, my mom, Renée—they think I *enjoy* hurting other people. This isn't within my power. It's something darker than me. It's manipulative."

"You'd be surprised how many people assign personalities to parts of themselves that they can't accept—"

"I can accept it," I bark, "I just don't like it. I want to be rid of it, once and for all."

"Then you've got to work," she says. "No one can come in and cure you, Locke. There's no deus ex machina here. If you want help with your feelings, you need to show those around you that this help will lead to something. So far, it seems like you've gone behind their backs, lied about what you're actually experiencing. It must confuse your friends quite a bit."

I snort. She has a serious point here, but it's still shrink talk. "Well, at least someone's giving me advice."

"Not advice. Just my opinion. Right now, someone else telling you what to do is the last thing you need."

Class crawls by at a snail's pace on Tuesday, considering the insanity of my nonacademic life. The idea of paying attention to my history professor is absolutely meaningless. With the introspective nightmare I just went through, the views on Napoléon coming out of the graying little man in front of me just don't hold that much true significance. Randall jots notes down halfheartedly, but I can tell he's thinking the same thing. Part of me wants to get up and just scream that this has nothing to do with real life, that we didn't care and really shouldn't *have to*. For the first time that I can remember, I think about the universal teenager-versus-school question: Why should this matter to me? Will a serious knowledge of the cotton gin help with my unstable relationship with the woman of my dreams? Will learning that Napoléon and Hitler made the same stupid mistake change the fact that this weekend, I pulped the face of one of my best friends? This is all very interesting, but it has no bearing in my world. Who gives a fuck?

The minute class is over, I go to my usual smoking spot on the steps outside. Randall's waiting for me. His eyes sag with exhaustion. Sleep has not been a part of his life lately. When I sit down, he mumbles, "And how's the venom today?"

Hearing him mention it is odd. It'd always been my taboo subject, and now it's a point of order. "It's on and off. One minute I hear it commenting on my life, and the next I'm trying desperately to speak to it and getting no response." There's a silence, so I jump on it. "Randall, I'm so sorry. A million times, I'm sorry. I owe you so much more than this."

He waves me aside and lights his cigarette. "Well, Saturday was certainly the worst I've ever seen you," he says. "Maybe the venom just ran its course, like a disease."

"That's what I figured, that there was one last gasp and then it was dead, or at least retired. The other day, though, talking to my mom . . . I don't know, maybe I'm doing this wrong. *I'm* the venom's host, so it has to be within my control. But I'm not feeling angry or upset lately, just hopeless. I just want a sign that it wasn't all a bunch of bullshit, that there's actually something more to me than a . . . toxic concept. I want to feel something true."

"Okay!" chirps Randall, and puts his smoke out on my neck.

My insides whirl. There's a blur of coat and hair and collision, and the next thing I know I'm crouching on top of Randall, teeth gritted, one fist raised and the other behind his head clutching a handful of hair. Randall's got a smug look on his face, and his breathing is ragged but calm. I make a little cry out of my throat when I try to talk. There's none of the sweeping vengeance, none of the seeing red. This isn't a war. I'm crouched on top of my best friend, ready to punch him in the face. And I'm fucking TERRIFIED and really don't want to hit him.

This is pathetic. I feel sick.

"If you're gonna hit me," he coughs, "then fucking hit me."

"STOP IT," I cry, more sob than bellow. "You ENJOYED that."

He smirks. "Yeah, I took a little pleasure from it, considering the shit you pulled this weekend. What of it, Stockenbarrel?"

I sit back on my haunches, frozen, unable to move or scream. I keep waiting for the pounding heat, the raw power, but there's nothing, only embarrassment. Christ, my neck hurts.

Randall sighs and climbs to his feet. "Welcome to human emotions, Stockenbarrel. They're not fun, they're not cool, and you have a lot of fucking catching up to do."

He sits down next to me, and I'm grateful for it.

When Casey answers the phone, he seems genuinely surprised that I want to see him. We make arrangements, and I walk over to his house.

He answers the door, and I can't help but wince. He looks bad, just as bad as me, if not worse. His lips are crazy swollen, and there are bruises lining his cheekbones. There's a scab on his chin surrounded by a thick purple bruise, probably evidence of my boot. Every step and movement is deliberate and careful. It's like we're two old men, hobbling around the room, nursing our war wounds. Sooner or later, one of us is going to start reminiscing about a nurse.

His apartment is much nicer than I would have guessed—stone countertops, white walls, simple-yet-elegant carpeting, a distinct change from my lived-in crunchy home life. His bedroom has a bit more character. The walls are a deep navy blue, and the furniture has sort of an art-deco feel to it. The only light is one that hangs from the ceiling, the type that you always see in cop dramas, hanging over the interrogation table. Casey takes a seat at his desk in one of those basic swivel chairs.

We both look at our feet for a few minutes, and then I look up and try to smile.

"How are you?" It sounds plastic and forced, I'm sure, but it's the only thing I can think of.

"Sore," he says, and then looks at me. "I'm sorry about your eye."

"I'm sorry about your mouth."

"It's fine. You didn't knock any teeth out, though one of them's loose."

"I know. I talked to Randall."

"My folks aren't going to press charges," he says. "What about yours?"

"My mom figures this is my fault, and I should fix it myself. Besides, neither of us is in the hospital, it doesn't seem *that* necessary."

"Right."

There's a pregnant pause. Both of us want to speak, but neither of us know how to put it.

"Look," he finally says, "I'm sorry about how everything went down. Just . . . with my whole cover blown, it was like the black was the only thing that made sense, and I bet *you* know what that feels like. But you're not getting out of this, Locke. I will not let you out of this. You fucked up badly, and being sorry for something like this doesn't make it any better."

"Of course, but, Case—"

"No. Shut up. Let me finish. You've gotta understand, I've known Randall for . . . forever. And it took me a long time before I realized how I felt about him. It was hopeless from the beginning, so, whatever, I convinced myself that it wasn't anything big, that I was just lonely and horny. It wasn't that, though, not hormones and confusion but LOVE, bottom of the heart. So I couldn't tell him. Occasional attraction is one thing, but love . . . Tell him that, it would change everything. And no matter what you say now, there's going to be that change in our friendship, the change that you started. Randall and I will NEVER be the same friends we were. I overreacted, yeah, and things will get better, but that doesn't mean they'll be perfect, or AS GOOD. That's the last thing I wanted, was for Randall to have something else to, I don't know, write a song about, right?"

"Right. That wasn't my intention."

"'Course not. None of us expected a kid like you to come into the picture, for better or for worse. *I* didn't, and I doubt Renée did. But you showed up, and suddenly I had a comrade, and Renée had a lover, and none of us realized that we were sitting on top of a big tower of mystery and lies until you hopped up there with us and the whole thing collapsed."

"Sorry I ruined your romantic conspiracy."

"You didn't ruin anything," he says. "Everyone's to blame, no one's to blame, yadda yadda yadda. But no matter whose fault it was, you screwed up, whether you knew it or not. It was a mistake, but the intentions behind it weren't noble. I don't know how I feel about you anymore, Locke, but I will say that you have some apologies to make. Me, I'm flexible. I can bounce back from this. But Randall and Renée both love you, and you don't currently deserve that love. Neither do I, for that matter. You do realize how much they care about you, right?"

"Yeah, I have an idea." I puff heavily on my cigarette and try to fill Casey's room with smoke. His ceiling fan makes it quiver, then disappear in a flurry of thin wisps. "So what're you going to do now?"

He takes a minute and then smiles sadly. "I don't know. I don't think I'm going to try and make a strategy about this.

No more plans and hiding and conspiracy. Just take everything one step at a time and have a good time. Drink a little more. Meet some boys, get on with life. We'll see where we end up after this, as friends. I like you, Locke, but after all of this, I don't trust you. Even more, I don't trust myself around you."

I keep my head down, trying to contact some of the venom, the dark bond that made us friends. It's gone, though, tossed away by Casey in favor of common sense, and I can't blame him. The venom and I are alone in this one, back where we started.

One left to go.

I TURNED off the faucet and rolled up my sleeves. The razor felt cold in my hand as I pushed my fists into the warm water filling the sink. My eyes went up to my reflection in the bathroom mirror: Locke Vinetti, superhero, protector, brother, friend. Take a good look, you miserable bastard.

"I'm giving you to the count of three," I said to my reflection. "Then I cut myself to ribbons and die, and something tells me that'll piss you off."

No change. I pressed the blade's edge to my wrist.

"One."

Nothing.

"Two."

The mirror seemed to vibrate. I closed my eyes.

"Three."

I opened them and there it was. The song of the city personified, my dark power—the venom. It was horrible, spidery, like a mass of shadow trying to imitate a real person. About eight glossy eyes stared back at me, glinting with just the slightest hint of crimson, blinking in random sequence.

"Leave."

"Who are you to give orders to me?"

"I want you out, you hear me? Leave me and never come back."

"Did that thing from the future frighten you? You're Blacklight. You don't need to be afraid of anything."

"Just leave. I can be Blacklight without you."

Laughter boomed throughout the bathroom. "Idiot," snarled the thing in the mirror. "Blind, sad little boy. The city's song is always present, but the only way you harness it is through me. I am the doorway, the conduit. All you provide is a host, a being to make my power tangible." Its eyes flared bright. "We can do such things together, Locke. Your brother? Renée? Forget them. Humans. They want a weak, usable version of you, but I love you just the way you are. We can do whatever we want. Steal and kill and rule. Sounds fun, huh?"

I pressed the razor down harder. Ignore it. "Go now."

It stared at me for a second and muttered, "As you wish." It slunk off my form, twisting and scuttling until it got to the bathroom door. It turned and stared back at me through the mirror. "Enjoy your decision. Have fun living and dying as nothing special."

It slipped under the reflection of the bathroom door, and it was gone. I'd gotten rid of it, finally, for good. I was no longer a monster, a superhero; I wasn't outstanding or different.

It took me far too long to take the razor off my wrist.

CHAPTER FOURTEEN

"BE CAREFUL," SAYS Andrew as he ushers me into his apartment. "Like I said, kid gloves and all that, right?"

"Right," I whisper. Each step makes me feel a little colder, and a little older, in my flesh. I am not going to be able to make everything better in a couple of minutes, and I need to remember that. In the meantime, be ready for anything and everything.

Her door is closed, but the halo of light around its borders tells me that she's inside. Taped to the door is a piece of paper, reading, in scrawled handwriting, "I AM THE ROUGH BEAST. I SLOUCH TOWARD BETHLEHEM TO BE BORN." Yeats. Not promising.

I raise my fist, which weighs about six million tons, and rap it three times against her door.

"Who is it?" comes a muffled voice.

"Renée, it's me," I say softly.

Silence.

"I wanted to come by to see you. I know you're not happy with me, but I miss you. I'm terrified that you'll never talk to me again, and I don't think I could live with that. I love you, and I'm so, so sorry."

More silence. The clink and shuffle of slight movement, not much else.

"I can leave if you want--"

The door flies open, and there she is. All the prepared speeches I had backlogged in my mind melt instantly. She's a mess. All she wears is a black wife-beater and a pair of panties. Her eyes are tinged red and sunken into her face, surrounded by clumps of dried makeup. Her hair's ragged, spiky, shooting in a million different directions at once; one look at it lets me know that there was no method--she just grabbed a pair of scissors and went for it. But it's her lips, her perfect lips, that send me back—cracked in places, with a white film of semi-dead skin over them, like the way you imagine crackheads or people in the old folks' home or all those other kinds of people who you find instinctually repulsive, no matter how nice they are.

"Afternoon," she says, looking into my eyes with the expression of a snake. She can see my feelings, as hard as I try to hide them. "Sorry I repulse you, didn't know I had company. Can I offer you a drink?"

"Can I come in?"

She turns and walks into her room, leaving the door open as a sign that she doesn't care *what* I do. I try to make as little noise as possible in some feeble attempt to keep this low-key. She makes a round of her dressers and cabinets and bedposts, lighting every candle in the room.

"How have you been?"

"Well!" she chimes, whipping toward me with a maniacal smile on her face. "I flushed all my medication down the toilet. I haven't slept in two days, which is weird, 'cause I've been drinking like a fiend. How do you think I've been?" With the last sentence, she tosses a third-full bottle of gin at me. I just manage to catch it and set it down on her bed. I see. So this is bugfuck.

"You know you shouldn't be drinking."

"Oh, you're *right*!" she snaps, her voice betraying her unwavering smile. "I should . . . I should go find one of my friends and *beat the shit out of them*! *THAT* will help! That's the . . . the . . . the only way to *do it*, right? Well, guess what, sweetheart, not all of us have some expendable kinda *supply* of hate in us, y'know? We can't all summon our inner demon to make everything *better.* Would you prefer it if I was cutting, maybe?"

The words yank at my heart, and for a second I feel something familiar.

"That's unfair."

"So's LIFE!" she bellows, and in a single movement throws a lit candle at me. I dodge, but a drop of wax hits me in the cheek, sending a jolt of pain through my face. "Things never go right. People never stop hurting one another. It's all bullshit, and I was a moron to think you would be any different."

"Renée," I say, measuring my sentence, "when I was dealing with the venom, I didn't know—"

"Why do *you* get it?" she yells, throwing her arms out behind her. "Why do you get the venom? Why can't *I* call *my* dark side some superhero name and give it a personality? *I* just have to be plain old crazy, while you, you and fucking Casey get to be monsters and all of this shit? Christ, maybe I should just fucking design a fucking costume! Or maybe you should go on the fucking pills! Sure! For a week, *I'd* have the parasitic emotional entity, and *you* can have the Zoloft and the Dexedrine. And let me tell you, all your soul-searching bullshit can be performed with a single capsule."

"Stop it," I say through gritted teeth. "This isn't you."

"You're *right*!" she says, waving her hands in the air. "It's my evil twin! My dark side! It's the black, or the venom, or whatever the fuck I'd like it to be! How dare you talk to *me* like this is a fucking therapy session? Guess what, Locke, I'm not some big-titted shrink chick, *I'm someone who hurts too*!" Her face is inches away from mine now. "Answer me! You haven't answered me! Why do I have to be crazy?" She screams, somewhere between weeping and laughing. "Why do I have to be medicated? Why do *I* have to look after *you*?"

I feel it flex. I can almost hear it crack its knuckles.

"That's not *fair*, Renée."

"You said that already. Fuck you. Fuck fair. It's the truth. I'm just as fucked-up and miserable and ready to die at any fucking second as you are, and it's not because of the goddamn venom, it's because there's something fucking wrong with me. THAT'S the truth. How does it feel?"

"It feels like something you don't mean to say," I whisper, trying to be the bigger man despite the blood pounding through my face. "It feels like air. Like nothing."

Her mouth bunches up in a grimace and her right shoulder goes back and her hand goes flat, which means, no, hell no, she wouldn't dare—

CRACK!

"Feel *that*?"

Whoosh. Venom.

I have her wrists gripped in my hands just a little too tight, considering the cry she gives when I grab them. I let out a noise of rage and confusion and thrust my face right at hers. Her eyes turn from malevolent to terrified in a matter of seconds, and we're standing there, frozen, her breath ragged with fear and sorrow and mine heavy with pure hatred.

"Well, go ahead," she snarls. "Just fuckin' hit me."

"I don't want to hit you," I yell back. "I love you so fucking much. I came here to tell you that, and instead—"

"THEN DO SOMETHING ABOUT IT," she screams, wrenching against my grip. "If you love me so fucking much, LET ME IN! PUT ME BEFORE THE BULLSHIT, *AND LET ME IN*!"

She gives me one final shove and I stumble to the floor, my war wounds crying out in agony. She's on top of me, clawing at my clothes, screaming bloody murder into my face. I try to pull her off, but she bears down hard, pushing, screaming, her face all black tears and open mouth. Finally I let go and let her empty her anger out on me, pushing her face into mine until her mouth clamps onto mine, and suddenly we're kissing, gripping each other in both anger and love, pushing our faces together like blind people trying to find each other. My mouth breaks off and latches onto the side of her neck, and she moans softly under her breath. We start tearing clothes off until we're a mass of sweating flesh, snot, tears. We make love like animals, screeching and groaning. Our noises rise and rise and peak at the exact same moment, and we stay there, together, with nothing in the world to care about but each other.

Hours later I hear a rattle and look up to see Renée, curled in a fetal position at the end of her bed, smoking one of my cigarettes.

"Renée?"

She doesn't look up, just stares at her smoke.

I crawl over to her and put a hand on her knee. She flinches at first, but then settles under my touch. "Renée, what're we gonna do?" I ask.

She finally looks me in the eye and shrugs. "I don't know, Locke. I love you, but if you can't . . ." She gathers her words. "I can't take the venom anymore, hon. And I don't know if you can give it up. It's a part of you, like you said."

"The venom doesn't matter. I'm in control."

"Are you?" she says, motioning to the room around her. "Someone hits you—are you going to kill them? Is the venom going to whisper evil thoughts into your ear?"

"I don't know," I say, running my other hand through her hair. "That's the thing, Renée. There's no simple answer in this situation, I just have to work on it."

Renée's eyes close, and she smiles, and it's beautiful. "Taking you back would be a risk, and it might not be worth it, all things considered. At one point, maybe. Risky used to be sexy. Now, after this . . ."

"I know."

She stares at me a bit longer and then we kiss, long and soft. Pulling back, she speaks into my mouth, her breath smelling of smoke and sweat. "It was a strange day when you wandered into my life, Locke Vinetti."

"Likewise, Renée Tomas."

"I should probably call my doctor and get my prescriptions refilled." She sighs, putting out her smoke in an empty bottle. "He's gonna be pissed when he hears I ruined another order, but I think I'd rather be embarrassed and medicated than otherwise."

"That'd be a good idea."

"I don't know why I flushed them. I guess I was tired of feeling like I could control and structure things. I wanted to get rid of any scaffolding to my life and just . . . see where the pieces fell when things collapse. Does that make sense?"

"Absolutely."

She gets up to get her cell phone, and watching her, I realize that it's all a scaffolding, a form of preset preparation. The venom is as much a part of me as my friendship with Randall or wearing glasses. Everyone can be poisonous, whether or not they're psychotically angry, and I'm no different, save for being way too imaginative for my own good. The venom's just my way of not being scared of possibility, of all of the crazy shit that can happen to a kid, dads leaving and friends deserting you and so on. With the venom, the outcome is easier to predict, the deck is always fixed. It's nothing special, but I am, so maybe it's all been bullshit all along. Maybe I just need to gamble a little and see.

"Okay. Thanks so much, doc, I'll try to make sure it doesn't happen again. Okay. Bye." Renée snaps her phone shut and faces me, eyes worried but sympathetic.

"Take a risk," I say.

"Pregnant women and people with severe heart conditions should leave the room!" My mom steps out into the living room, lifts her arms, and gives a mighty "TA-DAAAA!" Lon walks in, and everyone gasps in mock terror while I begin to choke up.

He wears a trench coat stitched together from torn black vinyl à la Michelle Pfeiffer's Catwoman. Torn pieces of gauze smeared black and red dangle from his hands. He stands a full two inches taller than normal, thanks to Renée's donated combat boots. On his face he wears a black stocking, opaque, with evil-looking red eyes and a torn scarecrow's mouth.

"The night is mine!" he growls in the lowest voice he can muster. "The city's song calls to me in a . . . a . . ."

He looks at me pleadingly.

"Funeral dirge."

"A funeral church! I! Am! *Blacklight!*"

Appropriately uproarious laughter and applause ensue. Halloween's a big day around this household, as it's both Lon's birthday and the creepy kid's Mardi Gras. Each year my mom and I spend countless hours designing and piecing together Lon's getup, and every Halloween it's bigger and better (the Swamp Thing costume was a bitch, for the record). This year he'd asked for something different—"scary but original," he'd said. "Something that most people won't get." So Renée and I sat down, drew up some designs, talked to my mom, and, well, here we are.

While Renée and Mom get the cake out of the oven and I put the finishing touches on my face paint (Gene Simmons, thank you very much), I motion for Lon to come into my room.

"Close the door behind you," I say with my back to him. I hear it click shut and then take off my shirt.

He whips off his mask and gapes. "Oh my *GOD*," he whispers. "Does Mom know?"

In the middle of my lower back is Lon's birthday present: my first tattoo. It's a blocky outline of a spider's body, the legs jaggedly bending out from either side of it—the symbol that Spider-Man Venom bears on his chest and back in the comics. In the center of the symbol, on the abdomen, it reads simply: LON

"No, of course not. Not yet, anyway. That's why I brought you in here all secretly—Renée's the only other person who knows." I look over my shoulder and smile at him. "C'mon, check it out up close. You can touch it if you like, just be careful."

He nervously inches up to me, and I feel his cold fingertips tracing the design on my back. "Oh, man . . . I can't believe you did this. Did it hurt?"

"A little," I say, remembering the way my hand tightened over Renée's as the first flush of pressure turned into fiery pain. It wasn't as bad as getting the crap kicked out of me by Casey, but it was pretty fuckin' bad. Renée's artist was gentle, though, and had a huge Spider-Man obsession. "Not as bad as everyone makes it out to be, though. It was totally worth it too. Happy birthday."

"This is my present?" he squeaks, his eyes growing massive. "You got this for *me*?"

"What . . . of course I got it for you! That's your name there! It doesn't say 'George' or—or 'Bub' on there, it says '*Lon*'!"

"Wow. I don't . . . I mean . . . I . . ." Suddenly Lon's crying like an old lady at a wedding, his hands clapped to his mouth and tears pouring down his face. I turn around and grip him in a big hug, squeezing him tight enough to wring the juices out of him.

"Thank you," he blubbers, his face sticky and wet against my bare chest. "Thank you so much, Locke. I can't believe you did this. I can't believe it."

"You doofus," I say. "You know why I got the Venom symbol around your name, right?" I feel him shake his head against my chest. "When we were at Chapter and Verse, and I flipped out? You remember that?" I feel a nod. "Right, well, at the end of that day, after I flipped out at the woman behind the counter, I told myself that I was going to get rid of all of that stupid anger and hatred for you. There were very few things that made me really want to get rid of the venom, but you were always at the top of the list. It hurt you, man, and I was always scared. . . ." I take a deep breath, preparing myself to say something that I wouldn't ever dare admit. "I was always scared that one day you'd accidentally do the wrong thing, and I'd really hurt you. And that idea was too much, y'know?" I pull him away and look into his puffy red eyes. "I haven't had an angry in over a month, kid. Thank you for making that possible."

Lon bursts into tears again, so I clutch him for a while longer until he stops. We clean ourselves up, him wiping tears and snot from his face while I wipe the same from my sternum. I get my shirt on, Locke yanks his mask on, and we emerge from my room with a knowing nod. Lon, my friend, my brother. You will always be my inspiration.

"Guys," I hear my mom call out, "there's someone here to see you."

I turn around, expecting one of Lon's school friends—

But no. It's just my father.

Lon runs over to the man in the suit, the man holding a big box wrapped in orange, the man who abandoned him, and gives him a grappling hug. My dad growls playfully as he swings Lon in his arms, giving him a hard pat on the back. Knowing Lon, it probably hurts, but he doesn't seem to care. He looks good, Rick does; he has a bit of the distinguished-older-man thing going on right now, sort of like Jeff Goldblum, only a little grayer. A pointed wizard's hat sits on his head. This is his idea of a costume.

After handing Lon his present and asking the usual introductory questions, he marches up to me with a crooked smile on his face. "Locke. How're you doing, son?" His hand jabs out.

There's the stirring, the flexing, the twitching of something solid and alive inside me. A murky cloud stirs up, and a clawed hand reaches up through it.

I put my hand into his. We have a few hard shakes

before breaking it off. "I'm doing okay. How's life on your end?"

"Ah, y'know, life is life," he says, glancing casually around the apartment. "Work, family, sleep, eat, whatever. Nice make-up, by the way; shout it, shout it out *loud*!"

How dare you speak to me about family, you absentee shit? "Thanks, but I just do it for the chicks. You want your tux back?"

He looks me up and down. "You're not wearing it today?"

"It was for a party a couple of weeks ago. Besides, I don't think Ace and Paul would be cool with it."

"Huh. How well did it fit you?"

"Perfectly."

"Then keep it," he says, as if he's giving me the key to the city. "I haven't had much use for it any time recently." His Used Car Salesman smile pops up. "And I bet you looked good in it."

"Thanks. I did. How's the baby?"

He hisses between his teeth, and I gain no decent amount of pleasure imagining five-in-the-morning vomit runs on Rick's part. "Brian's a bit of a hellraiser, but it's all good. Bethany wants to get to know you better, by the way. I think she's a little intimidated by you."

"Understandable. I'm a little intimidating."

My dad chuckles, taken aback, wondering what to say to that, when I see Renée standing behind him wearing a baffled expression (her costume: Eleanor Rigby. A dead Victorian mistress. How cool is that?). I motion her over, and she struts up to me and gives me a kiss on the cheek, leaving a smear of glitter-laced black. "Dad, this is Renée, my girlfriend. Renée, this is my father."

"Oh, really?" she says, her eyebrows jumping a foot. She shakes hands with him and says, in a voice that drips with both sugary sweetness and Bambi's blood, "I've heard *so* much about you, Mr. Vinetti. It's nice to *finally* meet you."

The red in his face betrays his loss of composure, but he smiles and shakes her hand with a little bow toward her. "Call me Rick. Locke didn't tell me he had a girlfriend, much less one as beautiful as yourself."

"Oh, bah," she says, tugging at her bondage straps. "He just keeps me secret so other guys don't come gunning for me."

"Well, we'd better be off," I say, throwing a little salute to the man who was never there for me. "I'll see you later, Dad."

"All right, talk to you later, son. Nice meeting you, Renée."

"Oh, likewise, Rick!"

As I'm about to leave, I stop and trot back over to my

dad. "Hey, Dad, quickly—I'm sorry about being kind of rude, the day I came to get the tux. I was in a weird mood, and my head was . . . Anyway, just wanted to apologize. I was out of line."

He looks at me, half-puzzled, and says, "Well, thank you, Locke. I totally forgot about that, but . . . thanks."

We say our good-byes all around and make our way out into the street.

"You bastard," Renée snarls. "Nice meeting you, you schmuck. You fucking *waste* of a parent."

"Yeah, pretty much."

"Do you still hate him?"

I shrug. "Sure. I'll always hate him. But, y'know . . . that's it. He's an asshole, but he's still my father. I owe him that much. Besides, Lon adores him."

"On that note—Lon like his present?" she asks.

I grin from ear to ear. "He loved it. He started crying like a *baby* about it."

She giggles and bounces up and down. "Perfect! You, come here right now!" She grabs my face between her palms, and we share a prolonged, deep kiss in the middle of the street, smearing my demon face paint every which way. Then we're off down the street, arm in arm, taking in the autumn air and the smell of pumpkin. Parents and children covered in cheap lace and greasepaint are everywhere to be seen, fixing hats and holding out pillowcases. Everything is orange, black, red, and green. This might be the best day of the year to be a teenager—looking ridiculous and getting up to no good are part of the game plan.

When we get to the park, the tarot kids are all sitting on or around the rock where I met them, talking among themselves and having a good time. They've brought blankets and pillows and beanbags, as well as more pots of soup and Thermoses of hot chocolate and coffee than I can count. One of them, a towering raver with pink hair and platform boots, is serving what appears to be eggnog with Count Chocula floating in it from a big glass bowl. And all around it's costumes and candy, mummies and werewolves and Power Rangers hitting joints and swinging bottles.

We sidle up to Randall, Casey, and Tollevin (Freddy Krueger, Austin Powers, and Rick James, respectively), who're sitting in the middle of the crowd, laughing loudly over glasses of apple cider. Randall and Casey are still more reserved around each other than they've ever been, occasionally stealing glances out of the corner of their eyes. Randall has especially taken his time letting Casey and me back into his good graces, but it seems to be wearing on him, and he's almost back to his old self. We realized, after everything exploded into insanity, that we couldn't help but be friends at this point. It was a dirty job, yeah, but who else would we want to spend time with? Without one another, what was there?

They hail us over when we're seen and start firing questions at me about Lon's birthday party. But there's one thing that everyone's curious about.

"For fuck's sake, Stockenbarrel," whines Randall, "can we *see it*?"

I turn around and lift my shirt, feeling the weather run its biting fingers down my spine. Everyone *oohs* and *aahs* at the tattoo, one or two of them reaching out and touching it. When I turn around, they all sound their approval.

"Cute," says Casey, smiling crookedly. "If only there was a superhero named the Black. There'd probably be some sort of racial protest, though, I'm sure."

"Nice job, Stockenbarrel. If there was ever a dude who needed a tramp stamp, it's you."

"Well, now that we're done jerking each other off," says Tollevin, laying his hands on the bongos in his lap. He starts tapping out an almost tribal beat, and then from somewhere in the crowd of misfits and crazies, another set of drums joins him, and then another, and then another.

Randall pulls his guitar out of its case and begins plucking. His eyes shoot to Casey, and he says, "You're gonna sing this one for me, right?"

Casey sighs dramatically. "If you insist." Looking upward, he yells out, "IT BEGINS!"

A sound starts going, but not the normally jovial one that I remember from the first night here. This one is darker, with a little more of a bite to it. Casey closes his eyes and starts singing in a deep, slippery voice.

"'Here come the man . . . look in his eye . . .'"

The crowd starts hooting and hollering, and more and more people join in. I don't know the song, but Renée does, and she squeezes my arm as the first chorus comes up. The words hit me, and I can't help laughing.

"'The devil inside, the devil inside, every single one of us the devil inside . . .'" Casey's eyes pop open onto me, and he winks once, conspiratorially. I wink back and start singing with the rest of the group.

The whole thing seems dark and ritualistic, but it feels like home. I can't bring myself to feel awkward or strange or upset around these people, and even though a little part of me almost wants to complain about something—the cold, the song, anything—I can't. Every person before me is a person, but they're a world before that. We are all time bombs and angels, poisons and antidotes, question marks and commas, and it suits me just fine.

As the chorus finally swells, I look up into the sky, which is a perfect, miserable gray. I can't help it, and I start crying softly, tears crawling down my cheek while my voice never wavers. I look over at Casey and see that he's crying too. Renée lights two cigarettes and hands one to me, which I smoke happily.

And when the song finishes, I'm still here. And for once, I don't think that makes anything worse.

I SAW it before it saw me. That made me incredibly happy.

There was no mistaking it. To everyone else in the park, it probably resembled a grandmother, a hobo, a stoner kid playing Frisbee, but I could see it. The shadowy body. The eyes, blinking in random patterns. The mouth, a burbling gash in its pitch-black face. It had been skulking around town, trying to find a new host, to recreate what we had. Stupid. I could see it. It was mine.

Just as my eyes hit it, it got its first look at me. It stayed frozen in place, hoping I wouldn't be able to tell what it was, who it was. That was bullshit, of course. When you had a relationship like ours, there's no chance of staying hidden. I'd followed it to the park, and there it was, slithering its way across a warm Sheep Meadow in broad daylight.

"Get back here!" I screamed, and then I was barreling across the grass, putting my shoulder down. As I got close, it reared up to its full height and stretched its arms out. Maybe it was trying to scare me off. Maybe it was trying to grow wings and flap away like the batty monster it was. I couldn't tell. All I knew was that it looked weaker, more vulnerable, than it had ever appeared before.

I slammed into it like a refrigerator, sending both of us sprawling into a heap. The minute I got my bearings, I was up on my knees, straddling it, my hand around its thin black throat. It made a shrieking noise and raked at me with its claws, but their taloned ends snapped and shattered when they connected with my flesh.

"You little shit," I hissed through my teeth. "You thought you could get away with all this, didn't you? You thought you didn't need me?"

My other hand clenched into a fist and smashed into the thing's twisted face. The blow sank into its countenance, like the monster was made out of pudding.

"Well, it ain't gonna happen, and y'know why?"

The thing made a sound, like a rabbit that's been hit by a car, and writhed beneath my fist.

I closed my eyes and took a deep breath.

This was my fist. My skin, my bone, my sweat. This was my *victory and also* my *fault.*

"BECAUSE," I said, leaning in and hissing right in its fucking face, "I'M BLACKLIGHT, *YOU HIGHFALUTIN SON OF A BITCH, AND YOU'LL DO WELL TO FUCKING REMEMBER IT!"*

My hand came out of its head with a horrible little plop. I shook the grass and dirt off my shirt, and got to my feet. When I was finally a little less unkempt, I looked down at the beast at my feet, inching away like a wounded animal, claws shielding its eyes.

"C'mon," I said, hiking my thumb back toward the city, "let's go back."

The thing lowered its claws a little bit and blinked at me in puzzlement.

"Are you coming with me or not?"

It tilted its head.

"Well, I'm going," I said. "Come if you like."

I turned back to the skyline and began to trot slowly over the grass, basking in the sunlight and the smells of the park, the burning heat of the light off the city's million windows. After a moment or two, I heard it get up and begin to follow me a few paces behind, just a little scared of what it might have created.